The Puttermans Are in the House

The Puttermans Are in the House

Jacquetta Nammar Feldman

HARPER

An Imprint of HarperCollinsPublishers

Names: Feldman, Jacquetta Nammar, author.
Title: The Puttermans are in the house / Jacquetta Nammar Feldman.
Description: First edition. | New York, NY : Harper, an imprint of HarperCollins
    Publishers, [2023] | Audience: Ages 8-12. | Audience: Grades 4-6. | Summary:
    Told from different points of view, the Putterman cousins, twins Sammy
    and Matty, and Becky, have been at odds, but when Hurricane Harvey
    hits Houston, they soon find that they need each other more than ever.
Identifiers: LCCN 2022044844 | ISBN 978-0-06-303443-3 (hardback)
Subjects: LCSH: Hurricane Harvey, 2017—Juvenile literature. |
    CYAC: Hurricane Harvey, 2017—Fiction. | Baseball—Fiction. |
    Family life—Fiction. | Cousins—Fiction. | LCGFT: Novels.
Classification: LCC PZ7.1.F445 Pu 2023 | DDC [Fic]—dc23
LC record available at https://lccn.loc.gov/2022044844

22 23 24 25 26 LBC 5 4 3 2 1

First Edition

To David, Isaac, and Daniel—may you cheer your hearts out

Before

Sammy

It's a perfect end-of-May day at the ballpark, and my baseball team's clinching our semifinal playoff game.

I've been at first base like always. Calm and cool. Stretch and catch. My twin brother, Matty, has been pitching, shutting batters down like a routine matter of business: strike one, strike two, strike three, you're out!

My whole family's been in the stands cheering us on like usual.

We're their star twin team: Sammy Putterman, the only girl still holding her own in the Houston, Texas, twelve-and-under baseball league, and Matty Putterman, whose lefty southpaw arm's going to take him all the way to the major leagues someday.

Our team's up 6–0 at the top of the fifth inning,

easy-peasy lemon squeezy. It's been a near-perfect game . . . until now.

My brother is gone.

I squint at the stands. My dad's spitting out a mouthful of sunflower seeds, his eyes darting around. My mom is speed texting, her brow cut into a deep V shape. My grandparents, Bubbe and Papa Putterman, are whispering to each other while plastering big supportive smiles my way. My uncle Mike and aunt Deb are shifting around in their seats and shrugging to each other.

And my first cousin, Becky, who didn't want to be here anyway, is eyeing the car.

The ballpark's mic screeches alive and the guy who's been playing the walk-up batter's music says, "Matthew Putterman, Matthew Putterman, please return to field number three, you are needed on the mound to resume play."

But there's still no Matty.

The last time I saw my brother, it was the bottom of the fourth and I was outside the batter's box. He'd just smacked a single and driven in two runs! With our team's bats on fire and Matty's dominant fastball, it was sure to be another blowout win that would take us to the finals next Saturday.

I'd taken a few practice swings, grinned at him on first base, and said with our twin telepathy, *Get ready, Matty! I'm bringing you home!*

The fastball had come middle-in over the plate, right where I like it, and I'd barreled it. It sailed to left center, and I ran as fast as I could as the ball struck the fence. Then I stopped at second with a double and watched my brother slide into home plate, scoring another run.

But after our team took the field again, he never came back out of the dugout to pitch. I figured he ran quick to the bathroom like he does sometimes, and he'd come back any second. He didn't.

Now everyone's staring at me—my family and my coach, all the parents in the stands, my whole team, and a bunch of players from the team we're up against. They're looking at me like I must know what's going on with my brother, where he is. And usually I would.

But somehow I don't.

It's like this: one minute, you're having this great conversation on the phone. You're talking and laughing and talking and laughing. Then the call gets dropped, but you don't know it, so you keep talking. Then you realize there's no one on the other end, there's only silence.

And you think—maybe if you'd been listening a little bit closer, maybe you would've heard the cut connection. Maybe you wouldn't be standing on first base punching your mitt, all confused.

That's how I feel right now. Just like that.

I stare at the hill where Matty should be and blink, just to make sure this isn't some kind of mind-trick joke. I wave to Matty's best friend and our catcher, Ethan Goldberg, to get his attention, but he's hanging his head and kicking at home plate with his cleats.

He's upset that Matty's not here, too.

Coach calls, "Hey, Sammy! Keep everybody warm!" and hurls me a ball. Then I throw grounders to the other infielders while we wait.

But my brother never shows.

The other team's coach jogs over to my coach and points to his watch. My coach calls in another pitcher, and my eyes jump to my parents.

They gesture to their phones and shoot me identical thumbs-ups, like they're the twins, to make it seem okay that my brother's gone. So I grind my cleats into the clay and get ready at first, trying to stay calm and cool, even though I want to sink to the dirt and cry.

My team plays on, going through the motions. Matty's reliever walks the bases loaded, and our defense crumbles. We lose, giving up eight runs in the next two innings, and I strike out on the last at-bat of the game. We're not heading to the finals next Saturday, but if Matty had been here, with me . . . we would be!

I throw my gear into my baseball bag and text my brother.

Me: Where did you go? Why aren't you here?

He doesn't text me back.

I stomp to our car and climb into the back seat behind my parents. My mom and dad stare straight ahead, tight-lipped and quiet. I squeak, "Mom, did Matty text *you* back?"

She frowns over her shoulder and nods.

4

My dad clears his throat. "Sammy, uhh, your brother walked home. Says he . . . uhh . . . hates baseball now. Says he doesn't want to play anymore."

I shake my head and squeeze my eyes shut. My voice gets way louder than I mean it to. "That's not true! Matty loves baseball just like me! Maybe even more! And I know what he thinks better than anyone!"

But as soon as the words come out of my mouth, I worry they're not true anymore either, since our connection's been cut.

We drive home in silence, and as soon as we get there, I kick off my cleats and run up the steps of our split-level Meyerland ranch house.

I rap on my brother's bedroom door till my knuckles turn red, and my voice gets even louder than it was in the car. "Open up, Matty! Why did you leave? We lost!"

He doesn't make a sound.

Then my parents are right behind me. Dad puts his hand on my shoulder and says, "Honey, why don't you let us try?"

I shake my head and keep rapping. I yell into the door, "Matty needs to talk to me! He needs to tell me why he quit baseball! Our team needed him! I . . . I needed him!"

Dad takes both my shoulders and says, "Sammy baby, I'm sure your brother will tell you what happened when he's ready. Go rest now."

I nod, but none of it makes any sense. Matty and I are twins! I'm not used to waiting for him to tell me important things. I'm used to just . . . knowing them.

But our telepathy isn't working at all.

I drag to my room and sit down on my bed in my grass-and clay-stained baseball uniform. I press my back into my headboard. My skin's still sweat sticky and ballpark gritty, but I'm too numb to hit the shower.

Then I wait. I wait for Matty to come out of his room and tell me what's wrong. I wait for him to explain why he told our parents he's quitting baseball. I wait for our telepathy to kick in again, so I'll know the things I'd usually know.

I wait, and wait, and wait.

Finally I reach for my laptop and click on my favorite Astros game replay like I've done a thousand times before. The commentator says, "Swing and a drive to the left field . . . way back . . . this one is GOOOONE! The Astros win it! It's Chris Burke with a game-winning walk-off home run to make Roger Clemens the winner and send the Houston Astros to the National League Championship Series in eighteen innings!" and the cheering fills me up.

It's the time when the 'Stros played the longest game in the history of Major League Baseball's postseason, the winning game against the Atlanta Braves in the National League Division Series. It's the time when my dad held me in our season-ticket seats at Houston's Minute Maid Park, tears streaming down his face.

I don't remember that game, since I was just a baby. But

I was there—there's a framed picture of me and Dad on my nightstand to prove it.

The way he tells it, the real story behind that game was all about *me*. I stayed awake the whole night while Matty slept in Mom's arms. I was destined to become a die-hard Astros superfan.

It's some great story . . . unlike today.

I rewind the game and turn the volume on my laptop up as high as it will go to drown out all the things I'm waiting for, all the things I don't know or understand. The crowd in Minute Maid Park roars into my room as Clemens throws another perfect pitch, just like the ones my brother throws. When the ump yells, "You're out!" Matty finally texts me back.

Matty: Leave me alone, Sammy.

I'm the one who's out, but I don't know why. Nothing feels right anymore. Now that Matty's quit baseball, everything's all wrong.

Because we're Puttermans. We're a part of the biggest baseball family ever. And in our family—you don't just walk out on your team.

Now

Sammy

"Sammy . . ."

I hear my mom's voice, but I can't seem to open my eyes. "Hmm?"

Her voice gets more urgent. "Sammy!"

"Hmm?"

The insides of my eyelids glow hot pink, and I blink. My mom's leaning over my bed with a flashlight beamed right at my face.

When she's sure I'm awake, she rushes over to my dresser and tears through my drawers. She throws a bunch of my clothes into a big duffel, then flings a few things toward my bed: a swimsuit, a thermal underwear set from last winter, my water shoes from our trip to Kauai, and my subtropical Houston-grade bright yellow raincoat.

8

But she doesn't have aim—there's a growing heap on the floor.

Even though it's daybreak, the world outside my windows is steely gray. Two days ago, Hurricane Harvey made landfall from the Gulf of Mexico as a Category 4 storm near the coastal town of Rockport, Texas.

It's been raining ever since.

"What time is it, Mom?"

She doesn't answer my question; she doesn't even talk in complete sentences. "Rain's letting up . . . water's still rising . . . leaving . . . kayaks . . . oh my . . . can't believe . . ."

I sit up. "Mom? Are you okay?"

She steadies herself against my dresser and takes a big breath. "Please get ready, Sammy!" she says, then hurries out of my room.

My fingers and toes start to tingle, this weird jumpy feeling like I need to do something, quick. But what that is, I haven't got a clue.

I grope for my laptop amid my covers, hoping it still has some power.

The game replay I was watching last night is frozen, the hands of happy-faced fans in Minute Maid Park raised in mid-cheer. I can almost hear them; I can almost feel their excitement. The tingling fades, for just a second, then my screen goes dark. Game over.

It's Sunday, August 27, three long summer months after my brother quit baseball, three months where he's avoided me at home and at camp, three months where I've watched the team we've always cheered for together, the Houston Astros, without him.

All yesterday, murky floodwater spilled out of Brays Bayou and covered our street. When Matty and I went to bed last night, the water had reached the sidewalk in front of our house.

My parents stayed up to keep watch, and I guess they've finally made the hard call: we're going to evacuate. They're mobilizing in the face of emergency, like they always do. They say that parents of twins can handle just about anything.

There's a shrill screech outside.

I kick off my covers and run to my window. Our elderly next-door neighbor, Mrs. Sokoloff, who's been joining us for holidays since her daughter moved to Florida, perches in her stocking feet on the tall brick wall at the edge of her yard. Muddy brown water swirls around her, and she's holding the hem of her long skirt up to her knees. A plastic shower cap covers her purplish-gray hair.

Another loud screech emanates from a small wire cage at her feet. It holds her sopping-wet cat, Bartholomew. He doesn't exactly look like a cat anymore, but more like a giant, angry-eyed rat. Mrs. Sokoloff has four bright red scratches clear across her cheek.

"Children, prepare for the inevitable! These are biblical times!" Dad bellows through the house. "Annie, we're all set! Gather the troops!"

"Sammy-Matty! Let's go, now!" Mom's voice rings down the hall.

I weave my hair into a quick braid down my back, then pull on the clothes my mom threw on the floor.

Before I leave my room, I stash the nightstand photo of me and Dad, and my laptop, in the highest drawer of my dresser for safekeeping and grab the World Series baseball that I got for my twelfth birthday last April for good luck.

It's signed by all the Astros greats: Roger Clemens, Jeff Bagwell, Craig Biggio, and Lance Berkman. I've double-Ziploc bagged it for good measure.

Then I fold my favorite Astros cap into the big Velcro pocket of my raincoat and dash down our long family-photo-lined hall.

Just as I'm about to leap down the short run of steps from our bedrooms to the main house, I stop short. The rest of my family stands in the living room in a half foot of the same brown water that's rising around poor Mrs. Sokoloff in the yard.

The water from *outside* is *inside*!

My dad wears his high rubber waders and full back-country fishing gear. He sloshes over to two double kayaks floating in the middle of our living room, outfitted with two life vests apiece, umbrellas, coolers, our duffels, flash-lights, and beach towels.

He straps things down while barking into his phone, "Don't freak out, Mike! We're paddling to that big church near us. Yes, thank god we have the kayaks!"

Uncle Mike is Dad's older brother—my cousin Becky's father. He and my dad mostly get along, but not always. Baseball season always brings them together, though.

Becky doesn't get along with Matty and me anymore, baseball season or not.

My brother's dressed in the same fishing clothes as Dad, like he's his mini-me. Matty looks miserable. Hurricane evacuation aside, he hates fishing. After our one and only family fishing trip to Galveston, we ended up with two kayaks, some ridiculous-looking outfits, and Matty stopped eating fish.

He clutches a knotted kitchen trash bag with what must be his art supplies tight to his chest while water seeps up our curtains and walls. I lock eyes with him and try to use our twin telepathy to tell him that this Houston flood seems way worse than the last one.

But he glances away.

Our seven-year-old golden retriever, Bialy, pants and drools on his leash next to my mom. The top of him is dry, but the bottom of him is wet, since he's sitting on our living-room rug that's now—I blink to make sure I'm seeing all this correctly—covered with water.

My mom's ensemble closely resembles mine: bathing suit straps peeking from under a long-sleeved shirt, dark leggings, and water shoes. Her wide eyes dart around the living room and rest in disbelief as Bialy's half-full food container floats from the kitchen and bumps into the wall in front of her. She says, "Goodness gracious," then she starts crying.

The tingling in my fingers and toes seeps up my arms and legs like the water seeping up our walls.

What if parents of twins can't handle *this*?

My dad pulls my mom close and puts his forehead to hers. "Annie . . . let's just pretend I'm Noah, to the rescue, and these two kayaks are our arks."

Mom cries harder and Bialy whines and encircles her legs with his leash. Dad gently unwraps her, and she dries her face with her sleeve. He hands each of us a life vest and we strap them on. Then he pushes the kayaks toward our double front doors, and we all splash after him.

As my dad pulls the doors open against the rising flood-water, a buzzing noise gets louder and louder. A small motorized dingy with a Texas flag hoisted off the back whips down what used to be Braeswood Boulevard along the bayou and passes our house.

Two largish men in cabana-striped bathing suits wave to us. The one steering the motor at the stern wears a cowboy hat secured around his chin with a red bandanna, and the other one kneels at the bow in an enormous rain poncho.

They steer the dinghy up to Mrs. Sokoloff on the wall. "Ahoy, ma'am!" the poncho man yells to her.

Her bluish lips mumble, but I can't imagine that any intelligible words come out.

He stands up and extends his hand to her. She immediately grabs her wire cat cage and drags it along the narrow wall away from the dingy. "You're much safer in our boat than on that wall," he says. "We'll shuttle you to a church shelter in no time—and that cat can come too."

The cowboy hat man idles the motor and reaches for her cat cage.

Mom yells, "Esther! Go with them! We're right behind you!" and Mrs. Sokoloff finally sits on the wall and lets the poncho man help her down.

"Y'all all right, too?" the poncho man calls to us. "You've got a handy setup there with those kayaks. The big church isn't far!"

My dad looks from the motorized dinghy to our kayaks and back again. He waits a few beats too long before giving the men a thumbs-up. Then he reaches into his pocket and pulls out a hunk of raw hamburger to coax Bialy into the first kayak while Matty pushes our dog's furry wet tuchus.

After Bialy jumps in to scarf down the meat, Mom climbs into the rear of the kayak and Matty takes the front. Then Dad hands Mom and Matty paddles and pushes the three of them out our front doors.

He looks at me with a smile that's forced. He's working really hard to make it seem like everything's going to be okay. "Sammy baby, hop on in!" he says.

So I do. I place my autographed baseball deep into the kayak's hull, where it will be safe, and grab a paddle. My dad tries to shut our front doors, but he can't—the water's already too high. He shrugs, then launches our kayak into the street while water pours into our house behind us.

The air outside is calm and heavy and still, like more rain is on the way.

I pull my paddle to each side of the kayak like a summer camp pro. I'm on autopilot, like I've done this drill before. Like it's perfectly natural to be kayaking down the middle of Braeswood Boulevard after an epic Houston hurricane.

We catch up to Mom, Matty, and Bialy, and I start thinking about the Astros getaway game later today in Anaheim against the Los Angeles Angels. This year, the 'Stros are even better than they were when they made it to the World Series when Matty and I were babies. I wonder if my favorite player, José Altuve, will hit any homers today. I wonder if there's any way we can watch.

I repeat Altuve's season stats over and over as I row: "Batting average .355, 19 homers; batting average .355, 19 homers; batting average .355, 19 homers."

I don't even realize I'm chanting them aloud.

My twin brother doesn't chant with me. He hates baseball now, but he didn't used to. He used to love it just like me.

My mom sniffles and clears her throat. She says, "Samantha, how can you be thinking about baseball at a time like this?"

I don't know what to tell her . . . my mind's always on the game.

I'm Samantha Putterman. I'm a die-hard Astros superfan. And I'm a girl who loves playing baseball.

15

Matty

Sammy and Dad glide their kayak in front of us to lead the way. Before I know it, I'm keeping time with my sister's strokes. Pull. Pull. Pull.

Of course I am. Following her lead is what I usually do.

It's always been our story: Sammy-Matty, Sammy-Matty, Sammy-Matty. In our little twin unit, Sammy's name always comes first since she was born first. Exactly eleven minutes and twenty-eight seconds first, we've been told like a million times.

Sammy rolled over first. She sat up first. She talked first, and she always talked for me. I let her, since mostly she knows what she's talking about. She even threw a baseball first, when we were three years old.

But I threw it harder and faster, and I'm a lefty—the first

Putterman lefty, in fact. My whole family thinks my golden southpaw arm is gonna be my ticket to the majors.

I used to think that, too. But me and the MLB . . . that might not happen anymore.

Even though Sammy and I are fraternal twins, and we're a boy and a girl, we've always had this connection. Sammy calls it our twin telepathy. It's how we've always known what the other likes and doesn't like, what we're both thinking without even asking.

Sometimes I still know what she's thinking, but a lot of the time—honestly—I don't. And lately, she almost never knows what I'm thinking.

But I don't tell her that.

Everybody thinks I hate baseball now, since I quit playing last May in the middle of our 12U—twelve-and-under—playoff game, cold turkey. Bottom of the fourth, after forty-five of my most perfect pitches, actually. Twelve up, twelve down, with five strikeouts. I even drove in two runs in my second at-bat.

But I just had to get out of there.

So I threw my stuff in my baseball bag, snuck out the back of the dugout, and started walking. I left Sammy running the bases, my best friend, Ethan, at the plate, and my dad with a mouthful of sunflower seeds in the stands.

It was kinda like you see in the movies—when the guy drives out of town with his windows rolled down, his left arm draped outside the car in the breeze. He doesn't look back, not even in the rearview mirror. "Good riddance! I'm done with this place," he mutters. Or "I'm movin' on, far away from here!" Or maybe even, "Sayonara, baby! See ya again . . . *never!*"

It was unbelievable how calm I was and how easy it was . . . after what happened *happened.* How I could just walk away from the game of baseball forever. I mean, I've played my whole life, since I'm my dad's only son and *he* was a star pitcher, and so was *his* dad, too.

And even more than all that, I'm a *Putterman,* and we're like the biggest baseball family, ever. Dad says it's written into our genes. Uncle Mike played through high school like I'll bet Sammy's gonna do, and my dad pitched for a year at the University of Texas till he tore his UCL. Papa made it all the way to AAA as a pitcher before going to school in New York, where he met Bubbe. He taught me his change-up grip!

So generations of Puttermans have either played baseball, or watched baseball, or both. Except for my cousin Becky—she just plays with her cat.

Apparently it took everybody a while to figure out that I had completely left my playoff game because at first they thought I'd disappeared into the bathroom since I have what my grandmother calls a "weakish bladder."

My dad tells her, "Mom, we've talked about this. Nothing's really wrong with Matty's bladder. And he's already outgrowing, ahem—its temperamentality." Dad's a pediatrician, so I trust him. Bubbe mostly trusts him, but with her, instincts run super strong. And since I quit base-ball, her instincts tell her something serious is up with me.

She might be right.

At the game, they checked the bathroom—no Matty. So after a while, Mom *and* Dad started texting me, and my dad hates texting. Plus, he stinks at it.

Mom: Honey! Where are you?

Dad: Matt! Buddy! What gives?

Mom: Honey! Now I'm worried.

Dad: Matt, is your arm okay? Over and out.

Mom: Matty, if you have your phone, please let us know you are okay. Please let us know where you are.

By then I was sitting at our kitchen table at home, trying not to cry. The cool guy in the car with his arm out the window thing was over, and actually, it was never really a thing. I was just trying to sound brave.

I left the game because I didn't know what else to do.

And now I felt bad, *really bad*. The game—*my game*—was going on without me, and I pictured Sammy freaking out at first, wondering where I was. And I pictured Ethan . . .

So I texted back.

Me: I hate baseball. I'm done playing. I've walked home.

After the game, Mom, Dad, and Sammy stood outside my bedroom door, but I was locked in tight.

Sammy knocked on my door for what felt like forever till she gave up, then Dad started in. Mom sent him away and asked if she could help somehow, then stood outside my door taking big breaths in and out for like fifteen minutes.

I didn't open my door for anyone.

The next morning, Sammy slid a note under my door.

Our twin telepathy isn't working anymore.

I didn't write back to her. Truth is . . . our twin telepathy hasn't been working for a good long time. 'Cause if it was, she'd know why I quit.

I don't hate baseball. Not even close!

It's just now that I've said it, and I've told my family that's the reason I quit even though it's not, there's no taking it back. Since I can't tell them the *real* reason I quit.

I can't even tell Sammy yet.

I actually love baseball—I love it more than just about anything. But now the game's all wrapped up in some seriously confusing stuff I can't figure out.

Another dinghy full of hurricane evacuees rushes past our kayaks, and the loud buzz of the motor brings me back to the present. I shift in my seat as we bobble in its wake.

Sammy mutters something over and over while she paddles, but I can't quite make it out. Maybe I don't want to. She glances back at me for a second, her eyes huge and searching, like I have the answer to the question she's trying to ask me.

I turn my face away. I don't have any answers. For her or me or anybody.

I dig my paddle into the water and pull extra hard side to side, like I practiced at summer camp, breaking time with my sister's strokes. Mom's and my kayak lurches forward to take the lead.

But my twin sister's so lost in her thoughts, she doesn't seem to notice I'm passing her by.

Becky

The sky is heavy looking, like a giant bucket of water is about to dump on Houston again. Thank goodness our new house is high and dry in the neighborhood of Bellaire.

I unplug my nightstand lamp and reposition it inside my studio, which is really just the corner of my bedroom. I asked my parents if I could use just one of the spare guest rooms in this ginormous house to make a real studio for my new business, but they said no.

They don't take my passions seriously—no one in my family does. Everyone thinks that I'm always up in my room doing some silly little activity with my cat, but I'm not.

My work with Jess is really important to me. Plus, she's all I have.

Pat! Pat! Pat! Great, the rain is starting up again.

I glance at the big box of decorations in the corner of my room—pink and gold streamers and shiny mylar balloons that say HAPPY 13TH! I'm supposed to have a birthday pool party this Thursday before school starts on Friday, but Hurricane Harvey might ruin it.

Story. Of. My. Life.

But the story is supposed to be great right now, since my bat mitzvah's this fall.

I've been waiting all year for my family to finally focus on *moi*, for conversations around our weekly Shabbat dinners to shift. Instead of Sammy-Matty *this* and Sammy-Matty *that*, it's going to be all about Becky, Becky, Becky!

Do you know what it's like being seven months and fifteen days older than my twin first cousins? It stinks big.

In family pictures before the twins were born, Bubbe and Papa Putterman are cooing at me from cloud nine. I was better than bagels and lox. I was sweeter than raisin challah. I was their first grandchild, and how can you ever top being the first?

I'll tell you how: twins.

If you look at our family pictures after Sammy and Matty are born, it's obvious—no one's even looking at me anymore. That first Passover, everyone's looking at the twins. That fall at Rosh Hashanah, they're still looking at the twins. And at Chanukah, it's still all about the twins.

The perfect, adorable twins.

They're not even perfect, but who's listening to me? If

I say anything, I get the I'm-so-disappointed-in-you look. Like I'm just a jealous person, or like I'm an attention hog or something.

And since I'm oldest—by less than a year, remember, and we're in the same grade—I'm always supposed to be the more mature one. I have to give stuff up or go second. "You go first, Sammy-Matty, I insist." When I do, they never even say thank you!

Things between us used to be better, when we were little—before my family moved out of our cozy house in Meyerland, before Sammy and Matty started playing baseball, before they stopped wanting to hang out with me—we'd run between our houses and play games in our yards like freeze tag and hide-and-seek.

We had so much fun. But they don't give me the time of day anymore.

Ugh, I can't stand them! At least we're not at the same schools, since I go to private, and they go to public. Though I *am* forced to tolerate them at religious school since our families go to the same synagogue.

I reach for a new glue stick for my hot glue gun, and Jess takes that as her cue to stand up and try to leave the studio. "Hold still!" I say and push her rump back down.

She flicks her long, rough tongue at me.

Usually she doesn't mind our sessions since I've been dressing her up since she was a kitten. But with all the thunder, lightning, and rain this week, she's a tad antsy. I know the feeling.

I snap a few pictures with my phone to check the light. Even with my nightstand lamp, shadows fall on her stripy tabby cat fur from the dark, looming sky outside. But maybe they'll lend a more mysterious quality to today's photo session theme, Film Noir, where I've cast Jess as a femme fatale.

You can do a lot with a hot glue gun, I've discovered. I asked my mother to bring me home some fabric scraps from her design clients, and I made Jess a cute little dress and a wide floppy hat out of some shimmery black taffeta.

I wiggle her into her new outfit and assess my work. She looks fabulous. Then I snap away and coo, "Très jolie, Jess!"

She purrs. She likes being the center of attention. We have that in common.

Long story short: I should have known my cousins would still be the main focus of our family, even in my bat mitzvah year.

In late February when the twins' baseball games started, Matty's arm was stronger than ever, something about puberty and increasing muscle mass, *blah*, *blah*, *blah*. He was pitching so great that the whole family was cheering him on at every game. Their excitement over Matty almost overshadowed their excitement for the Astros, and that was something near impossible to do, since the 'Stros led the American League West with a 16–9 hot start in April!

Even I know the Astros are the best team in the league

this year, and I could care less about baseball. But in my family, you kind of absorb the game, since it's everywhere, and talked about all the time.

Plus, I've got a knack for spotting talent where I see it, and the Astros are, by any objective standard, flippin' amazing. Notwithstanding their August doldrums, which I'm sure they're going to turn around soon.

To top it off, Sammy—who was the only 12U girl ballplayer this year, which kind of made her famous even though she totally played it down, how annoying—was their team's best hitter. She actually led the league in home runs!

Then Matty quit baseball during playoffs and all heck broke loose. I overheard my parents speculating that he had a god-awful fight with his best friend and teammate, Ethan, who goes to my school.

I've texted Matty about it, but he's locked up like Fort Knox. I've asked Sammy what the deal is, too, but she's tight-lipped. One of two things: Sammy doesn't know what happened . . . or she knows and she and Matty are doing their twin thing again, where they're an inseparable unit and I'm left out.

Either way, I'm mad at both of them for all the reasons aforementioned.

My door cracks open and my mother pops her head in. "Becky? Are you taking pictures of Jess again?"

I stop gluing. "Umm, yes."

"Shouldn't you be reviewing your prayers and writing

your d'var Torah so you can practice with the rabbi when religious school starts back up?"

"Umm, I have. I've already written a bunch of my speech," I lie, and start gluing again.

"Well . . . Dad got a call from Uncle Greg and he, Aunt Annie, and your cousins are evacuating their home right now. Bubbe and Papa are already safe at the shelter."

"Okay," I say, but she's silent, so I put down my glue gun and glance up at her.

"I just thought you should know, Becky," she says with a disappointed look.

"I *do* know, Mom," I say. "But what can *I* do about it?"

She shakes her head and closes the door.

I know how I sound, but you've got to realize what it's like for me! We're the *Puttermans*, and it's almost impossible to be your own person in this family. It's almost impossible to stand out if you're not extra special, like the twins.

Believe me—I've tried!

By the way, I hate the name Becky. It's not even my name, it's just what everyone started calling me because wasn't it so cute, since Samantha is Sammy and Matthew is Matty and Rebecca can be Becky.

Except I'm not, do you hear me? I'm not Becky! I'm Rebecca, and while I may be a Putterman, I'm still my own person! Rebecca! Rebecca! Rebecca!

No one seems to get that yet, but one way or another, they will soon.

Rain or shine, my bat mitzvah's just around the corner. I'll be in the spotlight at our synagogue. I'll read from the Torah and give my speech on my portion to our entire congregation. I'll become a Jewish adult.

I'll be first again, and my younger cousins, Sammy and Matty, won't.

Sammy

My family kayaks to the church in near silence while rescue and weather helicopters roar overhead.

A woman sits crying on the roof of her almost-submerged car. A packed pickup truck with giant wheels tries to make its way down a side street and gets stuck. Houstonians evacuate their homes in every imaginable flotation device: kayaks, like ours; inflatable beds, rafts, and long metal canoes; even Jet Skis and stand-up paddleboards.

Some people wade through the rising chest-deep water holding suitcases high above their heads. The water's filthy and dangerous, but for them, there's not much choice.

When Bialy sees a dog or a cat afloat like he is, his ears smooth back flat and he growls low, but he doesn't dare jump out.

Thwack! Thwack! Thwack! Matty makes a game of hitting stop signs on each corner with his paddle. On some of the streets, the metal signs are only two feet above the waterline now. The sound is nearly the same as a metal bat connecting with a baseball.

Usually my parents would be all over this kind of behavior. It would get a "Matty, do you think that's absolutely necessary?" But both of our parents stare straight ahead, trancelike. They don't seem to notice; they're on autopilot, too.

I wonder if the water will rise above the signs. I wonder if the water will cover the rooftops on Braeswood Boulevard. I wonder if the water will cover the world, just like the story of Noah's ark.

I catch Matty's eyes to see if he's as scared as I am, but he shrugs me off and looks away. So I pull my paddle side to side, side to side, and try to keep the rhythm of my strokes even.

Finally a double yellow stripe in the road appears through the water below our kayaks. The ground must be higher here.

My dad says, "It's good the whole city's not covered in water, but our neighborhood is totally . . . ruined." My mom's shoulders shake.

I shudder; I've never seen my parents so—hopeless.

We round the corner, and the church comes into view. My grandmother stands under the porte cochere, shifting from foot to foot. The bottom of her skirt is crumpled like it got wet, but the upper part is pressed and crisp, like always. She's squinting with one hand above her face like she's shielding it from the sun—but it hasn't been sunny for days.

I bet she's been waiting there awhile.

"Thank god! They're here!" she calls out in her New York accent. "Ira! Where are you?" She cups her face and yells toward the open door of the church, "Come quick! They're here!"

Papa shuffles through the doorway and stands next to her. He has a little hearing loss, so Mom says thank goodness Bubbe has a voice that carries. He looks like he's been wading in water, too. The lower parts of his pant legs are stained and wrinkled.

My dad paddles harder, sprinting our kayak toward the church in the final stretch. It scrapes against the asphalt parking lot like we're sliding into home plate. He steps out of his kayak into two-inch water and pulls it to a dry stop. "Annie and Matt, get some speed!" he calls.

Then Mom and Matty's kayak lurches onto the asphalt, too.

My grandparents stumble to the water's edge and embrace each one of us as we stretch out of our kayaks.

"Greggy, that's some getup!" my grandfather says, looking at my dad's outfit. He musses Dad's hair like he's a kid and winks at my brother, who wiggles like he's a fish caught on a line. For a second, I imagine scraping off

31

Matty's fishing gear like I'm descaling a floppy, suffocating fish.

My dad wraps his arms around my mom. "I wasn't sure, Annie. . . ." His voice cracks. "That we'd stay safe this time."

She strokes his hair and nods.

Our parents reach for me and Matty and we all hug tight.

Then I notice a huge pile of deflating air mattresses and swimming pool rafts that people floated here on, stacked high under the porte cochere. My fingers and toes start to tingle again.

How did other families stay *safe*, evacuating a Category 4 hurricane—like *that*?

Bubbe takes a deep breath and shakes her head. "Greggy, this hurricane's epic! It's so tragic that our city's built on a swamp!"

My dad nods, and my grandmother reaches for my mom's hand. "Annie doll, I have a great spot staked for our family. Come inside."

I grab my signed baseball from the hull of the kayak with my tingly fingers. Just holding it makes me feel a bit better. I put it in the big pocket of my raincoat, then Matty and I help Papa and Dad unload.

When the kayaks are empty, my dad ties them to a signpost that says RESERVED FOR THE ANDREWS FAMILY. He fumbles over making the knots. "That should do it!" he says, smacking his hands together. "Arks are secured!"

I catch Matty's eyes again and nod to the knots. This time, he doesn't shrug me off.

While Papa and Dad carry our things inside, we walk over to retie our kayaks like we learned at camp, since they would've floated off in the next gust of wind. Then we shuffle into the community hall behind our family.

It's hard to believe that the air inside the hall could be even more humid than the air outside, but it is. It's like breathing through water.

People's stuff is piled waist-high in soggy heaps: sleeping bags, pillows and blankets, small overflowing suitcases, and canvas camping chairs. Everyone's dripping-wet belongings try to dry out in the same enclosed space; the linoleum floor is slick.

Dad's walking away from our spot when we get there, on the phone with Uncle Mike again, telling him we've made it to the shelter safe. He raises his voice and says, "Mikey, what do you mean by *that*?"

I turn to Matty. "Did you remember your phone? I forgot mine!"

He shakes his head.

My mom stands stiff as cardboard in the middle of our shelter spot, taking in all the evacuated families. Little streams of water from her soaked leggings pool around her feet.

"Sit down and rest, Annie," Bubbe says, pointing to a camping chair draped with a beach towel. "It's bone-dry, since we came in the middle of the night." She raises her voice a little. "Didn't want to risk breaking through the roof like the last flood, right, Ira?"

Papa nods.

We all jump when Bialy emits one loud bark. I follow his gaze: my dad steers dripping-wet Mrs. Sokoloff over to our shelter spot by the elbow, her hissing cat in its cage tucked under his arm. He puts Bartholomew as far from Bialy's leashed reach as he can and helps our neighbor into the chair next to my mom.

Dad says, "Esther, I'll call your daughter Amy to let her know you're safe," and Mrs. Sokoloff nods.

Bubbe jumps up and hands her another towel.

"Thank you, Irene," Mrs. Sokoloff says, wrapping it around her shoulders. "Thank you all so much." Then she sighs and peels off her shower cap.

I strip off my yellow raincoat and soggy water shoes and dump them on the edge of our spot, but I hold on to my baseball tight. Then I plop down next to Matty on the floor between all our chairs and glance around the room.

Just like Bubbe said, our spot's a good one. We're as far away from the bathrooms as we can get, which will be hugely important. We're also opposite the wall of the church that's lined with plastic bags filled with relief supplies—pillows, blankets, diapers, bottled water, dog and cat food, and toilet paper.

I look at my parents and grandparents. I look at Matty

and Mrs. Sokoloff. Their eyes are glassy and no one's talking. Now that we're here, we're all waiting, but for what?

I shut my eyes and listen. People retell their evacuation stories, then take big gulping breaths. A woman assures a boy, "We'll be home in no time," with a shiver in her voice. A man sniffles and says that his brand-new dream house is a "total loss."

And I feel like I'm back in our kayak, but this time, we won't make it to the church.

I clutch my ball and squeeze my eyes shut harder. The tips of my fingers go completely numb. I replay my favorite Astros game in my head, and I can almost hear the commentator: "Swing and a drive to the left field . . . way back . . . this one is GOOOONE! The Astros win it!"

The game in my head plays and plays until I'm ready to open my eyes again.

When I do, I see that my dad has taken his feet out of his wet wading boots and has put on a pair of sneakers. My mom's towel-drying her hair and has slipped a dry shirt over her swimsuit. Matty has stripped off his fishing gear and opened the plastic trash bag he brought with him. He's lying on his stomach next to Bialy with his sketchbook and pencils, drawing.

Papa's reading a book, and Mrs. Sokoloff and Bubbe have started a game of gin.

I reach over to pet Bialy, who's finally gone to sleep, and his golden fur warms my fingers.

Some ladies from the church come around with a food cart stacked with foil-wrapped sandwiches and juice boxes, and we take enough for our family and Mrs. Sokoloff.

It almost seems like we're having a picnic, except we're inside a steamy, wet church.

My dad's phone dings, and he says, "Great news, everybody! Mack just texted and our Home Away from Home hasn't taken on much water. There's just a little in the service areas!"

At this news from Mack, our head-of-security friend at Minute Maid Park, a big happy feeling rises inside me. My lips form a small smile, the first in days. I nod to my dad, and his grin breaks as wide as mine.

If there's anything that can make us feel a teensy bit better right now, it's this: we've called the Houston Astros ballpark our Home Away from Home for as long as I can remember.

I open my signed baseball's Ziploc bags and bring the leather up to my nose. It smells like *home*.

Thank goodness our Home Away from Home didn't flood, too.

Matty

Mrs. Sokoloff has taken Bartholomew out of his cage and put him on a leash.

He's dry now, but he doesn't look much different from when he was wet, since he hardly has any fur. Every once in a while, he fixes his giant blue eyes on Bialy, bares his teeth, and runs his long tongue over his whiskers.

I tap her arm. "Excuse me. Do you or your cat need anything?"

Mrs. Sokoloff hugs her towel around her and smiles. "Thank you, dear, but we're all right now."

"Guess I won't need to mow your yard this week, will I?" I mumble.

Her eyes lock with mine. She shakes her head.

I take my sketchbook and pencils out of my trash bag and

stretch out in our spot on my stomach, but my feet stick into the aisle; we're all crammed into the shelter pretty tight.

Somebody near us broadcasts hurricane coverage way too loud on their phone. I wish they'd turn it the heck off. It's not like we don't all know what's happening out there—we all got to this shelter somehow.

The weathercasters drone on and on about how Hurricane Harvey's dumping more than fifty inches of rain on the city of Houston. About all the submerged highways and cars. About the Addicks and Barker reservoirs northwest of the city filling up way too fast.

Now it sounds like there's a panel of speakers—suits going back and forth discussing all the alarming details, just like they did in the Memorial Day flood when I was ten, just like they did in the Tax Day flood when I was eleven. They're probably commenting from like California, New York, or somewhere else that's safe, since they sure don't have Texan accents.

I'll bet their suits are dry.

"What a terrible tragedy, Bill," one guy says to another. "Our damage estimates are soaring! Hurricane Harvey could cost well over a hundred billion dollars, with as many as a hundred thousand homes lost!"

He responds, "Those are heartbreaking numbers, Dan. How can a city, even the size of Houston, ever recoup from such loss?"

What a ridiculous question. We can't.

I mean, my family had some water in our house during those other floods too, but we just needed some new floors, carpet, and baseboards.

This time, I think we're gonna need a heck of a lot more than that.

I glance down at my sketchbook, and blink—a familiar face stares back up at me that I didn't know I was drawing. My eyes shoot around to see if anybody noticed, then I crumple up the page and toss it into my trash bag. But the face is still there, in my head.

It's a face that I think about a lot, even when I try not to. A face that always makes me think about kissing now.

My first kiss happened in sixth-grade language arts last spring, right before Mrs. Allen flipped the lights back on after we watched this documentary about a girl named Malala Yousafzai.

Documentaries are about something real that happens instead of something made up, but they're still movies, so that was cool. And it was our second day watching it, which meant Mrs. Allen wasn't drilling us on vocabulary. So that was cool, too.

Malala's story is pretty sad, so maybe I was crying a little.

I wasn't the only one. A bunch of people were sniffling. A girl who was shot 'cause she wanted to go to school? C'mon. Before I saw the movie, I couldn't even imagine a world where somebody wouldn't think a girl like Malala was perfect.

Maybe I was crying the most. I dunno, but it's possible.

And maybe I started making these noises like say, a big piece of chicken got stuck in my throat.

All I know is that Sammy's friend Amanda really quiet-like scooted her desk closer to mine in the dark—maybe it wasn't so quiet, but with the chicken noise, I couldn't hear much—and reached over and held my hand.

It was nice.

The chicken feeling in my throat started to pass. I wiped my nose with the back of my hand—my other hand, of course—and she didn't seem to mind. Then we just sat there like that watching the movie.

After a while, to tell you the truth, I didn't so much notice that Amanda was holding my hand.

I mean, from what other guys have said, I was supposed to notice. I was supposed to be, like, focused intensely on the fact that a girl was holding my hand and we were actually touching, and wonder—what did it all mean?

Did she like me? Did she want to be my girlfriend or something? Was anybody watching? Naw, too dark.

Etc., etc. You get it.

But that didn't happen. I stopped crying and we watched the movie. And it was nice, that's all. She's nice.

You know how you can tell a movie's ending, when all the story lines start to wrap up and the story gets to its point—well, that was happening. Everybody in class started shifting around in their chairs and stretching, making sure their faces were dry.

I noticed Amanda was squeezing my hand tighter. So what did I do? Well, I squeezed hers back. It seemed like the right thing to do at the time.

Wrong choice.

The movie ended and the screen went dark, and I felt a warm breeze on my ear, so I turned to see where it was coming from.

Also wrong choice.

I turned straight into a pucker. Amanda planted one on my lips, hard and fast, then she real quick dropped my hand and scooted her desk back.

What did it feel like? A cross between the time when I accidentally mashed my lips into my braces on the door-frame of my room, and what I bet it would feel like if I couldn't dodge our two-year-old neighbor, Ronnie, when he grabs both sides of my face and says, "Wet me kiss your wips!"

They say you see stars during a real kiss, one that means something. But I didn't see any, even though environmentally speaking, it woulda been perfect since we were in the pitch-dark.

I also didn't get the woozy sensation, head to toe, that would cause that weak-in-the-knees thing they talk about in gushy teenage movies.

And I didn't want another kiss, that's for sure. One and done is kinda how I felt. I chalked it up to the fact that before that day, I'd never thought of Amanda, you know, *that way*, even though I should've seen the signs. I mean, she'd started looking at me funny when she came over to hang out with Sammy when sixth grade started: super fidgety, extra blinky, *way* too smiley.

Anyhow, when the lights came back on, she was pink in the face. Then she packed up her stuff and bolted from language arts.

Now my second kiss—that one's a whole different story. But I can't talk about it right now.

As we're finishing our sandwiches, a series of hoots and hollers erupts from the corner of the community hall. A man cries at the top of his lungs, "Let's go, Astros! Let's go!" and his cheer echoes across the building.

Sammy scrambles to her raincoat and stashes her signed ball in a pocket. She throws on an Astros baseball cap and threads her damp braid out the back.

My dad grabs my grandfather's hand, and before I can protest, Sammy grabs mine.

"Did you *hear* that, Matty?" she yells. Then the four of us run to the cheers in the corner of the hall.

Becky

By late afternoon, our whole backyard is a swirly brown rectangle. When I look out my bedroom window, I can't see our swimming pool anymore.

My father says it would take two epic hurricanes for our house to flood, since we built it up so high on our lot. But every once in a while, he goes outside in the rain to double-check the water level, like now. He plunges a long stick down to the ground and makes another mark on it with his Sharpie, and frowns.

Even from up here I can see he's running out of stick.

I try another new outfit on Jess and I'm super happy with it. It's a French-inspired ensemble with a silky cape and a tiny pink beret that will stay on her head if I slick her fur down and use a rubber band.

The look's kind of Pink Panther meets Katy Perry.

I start gathering props around my room for another photo session. Then I hear it: my parents' loud voices downstairs in the kitchen. I try to ignore them and keep working with Jess, but I can't—the volume's rising fast, like floodwater pouring into our house.

The hairs on my arms bristle as I walk to the top of the stairs to listen. "You really want the Whole World to stay here with us, Mike?" my mother asks. "The twins and Becky haven't gotten along since they were little, your mother has something to say about practically everything, and you and your brother—"

My father interrupts her. "Just think about it, Deb. They probably won't even stay for very long. And it's baseball season, so it'll be fine. Baseball always brings our family together!"

The Whole World here with us, in our house? Right— like that could ever happen. The Whole World is what my mother calls the extended Putterman family. As in, "The Whole World revolves around those Puttermans," which I've been hearing from her for, like, my whole life. Never mind she's a Putterman, too.

But I get what she means. This is how it usually goes for me.

"What did you say your name is?"

"Becky. Rebecca Putterman."

"Are you—"

"Yes."

"Is your grandmother—"

"Yes."

"Hey, our pediatrician is Dr. Gregory Putterman. Is he—"

"Yes!"

"So, you're related to those amazing twin athletes—"

"Yes! Yes! Yes!"

Just once, I'd like to leave it at Rebecca Putterman, and have that be enough. I'd like to be known for something that's just me, and not the whole world.

I pitched my idea for my exciting new business with Jess to my father recently, and he gave me a piece of advice that I've taken to heart. He said, "Becky, true success lies where innovation meets excellence."

That really resonated with me, you know?

I'm super creative, all my teachers say so. And excellence is attainable if I just put my mind to it. I can work really hard and go the distance for the right project, and I've found one!

This fall's events are going to create a perfect chain reaction.

Number one: my birthday party this week, where I'll get gifts, some of them cash. To be followed by . . .

Number two: my bat mitzvah party this October, where I'll get more gifts, some of them also cash. Which will lead to . . .

Number three: my innovative and excellent plan, which involves a little thing called social media (since I can have an account when I turn thirteen), an exceptional tabby cat named Jess, and my newfound resources, which will buy lots of necessary supplies.

I walk back to my room and scroll through some recent themes from my photo sessions with Jess, trying to ignore the commotion downstairs.

There's Pool Party Jess, where she's wearing cute heart-shaped sunglasses with a hot pink floaty around her middle. There's Catwalk Jess, where she's prancing on a tiny ramp under some bright flashing lights. And of course, there's Bat Mitzvah Jess, where she's sitting on a chair covered in streamers like I'll be in a couple of months when everyone dances the hora at my party.

I know I'm biased—but the photos are really, really good, and I can't wait to post them.

Someone out there will think they're special like I do, even if my family doesn't. Even if I have to remind my mother over and over that I need more fabric scraps. Even if my dad shakes his head every time I dress Jess up.

Someone out there will think that what I do my studio isn't silly at all . . . won't they?

My parents' voices are still way too loud. Their discussion sounds like a big deal now. Like floodwater rising even faster.

I slip Jess out of her outfit and nestle my face into her warm fur. She purrs, a steady hum that almost drowns out the fuss in the kitchen. When she's done cuddling, she stretches her front claws into my shoulder until I place her on her little cat bed. Then she immediately curls up into a tight, protected ball and falls asleep since sometimes our sessions kind of tire her out.

"I love you, Jess," I whisper.

I always wanted a sister, but I never got one. The kind of sister that was really a best friend. I imagined we'd share a room, and we'd finish each other's sentences. I imagined we'd trade clothes and fix each other's hair for parties. And when our parents worked late, we'd sit together on one of our twin beds and listen to Katy Perry songs over and over.

And it wouldn't be like now, where my parents are too busy to notice me—my father with his important business deals and triathlon training, and my mother with her job as a high-end designer and her tennis matches. Where even when we're home, we each keep to our own corner of this ginormous house, and I'm usually by myself.

If I had a sister, it would be us, always together. I imagined her name would be Jessica.

I walk over to my door and crack it open. My parents are way too quiet now. I'm worried that something important is being decided without me. I head downstairs.

My father is talking on the phone in the kitchen.

I put on a disguise of helpfulness and start unloading the dishwasher. Sometimes spritzing the countertops or folding a basket of laundry works—any assistance my mother can't, in her right mind, refuse. I'm good at paying attention without looking like I'm paying attention. It's another one of my talents.

"Of course, Greg. Of course!" my father says, nodding his head. "As long as you need. It goes without saying—we're family."

My mother stands on the other side of our center island and glares at him.

Even I can tell what she's thinking, and I'm no expert on relationships since I've never had a boyfriend. Her glare says, "You really should talk with me some more before you keep talking, Mike!"

But he ignores her. "I'm just so glad you're all safe with your houses so far under . . . oh my god. But I'm still pissed you didn't come here before the storm like we talked about. I know, I know! It doesn't do any good to say that now. What? Of course, I remember how hard it was evacuating Hurricane Rita when the twins were babies! It was hard with Becky, too!" His voice cracks. "Listen, Greggy. Hang tight. I'm coming to the shelter in the Suburban to get all of you just as soon as the weathermen give the all-clear that the water's receding, okay? Please tell Mom and Dad."

My mother's rubbing her temples in tiny circles with her fingertips, resigned, her eyes taking in the deep gray sky out the window.

Apparently the Whole World is coming to stay with us soon. Then they'll be in our house . . . indefinitely.

Sammy

About twenty people are huddled around four laptops lined up on a plastic folding table in the corner of the community hall. They've got the volume on the computers cranked up, and someone's detangling a bunch of wires, trying to hook up some portable speakers.

The Astros fans in the church are streaming the afternoon getaway game in Anaheim against the Los Angeles Angels!

"C'mon!" I pull Matty around some tall people standing near the back of the group to find an open spot front and center, while my dad and grandfather find an empty space off to the side.

A commercial cuts back to the game, and we're instantly glued to the screens.

Cameras pan the crowd in Angel Stadium, where small groups of Astros fans hold up makeshift signs that say things like HOUSTON STRONG! and GO AWAY, HURRICANE HARVEY! and WE'RE PRAYING FOR YOU, HOUSTON!

"Houston Strong," I whisper to Matty, and he nods.

It's the first inning, and José Altuve's at bat. I hold my breath as he hits one deep into left field and . . . it's gone! It's his twentieth home run, and the 'Stros take a two-nothing lead!

I start jumping up and down, and I'm not the only one. A hurricane-force feeling rushes through the community hall. More people drift over from their spots to watch. Our small crowd grows!

I start rooting, hard, and focus all my thoughts on my team.

When I was little, I used to cheer my heart out at games. I'd yell and yell and the next day my mom would say I sounded like her great-aunt Martha, who's a chain smoker. She'd tell me if I kept it up, I might always have a raspy voice.

My dad would tell me not to worry, and he knows best since he's a pediatrician. But he also said, "Sammy baby, there's no need to hurt yourself. Your superfan cheers are special. They'll reach your team wherever they are."

And he's right—my cheers always reach my team.

It doesn't matter if the Astros are down on the field at

Minute Maid Park and I'm in the stands, or if they're in another city at an away game, like now, in Los Angeles, and I'm watching them on TV.

My cheering matters.

I've been tuned in to my team all season long, and it's mostly working. While the Astros still have their best record ever, they've lost and won about the same number of games in August. They need my cheering now more than ever!

Maybe it sounds silly, but think of it like this: you make a wish on your birthday candles as you blow them out, or you stroke your lucky rabbit's foot before you run a big race.

Superfan wishes are powerful, just like that.

By the fifth inning, the Astros are up 4–3. Then the Angels hit one over George Springer's head and take their first lead of the game.

Now almost everyone in the hall has gathered in the corner. My mom, Bubbe, and Mrs. Sokoloff. Parents with their kids hoisted high on their shoulders. Older and younger people, and everyone in between.

Some people are standing on their toes to get a better view, and some people have brought their camping chairs to sit nearby and listen, even though they can't see the small screens.

We're all cheering for the Houston Astros. Together.

A newscaster cuts in during what would normally be a commercial break. He clears his throat, then says, "Our hearts go out to the fans in Houston who are evacuating flooded homes right now. Bob, can we cut to the footage?"

Everyone leans in closer as images of our city begin to scroll.

Aerial helicopter footage shows Beltway 8, the main toll highway around our city, covered in water to the tops of stranded 18-wheeler trucks. It shows the Addicks and Barker reservoirs full to the brim. In some neighborhoods, floodwaters reach the eaves of the houses now.

All around our city, what used to be land is now covered in water.

People around us start to sniffle and hug each other. A woman wipes the tears from a man's face and says, "We've been here before . . . we'll be all right."

I wrap my arms around my sides tight and scoot closer to Matty so our shoulders touch. He's staring at the screens, like everyone, but he's not reacting like we are. His face is flat and still, and his eyes have gone glassy.

After the news break, I turn back to the game and root for my team even harder. A win would mean everything to our flooded city!

And with Matty still not cheering, I have to cheer for both of us.

The crowd in the shelter roots louder and harder, too. They cheer and cheer, and it works.

By the eighth inning, the Astros have the bases loaded. Then they get a three-run triple for a 7–5 lead!

Everyone's smiling again. We're all wet and soggy, and we've probably lost almost everything we have—but we haven't lost the Astros.

Our team is here for us, still.

At the next Angels at-bat, the Astros get 'em out easy, and it's a ballgame! We win our seventy-ninth game of the regular season! Only thirty-two games to go!

I throw my hands in the air and start jumping up and down again. I could bounce to each corner of the community hall and back. I could jump up and down all night. "Way to go, Astros! Way to go, Astros! Houston Strong! Houston Strong!"

My cheers catch on, and soon the crowd is jumping and yelling "Houston Strong!" right along with me. I cheer my heart out, and don't care if I sound raspy tomorrow, or even the day after that. Every cheer is so worth it.

I finally stop to take a breath and look at everyone around me.

Mom, Bubbe, and Mrs. Sokoloff are holding hands. My dad stands hip to hip with my grandfather as he watches the final replays on the laptops. He tries to shake Papa's hand, but before he knows it, Papa rocks to his tippy toes and plants a kiss on his cheek instead. Then he musses Dad's hair again, and they both start laughing.

A white-haired lady with a little girl perched on her shoes dances to music only they can hear. The man next to them tilts his head to the ceiling, and the woman with him strokes the nape of his neck, and he smiles. A tiny poodle peeks its head out of her purse, and it's smiling, too.

Everyone is smiling like they'll never stop.

My cheeks hurt from smiling. My calves are sore from jumping. I stare at the final score on the laptops, 7–5, and my heart soars.

I close my eyes and listen to the cheering, and for a few minutes, it's almost like Hurricane Harvey never happened, and my house isn't underwater. It's almost like I've been transported to the game at Angel Stadium and I'm not in a shelter at all.

With my eyes closed, just listening, it's almost like all of us are there.

I imagine us in the stands at Anaheim. Dad and Papa have bits of peanut shells stuck to their shirts and Diet Cokes at their feet. I've got my glove on tight, and I'm ready for a big foul ball.

The man and lady with the poodle are sitting in front of us. She's hanging on his shoulder and whispering in his ear. Every once in a while, he *woot, woot, woot*s and pumps his fist in the air in a big circle and she pulls back for a second. They don't have their dog, of course.

The white-haired lady and the little girl are eating bright blue cotton candy. Their fingers are blue, and their smiley lips are blue, and even their teeth and the tips of their noses are blue. The lady winks when they take their last big bites, then she hands the little girl a wet wipe.

And my twin brother Matty—he's next to me in the stands, too.

We're doing what we always do at games: we're eating sloppy chili dogs with extra ballpark cheese; we're belting out "Take Me Out to the Ball Game" in the seventh-inning stretch; we're bumping fists and hips and shooting up from our seats in unison and standing and cheering until all the people in the rows behind us growl, "Sit down, kids, will ya?" But we don't care.

Because cheering for our team means everything, and maybe they've forgotten how important it is to never stop rooting, but *we* know. We'll never forget.

But my brother . . . did forget.

We were a twin team before, too—me and Matty. We were Sammy-Matty, and both of our 12U team jerseys said PUTTERMAN across the back. He didn't just forget about our 12U team. He didn't just forget about the Astros.

Matty forgot about us.

Then I'm back at our last playoff game again, standing on first base, punching my mitt, waiting for Matty to take the mound. And everyone's staring at me like I know where my brother is, why he left. Like we still have a connection.

I open my eyes.

Matty's clutching his pencil, swishing his hand back and forth in the air like he's recording something. But I don't think he sees what I see. He doesn't close his eyes and feel like the Astros have taken us out of the hurricane, not for a second.

I look down at my hand. There's no glove. It's underwater now, too.

I scream, "Dad! Dad!" and my face scrunches up tight.

He rushes over. "Oh, Sammy, oh, baby," he says, scooping me into his arms.

"We won, Dad, we won," I sob into his chest. "But we didn't. We really didn't."

"I know, honey," he whispers into my hair. "I know."

He pulls away and tears start running down his face, but this time, they're not like his tears at the game in my nightstand photo. It's not for the Astros he's crying.

My dad's face is mixed up happy-sad since our team may have won, but our city has lost.

I'm all mixed up now, too. My tears come faster and faster like the rain outside, like the overspilling reservoirs and bayous.

I cry for the Astros win in Anaheim, so far away. I cry because we're in a humid, wet shelter. I cry because the roof of our house may be covered in floodwater now. But even more than all that, I cry because Matty doesn't cry with me.

He's been transported someplace, too—but it's nowhere I am.

I will Matty to look into my eyes. I want to use our twin telepathy to explain to him why Dad and I are mixed up happy-sad, why we've been smiling and crying at the very same time.

I say, "Matty? Matty!" but he just looks down at his

sketchbook and the pencil in his hand. He doesn't even hear me. We're in different worlds now.

Maybe our twin telepathy is broken for good.

His eyes dart around the room for a second, then he turns and walks away from us just like when he left our playoff game and walked away from baseball forever.

But this time, I watch him go.

Matty

When I finally get back to my family's spot, it's past dinnertime and my mom and dad are laying out sleeping bags, pillows, and blankets, making beds for everybody.

I guess we're spending the night here.

Sammy and I were supposed to start seventh grade tomorrow, but I'll bet our Meyerland public school's under water now, too.

"Where did you go?" Sammy grills me.

I hug my sketchbook and pencils to my chest. "Bathroom," I lie. Usually the mention of the facilities is enough to make anybody in my family stop asking questions.

My sister searches my eyes for a second, then she lowers her face. Her knuckles get white as she squeezes her signed baseball. Our twin telepathy is working perfectly right now—Sammy knows I wasn't really in the bathroom.

But I don't want her in my head anymore.

I turn away from her, and my mom hands me another sandwich, a juice box, and a banana, since I missed the second food cart that came around. Then I sink down to the floor next to Bialy. He's snoozing again and Mom's got his leash looped onto her camp chair so he can't go anywhere, but every once in a while, his legs run in place.

I dunno where he dreams he's going, since we're all trapped here. But sleeping through all this is a really smart choice.

Bialy got his name because he's a bagel-shop dog. When Sammy and I were five, our parents did their usual Sunday morning bagel run, and there was the most incredible thing at the shop that day: a litter of golden retriever puppies.

The owner's dog was their mother, and he thought that the best way to find homes for them was to bring them to his shop on a Sunday.

Boy, was he right.

They were all nestled in a wire enclosure in the front corner of the store, and people were standing around eating and *ooh*ing and *ahh*ing. A few kids were whining to their parents. "Please . . . I need a puppy. I really, really need one."

I may have been one of those kids.

'Cause the minute I stroked Bialy's soft golden fur and put my hand on his round little chest and felt his heartbeat, that's how I felt: I needed him.

I became inconsolable, and Sammy was alternately jumping up and down outside the enclosure and climbing in and rolling around with the puppies and nuzzling them and squealing. The shop owner told Mom and Dad to get a handle on things if they wanted to stay there and eat.

Sammy and I worked on Mom, since she's the most likely one to cave to us, still. Eventually she got that soft look on her face that Dad can't resist. She scooted up close to him and started hanging on him, and said, "Oh my, Greg. Just look at these *babies*!"

There was no way we were leaving without a puppy.

We named him Bialy—which is like a bagel without a hole. At the time, we all just thought it was a cute name that would always remind us of his beginnings at the shop. But before we got him, we had a hole—our family—and Bialy filled it.

Right as I'm finishing my sandwich, his eyes pop open. He jumps up and starts sniffing and digging through our stuff, grunting and turning it over with his nose. He gets this desperate look in his eyes. He's practically dragging my mom around on her chair.

"What's the matter, boy?" I ask. Then I get this sick feeling in the pit of my stomach.

I say, "Dad! Did we bring Bialy's tennis ball?" He looks confused.

"Mom!" I say. "Do you know if we brought Bialy's ball from the house?" She stares at me and blinks.

Bialy's breathing heavy and panting now, and his furry dog eyebrows keep shooting up above his big brown eyes. He starts whining and walking in circles again, just like he did in our living room when it was filling with floodwater.

My mom says, "So much was going on, Matty. . . ."

And Dad says, "We talked about it, but I'm just not sure."

Sammy claps a hand over her mouth.

Bubbe sideways-looks at Papa like *Here we go—all heck's about to break loose!*

She's probably right.

I start digging with Bialy. I dump everything out of our duffels, and I sift inside our coolers. I feel under the blankets and sleeping bags that we've laid over our small square of floor. I check all our pockets—in every raincoat and every pair of pants and shorts—and even Bubbe and Papa's pockets. I put my hand into every pair of shoes to see if somehow Bialy's favorite ball is here.

Right now, Bialy's ball is a tennis ball, but before that it was a lacrosse ball. And when he was little, it was an orange squeaky ball. Sometimes he likes baseballs because they're leather, and they smell like his rawhide jerky. But we redirect him because baseballs are for baseball, and that's really important in our family.

Bialy loves his tennis ball so, so much. He carries it with him everywhere. He even sleeps with it. It's usually covered in slobber from all his mouthing and it's kinda smelly, but we don't care.

My mom calls his ball his lovey. It's kinda what he's about.

Bialy starts panting harder. He whips around and around in circles with his tail tucked between his legs. "Bialy, stop!" I say. "Mom! Dad! Get him to stop!"

They try, but it's no use.

When he's exhausted, he collapses on his side and his tongue hangs on the floor. I put my hand on his chest—his heart's beating way too fast.

I slide my feet into my fishing boots and run for the blinking red exit sign at the front of the community hall. My dad calls, "Matt! Wait! What are you . . ."

And I call back, "Kayaks!"

Outside the church, it's already dim: the sun's about to set and the parking lot lights have flipped on. Falling raindrops look like party glitter in the artificial light. But this—the hurricane and the shelter—is no party I wanna be at.

Our kayaks are still tied up where we left them. They're floating up near the signpost now.

I don't have my fishing waders on over my pajama bottoms, but I rush through the chilly floodwater anyway. I have to find Bialy's ball!

My dad follows me outside. He yells from under the porte cochere, "Matt! Be careful!" and stands watch.

I run my hands inside both hulls, over and over. But there's nothing there. Bialy's ball didn't make it.

I spin around in a slow circle, and my eyes take in all

the flooded houses, sidewalks, and streets. Our neighbor-hood didn't make it either. Everything is gone: our cars, our house, our life like it was before—everything's been lost in the hurricane.

"Dad?" Big chicken sounds fill my throat again. "W-what will Bialy do without his ball?"

Then my dad is next to me with his hand steady on my back. "He'll find another, Matt," he says. "He'll be okay."

We stand like that for a few minutes, the glitter raindrops damp on our faces, the floodwater wicking cold against our skin through our clothes.

"Will he really, Dad?" I ask. "Will Bialy really be okay?"

He nods. "And we will, too, Matty," he says. "We will, too."

But when I look up into his eyes, for the first time ever, he doesn't seem so sure.

Becky

Tuesday after breakfast, my father shuts his laptop and says, "Okay, girls, I'm going to get them! Every single site I searched says the floodwaters are down significantly this morning. It's all clear!"

He turns to my mother. "Deb, where do we keep the keys to the Suburban anyway?"

She pushes back from the kitchen table and goes to find them while my father makes sure his phone is charged and slides on his Galveston beach water shoes, just in case he gets stuck. Then he smiles big at us as he backs out of our garage like he's going on an off-road adventure.

Our Suburban is the extra car my parents bought for family road trips we never take. The purchase was really my father's idea. "An extravagance on top of all our other extravagances," my mother's noted more than once.

She frowns as she pushes the button to close the garage door after he's backed out, then heads upstairs to start making spare beds. I follow her up.

I guess *never* isn't completely accurate. We tried taking a road trip for the first time this summer, just the three of us. We drove to Colorado. It was an important attempt for a number of reasons.

Number one: we wanted to beat the Houston summer heat wave. Since our city's just about at sea level on the Gulf of Mexico, it heats up in the summers well over a hundred degrees, but that's only part of the problem. The real problem is the humidity, which my hair absolutely hates.

Number two: we were taking a break from the larger Putterman family, a reset from weekly Shabbat dinners at our house. *Time for just our little family*, my father said, *time to just be us.* I said that our family included Jess, of course, and after some negotiating—she got to come! Her fur hates humidity, too.

Number three: we were addressing my mother's recent obsession with the passage of time. During sixth grade, a pattern emerged. She'd look at me and cry, "You're practically a woman, with your bat mitzvah coming next year!" Then she'd look at my father and say, "Mike, are you listening? We need to become a glue family before she goes to college! We need to bond!"

A glue family, I learned, is a family where the kids want

to keep in touch after college. Not a family where everyone spreads out across America and hardly ever calls or visits each other, like my mother's family did. Where they hardly get together and when they do, they barely have much to say because they barely know each other.

I don't think the three of us are the sticky type either, but I don't say it.

But what do my parents expect, anyway? I'm the only one in our family who's ever bought any glue!

Long story short: my parents worked the whole way to Colorado and back and there wasn't any bonding. My father negotiated the biggest deal of his career and my mother put together a winning proposal for a semi-famous new client.

Jess and I watched videos and listened to podcasts in the wayback of the Suburban and got terribly carsick. And after we got back, we all needed a reset from our road trip. We came home completely unglued! It was très mauvais.

My mother calls down the hall, "Becky, can you please make up the spare bed in your room?"

I freeze. *The spare bed in my room, with my studio?* "For who, Mom?" I squeak.

She pops into my doorway with an armful of blankets and sheets. "For your cousin Sammy, who did you think?"

"I just thought that since our house is so big, we'd have enough space for her to sleep in another room."

My mother shakes her head. "Count, Becky. We have the pullout in your father's library for Matty, and the two spare bedrooms for your aunt and uncle and grandparents.

And . . ." She shakes her head again. "They're bringing Mrs. Sokoloff. Apparently, her daughter Amy just had major surgery. Your aunt and uncle aren't sure when she can come from Florida to pick her mother up."

I stare at her, blank. "Who's Mrs. Sokoloff again?"

"You remember, Becky . . . your cousins' elderly neighbor who came to our last Yom Kippur break fast and Passover? The one who makes that amazing rugelach and matzoh candy. I guess she'll take the living-room sofa."

I nod. Oh, yeah, her desserts *were* amazing.

Then, before I can help myself, I blurt, "Our sectional sofa is huge, so maybe Sammy could take one end and Mrs. Sokoloff could take the other."

My mother frowns and gives me another I'm-so-disappointed-in-you look. "Becky, it's an epic hurricane. It's time for everyone to put forth their best self, don't you think?"

I nod. I guess everyone means me since other people in my family—I'm not saying names—think they're clearly their very best selves since they're baseball stars.

They think I'm the only one who's not.

But like I said, Sammy and Matty aren't as perfect as they appear to be.

Take their relationship, for instance: Sammy's always the leader and Matty's always the follower. He can't even get a word in edgewise. It's always, "Matty likes *this* and Matty hates *that*."

If that's how they like it, that's *their* business, but I'm not about to let Sammy boss *me* around.

But every year, for the four and a half months when Sammy and I are the same age, she tries. When we were five, she insisted she was the teacher and Matty and I were her students for the whole lousy summer!

It got really old. *I* wanted to be the teacher. *I* wanted to be the one standing up at the chalkboard while Sammy and Matty sat down. *I* wanted to be the leader. *I* wanted to shine.

I remember wrestling Sammy to the ground for the chalk. I remember pulling a big chunk of her hair out near her temple when I yanked off the teacher glasses with the silver chain, and the angry red bald spot that was left. I remember Sammy screaming, then Matty screaming with her.

And I especially remember how everyone looked at me, like I was the bad one and they were the good ones. Even my own parents, who are supposed to be on my side, always.

I've seen the way Sammy catches Matty's eyes when I start talking about my photos of Jess at Shabbat dinner. I feel what passes between my cousins even if the adults can't. It's like there's invisible glass between us and they're on the inside and I'm always out.

And the most hurtful part is . . . Sammy seems to like it that way.

I pull the comforter off my spare twin bed and get some sheets out of my closet. The whole time, I stomp around, hoping my mother can hear me.

When the rest of my family gets here, I'm sure it'll be like it usually is when they come over, where everyone's paired up. Bubbe has Papa, my mother has my father, Uncle Greggy has Auntie Annie, Sammy has Matty, and who do I have? Who's there for me? No one!

At least I have my cat.

I make up the bed and clear off a few shelves in my closet and a few drawers in my dresser for my cousin. I try to put my best self forward.

But that's all Sammy's getting, this little part of my room. The studio is mine.

I tell myself that even though the Whole World's coming to stay with us, indefinitely, at least here in my corner . . . things will stay normal.

My studio is the only place in this ginormous house where I feel like it's easy to be my very best self, where I feel okay. It's the only place where I'm Rebecca, and I don't have to try to be Becky for anyone.

Sammy

The church's pastor makes a big announcement. Today, everyone in the shelter will get moved to the football stadium, where there are ample relief supplies and plenty of cots.

Some people pack their things in a hurry and crowd outside under the porte cochere for the first shuttles to arrive. Some people linger at their spots, a little attached. Either way, there are hugs and unexpected tears all around. There are *thank you*s and phone numbers exchanged.

We've been here less than two days, but our shelter neighbors feel like new friends. Bubbe and Mrs. Sokoloff have been inseparable with the older lady from the spot next to ours. They'd never met her before the hurricane, even though she lives close by.

"You play mah-jongg?" Bubbe asks the lady, right before the next wave of shuttles arrives, and she nods. "Then, doll," my grandmother says, "I have an opening in my group with your name on it!"

My mom has been quiet since Sunday night. After the Anaheim game, hurricane coverage ran over the laptops in the corner for hours. We all saw the aerial photos of Meyerland as the floodwaters finally crested—only a sea of rooftops remained.

I'd never cried so hard or so long. But now I'm finally drying out like Houston.

Matty's been quiet, too. He disappears to his secret spot with his sketchbook and pencils again this morning, and when he gets back, I ask, "What have you been working on?"

"Nothing important," he says, and knots his pencils and book back into his trash bag.

My dad walks outside with his phone and comes back smiling right before lunch. "Mike's on the way! His Suburban is an eight-seater, so we'll only need one trip!"

I look around our spot. There's not much here—just some empty coolers, stinky duffels, damp, mildewy bedding, and stained camping chairs. Everything we have left should fit into my uncle's car just fine.

My grandmother strains forward on her chair, almost tumbling off. "Ira! Did you hear? Mikey's coming!"

"Great!" Papa says, and starts packing his things.

Uncle Mike pulls up to the church, grinning ear to ear.

He's like a summer camp counselor directing seven tired campers onto the bus home after the long session. He puts Mrs. Sokoloff and her hissing cat in the front seat, and Mom, Matty, and me in the wayback. Bubbe and Papa sandwich in the middle row, with panting Bialy at their feet, and leave room for my dad.

Dad and Uncle Mike load our dirty gear in the trunk and strap our two kayaks up top, and Dad swings in next to his parents. Then off we go. Thank goodness we aren't going far, since we actually barely fit.

It's still drizzling and misting outside. Brays Bayou rushes with brown water, still swollen near its banks, but the bridges running over it are visible again. My uncle navigates us around stalled-out cars that line some of the roads, around intersections where cars are still partly submerged in floodwater.

I hope whoever was in them made it out safely.

I close my eyes and see water covering the street we're driving on, even though there isn't any. How could it all come and go so fast? How can some parts of the city be back to normal and some parts . . . I shiver . . . be how I imagine our house is now?

Even though the streets are mostly clear all the way to my aunt and uncle's house, there's mud, sticks, and debris everywhere. Waterlines mark some of the houses in Bellaire, too, but the flooding wasn't nearly as bad here as it was in Meyerland. There's not as much total loss.

We pull into their garage and start to unload while Aunt Deb and Becky stand in the doorway.

My cousin shifts from foot to foot, and my aunt presses her lips with her fingers. She raises her eyebrows at Uncle Mike as we unload our dirty gear.

He shuffles his feet and turns to my dad. "Uhh, Greg? No need to, uhh, bring the dirty stuff inside. We can wash it in batches."

Dad nods and starts stacking our stuff against the garage walls. "Sure, Mikey, whatever works," he says, getting a little teary. My uncle pats his back, and my dad says, "We're just so glad to be here."

I hug my duffel to my chest—there's no way I'm leaving it in the garage, dirty and stinky or not. Everything I have left is in it: my raincoat, my change of clothes, my Astros hat, my baseball, my . . . I guess that's about it.

But it's not nothing. It's just almost nothing.

We head inside to the living room and sink into the big sectional sofa, exhausted. My mom lets Bialy off his leash, and he runs around sniffing all the corners; Mrs. Sokoloff lets Bartholomew out of his cage, and he fixes his big blue eyes on Bialy and hisses.

Aunt Deb brings a tray of lemonade and cookies out to the coffee table and takes a long look at all of us. "I'm just so sorry." She nods to Uncle Mike and Becky. "*We* are just so sorry. You can all stay as long as you need to." She glances at Mrs. Sokoloff for a split second, but then she continues. "Our home is your home."

My parents sit smushed together on the sofa, tightly holding hands.

Aunt Deb sits down next to them. "Maybe the flooding in your part of Meyerland isn't as bad as you think."

My dad shakes his head. "I don't know, Deb, but we saw some footage and, uhh . . ." His voice cracks. "Our neighborhood was hit way harder this time than the last two floods. Mom and Dad's house probably took on a bit less water than ours and Mrs. Sokoloff's, but we'll find out soon enough."

Uncle Mike stands, feet apart, arms crossed firmly over his chest. "The Suburban is ready again when you are, Greg. Maybe the two of us should go in first."

It's like he's shifted his role from summer camp counselor to special ops coordinator now. I wonder what he'll be next. I smile at Matty and try to tell him with our telepathy how funny our uncle is. But he just raises his eyebrows at me and shakes his head, like he doesn't understand me at all. Becky's eyes dart between us.

Bubbe clears her throat and stands up. "Well, speaking of our houses, Ira and I have a quick announcement!" Papa smiles.

My dad and his brother shudder.

"We've decided we aren't going back to the Meyerland house, ever," she says. "At our age, three floods in three years are more than enough. Thank goodness our photos and heirlooms have stayed in storage!"

Aunt Deb makes a noise between a gasp and a yelp, and Uncle Mike's voice gets high. "Dad, Mom—where is it you think you're going?"

Bubbe gives him a stern look and points a finger at the floor. "Here, Michael! Where else would we be going? You have plenty of room and we'll be no trouble at all. We're so very quiet."

My aunt runs her fingers over her eyebrows and pulls her lips into a line. "I'll be in our bedroom, Michael," she says, hurrying from the room.

I smile at Matty again. We've never heard anyone call our uncle Mike Michael, and now it's two times in a row!

But Matty doesn't understand me this time either. He crosses him arms, shakes his head, and turns away.

"Hey . . ." Becky says, her eyes narrowing, still darting between us. "Are you two mad at each other or something?"

The whole room goes quiet, and everyone frowns, especially my parents.

Our awkward silence ends with Bialy's loud barks when he notices two cats approaching each other across the living room.

I do a double take as Becky's cat, Jess, sideways-scoots up against Mrs. Sokoloff's cat and practically roars like a tiger. Her tail flicks back and forth, then she starts licking the side of his wrinkly, hairless face.

Becky shrieks and scoops her up. "Oh my god, Jess! Eww! *What* are you doing?" She scrunches her nose at her dad. "Is that a cat? Is it sick? Where's all its fur?"

Uncle Mike gives her a stern look.

Mrs. Sokoloff says, "He's a hairless variety, dear—a sphynx. His name is Bartholomew."

Becky holds her cat away from her, eye to eye, and scowls. "Jess, I absolutely forbid you from socializing with that . . . *that creature*, ever again!"

Aunt Deb clears her throat. She's back in the living room. Her hair's swept off her neck and she's wearing a fresh coat of lipstick. "Maybe everyone should get settled where they'll be sleeping before dinnertime," she says. "I'm sure we could all use a rest. I know I can. Becky, why don't you get Sammy set up in your room?"

Becky clings to her cat and doesn't budge, and I sink deeper into the sofa—maybe I'll just disappear into the cushions.

"As in, right now, Becky," my aunt says.

"C'mon, Jess," my cousin says, and stalks up the stairs.

I'm still sinking. "Go on after her, honey," Aunt Deb says shaking her head, and I ease up off the sofa.

Upstairs, I stop at the entrance to Becky's room. "Wow. I haven't seen your room since . . ."

Becky gives me her first smile. "Well, my mother *is* a successful designer, you know." She sweeps her hand from one wall to the next. "*This* is my big present, since I'm having a *big* birthday this week. Isn't it fabulous?"

I nod and take it all in. Becky's room looks like something out of a magazine.

It has wall-to-wall hot-pink-and-purple geometric carpet and shimmery purple curtains that pool on the floor. It has twin canopy beds with matching fabrics, separated by a silver nightstand with sparkly cut-glass knobs. There's even a miniature matching four-poster bed near the corner of her room, where Jess has curled up.

It's nothing like my room is—or was—with my Houston Astros comforter and my favorite players' posters lining my walls.

I dump my dirty duffel on the bed closest to the door, sit down, and ignore Becky's grimace. "Why do you have two beds now?" I ask.

"You know—for sleepovers." She frowns at my duffel. "Not for something like *this*."

"Aren't I sleeping over?" I say. When we were little, Becky always wanted me to sleep over. We'd zip our sleeping bags together on the floor of her room and tell each other scary stories by flashlight until Aunt Deb made us stop. It was so much fun!

I'm not sure how everything changed. It just did.

"It's not the *same*, Sammy." Her fingers clench her hips. "You're my *cousin*."

Becky makes a show of taking a deep breath. "Okay, you can sleep here," she says, gesturing to the bed I'm already sitting on. "And there's an empty drawer in my dresser and some space in my closet." She glances at a small pink-and-purple pile on a shelf. "My mom said I should put some old clothes aside for you since yours are gone now."

I gulp and nod, then walk into the closet. I can't imagine wearing any of the clothes in the pile.

"You still have Itty Kitty!" I say, taking what used to be Becky's favorite stuffed animal down from a shelf.

"Of course I have her! She was my favorite cat . . . before Jess."

I stroke Itty Kitty's super-soft synthetic fur, like Becky let me do once when I was at her house and I skinned my knee. And maybe once more, when Matty played over at Ethan's every day for two whole weeks after I told him that three was a crowd and I wanted to have a girls-only play-date, just me and Becky. And maybe once, or twice more, after that.

Becky grabs her. "You've touched Itty Kitty enough, Sammy. And don't touch anything in my studio, okay?" she says, pointing to the far part of her room.

My eyes drift to the corner. There's a small area with some white poster board tacked on the walls and spread over the carpet. A little table with a bouquet of flowers and a miniature chair sits inside it.

There's also a tall set of shelves next to the poster board area, overflowing with all sorts of props, like the kinds they have at bar and bat mitzvah party photo booths, but smaller sized: short neon boas; a tiny black top hat; a miniature cane; doll-sized, rainbow clown hair and a cowboy hat; and some glittery Mardi Gras masks. What does she do with all this *stuff*?

"Your what?" I ask.

She barks, "My *studio*, Sammy! It's where Jess and I do our *work*!" Then she storms out the door.

I don't know how I'm going to stay with Becky in her room for very long. Her *studio*? What the heck is it, anyway? That little corner of her room? And what does she mean by her *work*? I won't call playing baseball my work unless I somehow become the first woman to play in the major leagues. And even then, baseball is still a game . . . it's just the best game.

I flop down onto my frilly new bed. We're polar opposites, me and Becky. We have been since Matty and I started T-ball when we were five years old.

I'm all about grassy green ballparks and sand in my cleats. I'm about ground-in red clay stains on my white uniform in all the right places. I'm about being a good sport whether we win or lose, and always being a team player. And I'm about cheering on the Astros with my brother, since we're a twin team. At least, we used to be.

Becky's about holing herself up in her room all the time with her cat, even right after Shabbat dinners when we're still over. She's about dropping silly French words that she learns online like she knows what she's talking about. And most of all, Becky's not about baseball. She's—I stare at the props on the shelves again—she's nothing like me at all.

We don't have a single thing in common and we never will. Game over.

When I get downstairs, Mrs. Sokoloff has fallen asleep on the sectional. "Is she still breathing?" Becky asks, and her dad gives her another stern look.

Bubbe takes over Aunt Deb's kitchen to make us dinner like she does every Shabbat. We hold our breath when she opens the refrigerator and says, "Deborah, where do you keep all your *food*?"

My aunt replies, "Irene, you are still the jokester, even after what you've just been through," and heads upstairs to reapply her lipstick, I'm sure.

We eat around the sectional, watching the Houston Astros play a home game against the Texas Rangers down in Tampa Bay because Minute Maid Park is closed from the hurricane. Our team loses big, 12–2, and it puts everyone in an even worse mood. All the hope I felt in the shelter when we won in Anaheim feels shaky now.

After dinner, before Becky comes up, I lay everything that's mine out on my new bed and make a mental list of what I still have, and what I've lost.

My throat gets tight. The list of what I've lost is so, so long.

Fall ball is supposed to start in two weeks, and I don't have my first baseman's glove that I broke in with shaving cream last year. I don't have my baseball pants, my practice jerseys, my cleats, or my knee-high socks. I don't have a bucket of practice balls, a tee, or my favorite bat.

I don't have my own clothes for when school starts back up. I don't have my phone or my laptop. I don't have my framed nightstand picture of Dad and me in the stands. I don't have a room of my own. I don't even have a home anymore.

Almost everything I had got taken away by Hurricane Harvey. There's hardly anything left.

Matty

My uncle's library isn't really a library. It's a man cave.

It's got a long wood desk with a leather swivel chair and some tall bookshelves like most libraries, but it's also got a plush pullout sofa and a giant TV. Framed Astros jerseys line the walls, and the shelves are filled with autographed baseball stuff. There are hardly any books.

My guess is that library-type activities barely happen in this room.

The first thing on the shelves that catches my eye, however, is a short row of books about famous ballplayers, and one in particular, *Sandy Koufax: A Lefty's Legacy*.

Figures my uncle would have it—I bet every Jewish guy who's a baseball fan has read that book, except for me. My dad gave me a copy for my twelfth birthday, and I meant to read it, but I'm sure it's underwater now.

Sandy Koufax is a Jewish pitcher—super famous, played for the Los Angeles Dodgers, the youngest ballplayer inducted into the Baseball Hall of Fame at age thirty-six, a real legend. Not *a thing* for a used-to-be young lefty pitcher like me to aspire to with him, no sirree.

No pressure at all.

The other books are fine where they are, but I move the stinkin' Koufax book up to the highest shelf, lay it flat, and push it all the way back so it won't glare down at me.

Pressure averted, for now, but I've got plenty of other stuff to worry about.

I pick up the bedding my aunt set out for the pullout. Great, it's Becky's old Little Mermaid sheet set. I ignore the obvious water theme and make up my bed.

Then I flip off the lights and climb in.

A sleepless hour goes by. Wire springs poke my spine through the pullout's thin layer of foam. The noises in this house sound too different to fool myself that I'm still home. A grandfather clock in the entryway chimes like every quarter hour, and the kitchen ice maker dumps ice in the basket every thirty minutes.

Plus, Bialy usually sleeps with me, but my parents took him to their room tonight. He's still frantically hunting for his tennis ball, and they worried he'd keep me up.

But I'm up anyway . . . staring at the ceiling . . . trying to forget the book on the high shelf . . . trying to forget my perfect southpaw pitches . . . trying not to think about kissing again.

The sky out the window is clear, and the stars shine bright. It's hard to believe an epic hurricane ever happened. I try to think of anything else but kissing—even baseball—but my second kiss, the starry *real* one, comes anyway. It's hard to believe *it* happened, too.

I'm gonna tell you the story of that kiss real quick, so I won't chicken out. So after I slid home off Sammy's double during our last playoff game . . . wait, lemme back up.

The story of my second kiss really started a week earlier, when the middle school winner of the annual Bayou City Art Contest was announced at school, and it was me. Me!

I was so proud. I mean, the winning part was great and all, but what was really great was that the judges saw my drawing of Bialy and his lovey tennis ball, and they liked it. They really liked it!

See, to win, I figure they had to feel something when they saw my drawing, just like I did when I drew it. I made that happen. Me. It was so cool!

I went home and told my family about my win that night over dinner. Mom said the predictable, "Matty, it's so nice that you're getting recognition for something you enjoy doing."

Sammy gave me a thumbs-up and said, "Way to go, bro!" and kept munching her fries.

Dad didn't say a thing. He was peeking at his phone under the table, probably scouring Astros baseball stats like he always does during baseball season, duh.

Mom cleared her throat, and he looked up all spacey-like. "What are we talking about here, Matt? Your 12U play-offs?" He winked. "Your southpaw's gonna dominate!"

I shook my head. That wasn't what I had been talking about at all! But he was already peeking at his phone again.

The next day at practice, I told Ethan about what had happened at dinner—how it didn't feel like my family cheered for me with my art the same way they cheer for me when I'm playing baseball. To compare the two . . . I can't even go there, it's too disappointing. And even though nobody seemed that excited about my contest that night, my dad's reaction hurt the worst.

'Cause I'm an artist just as much as I'm a ballplayer—but I can't explain that to him.

I mean, he knows I *do* art, but he doesn't *know*. He doesn't know about the sharp colors I see, or the layers and textures that appear for a second when light bounces off them and I have to catch them, fast. He doesn't know how I can see things in empty spaces, or how stuff sometimes pixelates into its tiniest details.

He doesn't know that I draw what I see so I can capture the way it feels, forever.

See, my dad's the kinda guy who thinks you make your pick—you know, sports or not sports, who your team is, Astros or Yankees—and you give your pick your all. You push everything else out so you can go all the way. He's also the kinda guy who really wished that he'd been given a left-handed arm like mine, so I'm like his do-over, his second chance as a player, you know?

I never wanted him to feel like I wasn't giving baseball my all, since I love baseball, too. And I never wanted to let him down, but I did. But not for art. I let him down when I walked away from baseball because of the second kiss.

So after I slid home off Sammy's double during our last playoff game, I had a mouthful of grit and dust. I grabbed my water bottle off the bench in the dugout to rinse it down, but it was empty.

Ethan said, "I need a refill, too!" and we ducked out back to the cooler. The rest of our team was still standing at the fence outside the dugout, cheering on the next batter.

Ethan grinned as I filled my bottle. "That was some speed, Matt!"

I chugged my water down, then grinned back. "Yeah, did you see my dad when I flew home? He was cheering like my superfan, hollering and spitting seeds!" Then I thought about Dad at dinner again, not cheering. My face twisted up; I couldn't even help it. "I wish he got excited like that . . . about my art."

"Matt, I'm sorry your dad doesn't see . . ." Ethan's voice cracked. "How great your drawings are, how they're something special."

I remember this feeling growing inside, strong and bright. It totally filled me up.

Then we kissed, kinda on the mouth, but more on the cheek. It was quick and right, and even though my eyes stayed wide open, and it was daytime, I saw stars—lots of them—unlike my first kiss with Amanda.

"Wow," I said.

"Really wow," Ethan said, then he flashed that smile of his that always makes me smile back. "I'm on deck next, Matt! See you out there!" he said, and slipped back into the dugout.

I stood there for a second, stunned, trying to figure it out: who kissed who. Maybe Ethan kissed me, or maybe I kissed him. Maybe we kissed each other.

Maybe we'd wanted to for a while.

But never in a zillion years would I have thought that our kiss would happen behind a dugout at a game, with my sister running the bases and my teammates nearby, with my whole family cheering in the stands.

But that's where it happened. It did. And there's no going back.

Right then, all I could think of was how, just like art, I had the feeling that me and Ethan are a big part of what I'm about. How I wanted to draw our kiss to make the feeling of it last forever. How if I followed Ethan back out to the game, the feeling might not last at all.

'Cause a ballplayer who *likes* another ballplayer—I've Googled out baseball players in the major leagues before, and it doesn't seem like there are any!

So now that our kiss happened, what are me and Ethan supposed to do? Hide how we feel about each other? Hide what we're about?

I pull my sheets up over my head tight. I squeeze my eyes shut. For a couple of minutes, I try to block out the memory of our starry kiss and how right it felt, but I can't. I don't even want to.

You really wanna know why I walked away from baseball? You really wanna know why I didn't I think I had a choice?

Because on the ballfield, it doesn't seem like me and Ethan will ever . . . stand a chance.

Becky

Thursday, the morning of my thirteenth birthday, I'm in the middle of a dream about the Houston Astros. God!

I'm standing in line in front of the team dugout. The boy in front of me moves up, and I inch my sandals forward on the rough pavement. A man in the stands behind me says, "Kid, you gotta move when the game starts. You know that, right?"

I turn around and shoot him a dirty look. *Doesn't he know how important this is?*

Bright lights beat down from the corners of Minute Maid Park. The retractable roof is wide open to the stars. The air's heavy and damp, terrible for hair like mine, but it's a concession I'm willing to make.

I clutch my new white baseball in my sweaty palm,

double-check my pocket for my Sharpie, and inch forward some more. I'm almost there!

"What's your name?" George Springer says, and I hand him my pen and ball.

I can't believe it. I can't believe it! I can't believe I'm standing with one of the Astros' star outfielders! I stare at his jersey that matches mine. I look into his bright eyes and smile. He's waiting. Oh my god! What did he ask me?

He clears his throat and repeats, "What's your name?"

Of course! "Becky Putterman—I mean, I'm Rebecca!"

He signs my ball "To Rebecca, from George Springer," and hands it back to me as raindrops fall on our faces. I tuck my signed baseball under my shirt to keep it safe, and smile.

The retractable roof begins to close, and the Astros take the field. George Springer looks at the long line behind me. "Well, kids," he says, and winks at me. "Looks like Rebecca's my last fan autograph tonight!" Then he runs out with his teammates.

I wipe at my damp face and call after him, "Have a great game, George! Of all the Astros, you're . . . you're my favorite!"

What on Earth is going on?

I wake up and run my hand over my dripping-wet face. I yell, "Gross, Bialy! Stop licking me! Jess! What the . . ."

Bark! Bark! Hiss! Hiss! Mmroww!

The animals jump into my bed for a standoff. I bolt up and flip on the lights.

Sammy's nowhere in sight, and everything in my studio is ransacked, like someone's been looking for the crown jewels, or maybe a squirrel. "Out, Bialy!" I shriek, and he slinks off with his tail tucked under him.

Jess settles her furry, shedding self onto my pillow like she owns it.

Great. Some thirteenth birthday this is going to be.

Even though Houston had sunny skies by Wednesday and our backyard drained, my pool party's a rain check since our pool is a mucky mess. I asked my mother, "Can't I at least have some people over to celebrate?"

"We have some people here already, Becky," she said, peering into our full living room.

"I mean like *friends*, Mom. Like Jenny and Rose."

She took a deep breath. "I think we should have a family party this year. This week has been a lot. You'll see Jenny and Rose at school tomorrow since, thank goodness, your school didn't flood."

I nodded, trying to put my best self forward in light of the epic hurricane. Of course we should have a family party—why would I need to invite anyone over when the Whole World's in our house?

Plus, Jenny developed a sudden allergy to cats over the summer, and Rose . . . I'm not even sure we're still friends since we discovered at the end of last year that we're both crushing on Yale, this super cute and funny boy from religious school.

I wash my face and comb out my frizzy hair. I don't try to straighten it, but I add some product and comb it to the side and clip it with a sparkly barrette. Then I put on a new outfit. It *is* my birthday, after all.

Downstairs, my father, my uncle, my grandfather, and Sammy are already on the sectional, tuned in to the pre-game TV coverage, even though the third Astros game against the Rangers won't be broadcast till lunchtime.

They're all debating who has the talent to go up against the Astros in the World Series if they make it. They're throwing out these *ridiculous* teams, like the Nationals and the Cubs. Clearly, they're sleep-deprived!

I walk by the sofa and spit out, "*Please*, people, it's the Dodgers. It's *only* the Los Angeles Dodgers!" Then I head to the kitchen.

Matty's at our table, doodling in his sketchbook while my grandmother and Mrs. Sokoloff play dominoes. She's got that awful cat Bartholomew on a leash by her feet.

He flicks his long tongue and hisses at me as I sit down. The feeling is mutual.

Bubbe pinches my cheek and slides me her dominoes. "Your turn, doll! Happy birthday!" she says, and heads for the kitchen.

"Where are you going? I haven't even had breakfast!" I squeak.

"Someone needs to make your lemon birthday cake!" my grandmother says. "I'll fry you some eggs. Be right back."

Matty lifts his face from his sketch, which looks like a Noah's Ark scene. "Happy birthday, Becky," he mutters, and starts doodling again.

Mrs. Sokoloff takes a sip of her coffee, then she leans over and lets that creature lap some from her cup. "Good kitty," she says, stroking his wrinkly bare skin.

I raise my eyebrows, and she raises hers back. Then she grins at me and shuffles the dominoes in the boneyard.

After I've eaten my eggs and lost at dominoes to Mrs. Sokoloff twice, I head back to the living room, where my birthday only gets worse. Sammy's cheering for the Astros like her life depends on it. Apparently her favorite player, José Altuve, just hit his 21st homer.

Uncle Greggy says, "Keep those cheers a-comin', Sammy! We're down in the series and we need 'em!"

"You bet, Dad!" Sammy says. "My superfan cheers'll help the 'Stros go all the way!"

I can't help rolling my eyes. Sammy Putterman's not an Astros *superfan*—she's just a girl.

Sure, she's a girl who can hit home runs, but lots of people do that, like Jeff Bagwell, Lance Berkman, and of course, George Springer. But look at the facts: the diamond gets bigger and the outfield gets farther away in the 14U—that's the fourteen-and-under—league she'll enter this fall.

Hate to say it, but those home run dingers of hers are going to turn into deep fly balls!

I stand by the sectional and get more and more irritated

the more she hollers. When the adults get up to refill their snack bowls, I hiss, "It doesn't matter if you cheer for the Astros, Sammy. They can't hear you, you know."

She stops mid-cheer and her lips quiver, and I know I should feel bad. *This* is the part of my personality that gets the frowns and my parents' comments about not being my best self.

But something's taken over. It's only been two days, but I'm already beyond sick of my cousin sharing my room— *invading my studio.*

That little corner was all mine, but it it's not anymore.

I look at Bialy and snap, "And keep your smelly dog out of my room and away from my cat!"

She blinks at me like she doesn't know what I'm talking about, and I suppose that's fair, since I was the only one who witnessed Bialy's crimes this morning.

"I was all set up for a birthday party studio session with Jess, and Bialy wrecked it!" I yell. "So the door to my room stays shut from now on. Get it?"

Sammy stammers, "O-okay, Becky. I-I'm so sorry. H-happy birthday. Bialy's just looking for his favorite tennis ball, but it was lost in the . . ." Her lips quiver again. "F-Flood."

God. Now *I* feel terrible, even though *I'm* the one with the messed-up studio.

I storm upstairs for my session, and later that afternoon, there's lots of celebrating. But not for my birthday.

The Astros win against the Rangers 5–1, probably from all Sammy's cheering, and there's a big rumor. My whole family is talking about it nonstop. Detroit Tigers star pitcher Justin Verlander is getting traded to the Astros!

Actually, if I didn't hate baseball so much, I'd think it was kind of brilliant.

The Astros *do* need a top starter, and since Verlander recovered from his June injury, he's put three miles per hour back on his fastball. I mean, if the 'Stros go all the way to the World Series this year, they'll *at least* have a fighting chance with an ace like Verlander, unlike when they got swept in their first World Series by the Chicago White Sox in four consecutive games when Sammy, Matty, and I were babies.

But, whatever.

There's a little party for me that night, but no one's really focusing on my birthday. There's the hurricane and our flooded city. There are my family's underwater houses. There's the Astros win today and our new star pitcher.

Sammy's frowning at me, and Matty's still scratching in his sketchbook. My father and Uncle Greggy check baseball stats when they think I won't notice. Mrs. Sokoloff's cat starts licking Jess back.

My mother, Bubbe, and Auntie Annie do their best. They put on smiles and go through the motions: "Becky's thirteen!" "Yippee! Our first teenager! Wow!" "Mazel tov, doll! You're such a big girl!"

Yeah. Yeah. Right.

I blow my thirteen candles out in one quick breath and eat some of my grandmother's lemon birthday cake. Then I head up to my studio and shut my door.

The party goes on downstairs without me.

There have to be people out there who like what I like, even if my family doesn't. People who'll think what Jess and I do in my studio is special . . . who can see my very best self.

I start setting up my new social media account so I can find them, and after a while, I forget the Whole World right below me.

Sammy

When I wake up Friday morning, something feels like it's missing. But of course I feel like that—a lot's missing lately.

Like my house. Like Bubbe and Papa's house. Like Mrs. Sokoloff's house. Like my clothes and my baseball gear. Like maybe even my brother, which sounds weird because how could someone who's right in front of you feel like they're missing?

But something *else* feels like it's missing. I just can't put my finger on it.

I leave Becky and Jess sleeping and head downstairs to the kitchen. Bubbe and Papa are at the table reading the Houston newspaper, and Matty's staring into his cereal bowl, shoveling big, milky bites into his mouth while Bialy begs at his feet. Mrs. Sokoloff's drinking a cup of coffee

97

with Bartholomew in her lap. His big blue eyes and pointy hairless ears peek above the line of the table as he sniffs her cup.

My grandmother smiles at me. "Good morning, doll. Hungry?"

"Morning, Bubbe," I say back, and she puts a bowl and spoon in front of me before I can tell her I'm not.

"Where's everyone else?" I ask Papa, raising my voice a little so he'll hear me better.

"Back to work!" he says, a bit loud. "Your dad's already at his clinic and your uncle just left for his office. Your aunt's dropping Becky to her first day of school in a half hour, and then she'll head to her design office."

I nod. "And my mom? Did she go to her job at the pathology lab?"

Bubbe shakes her head. "She's going back to work next week. She took that tank of a vehicle to the grocery store this morning. We've got quite a crowd to feed at dinner each night!"

"Hi, Matty," I say. At least he came out of Uncle Mike's library to eat with us, since sometimes this week . . . he hasn't. I reach down and pet Bialy. "Want to take him for a walk with me after breakfast?"

He looks up and shrugs, and I feel a teensy bit hopeful. I'll take that shrug as a maybe.

Papa slides me the sports section of the paper. "Check out this article about Justin Verlander's fastball!" Then he winks at my brother. "What an arm, right, Matt?"

Matty nods and pushes back from the table to stick his empty cereal bowl in the sink.

"Does that mean no for a walk?" I say.

His eyes meet mine as he turns toward the library, and it doesn't take twin telepathy to know the answer.

I read through the article. Yup, the 'Stros will be in great shape after their trade with the Tigers. Verlander's a big-game pitcher and his fastball's back.

Fastball . . . my signed baseball.

I don't remember seeing it on the nightstand where I left it! I run back to Becky's bedroom and flip on the light.

"Sammy, what the . . . ," she yells, bolting up.

I stare at the nightstand—there's nothing. I check under the covers—nothing. I check under the bed—nothing.

"Have you seen my ball?" I say.

"Go look in the garage for a ball," Becky grumbles. "My dad still has a bucket of baseballs from high school."

"I don't need just *any* baseball," I whimper. "I need *my* baseball . . . my special birthday present."

She pulls her comforter over her head and turns her back to me. "God, Sammy, turn off the light. I need more sleep! You're a guest and all, but you're being so rude!"

"Don't you start school today?"

"School? I have school!" she says, jumping out of bed. She runs into her bathroom and slams the door.

I grip the handrail at the top of the staircase and my

fingers start tingling. I call, "Bialy! Bialy? Did you take my ball?"

Of course he doesn't answer. He's a dog!

I search every room in the house. I check under the furniture and feel under the cushions. I even go to the garage and dump out my uncle's bucket of old baseballs, just in case someone tossed my ball in there.

But I already know—in a family of Astros fans—it's not going to be there. Every Putterman but Becky knows how important a ball signed by the greats is!

The only place I haven't looked is Uncle Mike's library . . . Matty's new room. I knock on the door and crack it open.

Matty's on his bed staring at the cover of a book. He hides it under his sheets, but not before I see the title. *Sandy Koufax: A Lefty's Legacy*. I've read that book!

I raise my eyebrows, and he raises his right back. "What, Sammy?" he says, then grabs a different book from the side table. It's about Jackie Robinson, who was the first Black baseball player to break the color barrier. I've read that book, too!

"You're going to love it," I say, nodding to the Robinson book. I let the Koufax book slide. "Have you seen my signed baseball?"

He shakes his head.

"I'm worried Bialy took it," I peep.

Matty's eyes get big. "He was in here before breakfast."

All my fingers are numb now, and my toes start in. If I had to catch or throw a ball or hit and run bases—I couldn't.

"That ball . . . means so much . . . since not much's left . . ."

Matty shoots up from the bed and we start looking. For a while, we're a team again, but I'm sad it took something as serious as this to bring us together.

We don't find my ball, and by Shabbat dinner that night, I'm a complete mess. But I'm not the only one.

After work, my mom and dad met my aunt and uncle at our flooded-out house while Bubbe made dinner. They checked out Mrs. Sokoloff and my grandparents' houses, too.

We sit down at the dining room table, and we're all grim. Mouths frowning. Eyes shifting. Napkins wringing. Barely talking.

Except for Becky. She's going on and on about her great first day of school.

My dad coughs and looks from Matty to me, to Bubbe, Papa, and then to Mrs. Sokoloff. "Uhh, the flood damage was more extensive than we thought. We, uhh, called a tow company to haul our ruined cars, but our houses, well—"

My mouth goes sour. I interrupt, "Dad? Are they . . . *a total loss?*"

He doesn't smile or make a joke to lighten things up like he usually does when something's really hard or scary—like he did when he pushed our kayak out of our house into the floodwater. "Not quite, Sammy," he says. "But they're gosh darn close."

"Can . . . can we go see?"

"Not yet, honey. We hired a contractor to clean things up a bit. Maybe it'll be safe enough to go on Labor Day, Monday. Let's focus on the Astros home games this weekend. We've still got our season tickets, and our team needs us to break out of their August slump."

I nod. I want to go see the flood damage, kind of, and kind of not. But our house—not *safe*? That doesn't make sense, since it's always been the safest place in the world. "What about school and religious school? When will we go back?"

My mom says, "The word is that your and Matty's middle school won't reopen until September 11. And our synagogue needs all-new carpet, so it'll be another few weeks before religious school classes start again for you, Matty, and Becky."

"Okay," I say. Then everyone but Becky gets quiet again.

Bubbe and Papa do their usual, trying to cheer us up. My grandfather cracks jokes, and my grandmother rushes in from the kitchen with all our favorite foods—homemade challah, roast chicken, and a big salad with green goddess dressing. She's even made another lemon cake for dessert.

We say blessings over the Shabbat candles, the wine, and the challah, but we barely hold it together.

My mom sniffles, and my dad stares at the ceiling. Mrs. Sokoloff lifts Bartholomew to her lap and pets him over and over. Uncle Mike and Aunt Deb pour the adults more wine. And Matty and I—we push our food around and refuse Bubbe's second helpings.

Then Becky looks from Matty to me and back again, and says, "Just so you know, Ethan stopped me in the hall at school to see if y'all are safe, since neither one of you texted him after the hurricane. He's super worried, but I told him you're fine."

Matty stares at a chicken wing like it might fly away, and numbness creeps into my hands again. I drop my fork on my plate with a *clang*. Neither of us is fine.

My brother looks up. "Our phones were lost in the flood, Becky."

Her eyes flicker. "Well, you *could* have texted him with your parents' phones, since he's *supposed* to be your best friend."

Bubbe looks at Becky. "Ethan Goldberg, Matty's ball-player friend from your school? He's such a nice boy, and he has such a nice mother! He'd be a perfect match for you!"

Becky squirms and mutters, "I barely know him, Bubbe."

I actually feel bad for Becky. Even *I* know she doesn't like Ethan *that way*, since she likes Yale from our religious school class, who's always doing these funny movie character impersonations. She can't hide how totally great she thinks he is—she gushes all over him.

Matty's squirming, too.

"Now, Mom," my uncle says. "We've talked about this. Just because Becky's having her bat mitzvah this fall, she's not *actually* becoming an adult, and we certainly aren't setting her up on *dates* already."

My grandmother gets up, puts another piece of chicken on his plate, and pats his cheek. "Calm down, Michael. We're just talking!" She turns to Matty. "Doesn't his family attend the other temple?"

Matty pushes his food around on his plate some more and nods.

"By the way, has anyone seen my baseball?" I ask.

Becky snaps, "Still with the baseball, Sammy? How could you have lost something already?" and Aunt Deb frowns at her.

Uncle Mike says, "Honey, there's a big bucket of baseballs in the garage. Take your pick!"

I shake my head. "It's my *signed baseball*, Uncle Mike. My birthday present."

He nods and gets all serious. "It'll turn up, Sammy. We'll keep an eye out."

Bubbe goes to the kitchen and brings back her lemon cake. She cuts thick slices and passes them around.

Bialy nudges me under the dining room table: eyes bright, tail wagging, slobber drooling off his pink lip that's wrapped around . . . *my baseball*.

"No!" I yell, and everyone jumps in their seats. "No, no, no, no! Bialy, what did you *do*?"

His tail pops between his legs, and he slinks farther under the table.

Matty says, "Don't yell at him like that, Sammy!"

My chin starts to shake as I crawl under the table after him to grab my ball.

It's ruined! It's muddy and covered with bite marks. The leather's coming apart at the red stitches, and the black signatures smear together into a purplish haze. What's left of a Ziploc bag clings to Bialy's slobber.

I spin to face Becky. "I-I thought your bedroom door was staying closed! Y-you told me to keep it shut, so your studio would stay safe! H-how did it get open?"

"I don't know! How was *I* supposed to know that he'd take your silly baseball? I thought he wasn't looking for his ball anymore! I thought he'd gotten over it!"

Bubbe and Papa clear their throats and grab the sides of their chairs like *Here it comes—meltdown, nuclear explosion, Putterman core breach!*

My insides heat up, and my voice gets loud. "*Gotten over it, Becky?* He lost his most precious thing . . . the thing that makes him feel good and safe! He can't get over it!"

"Sammy, I mean . . . he's a dog . . . and it's just a ball."

She runs to the kitchen and brings back Aunt Deb's can of new tennis balls. *Zip!* She pops the top, and tennis-ball smell wafts through the air.

"Here, Bialy! Take one of these!" She turns the can upside down, and the balls bounce around the dining room.

Bialy crawls out from under the table on his stomach and side-eyes Becky. He sniffs each ball, then sits by my feet with his ears smoothed back flat. His dog eyebrows lift high, and he stares at my baseball and whines.

Becky shrugs. "I guess he likes yours better."

Maybe it's not Becky's fault that Bialy took my base-ball . . . that the thing he loves most is gone . . . that my birthday baseball is all messed up . . . that everything's messed up now.

But maybe it is! Maybe she's rooting against me! She has been since we were little!

"You left your room open on purpose!" I yell.

"Like I care about your baseball!" she yells back. "And by the way, it's *ridiculous* you call yourself a *superfan*, Sammy Putterman! The Astros don't even know you *exist*!"

"Your studio is ridiculous!" I yell. "Your cat is ridiculous!"

"Well, you look ridiculous in my clothes!" she yells back.

Mom and Aunt Deb push back from the table and rush over to us. "Girls! Calm down!" My aunt puts her hands on Becky's shoulders, and my mom tries to do the same to me, but I jerk out of her reach.

She says, "I'm so sorry, Sammy. It was your birthday present. We'll get you another one."

"I don't want *another* one, Mom!" I scream. "I want *this* one!"

My dad says, "Sammy baby, it's not the only ball like that—the Astros made lots of them. And we've talked about that season, how it was tarnished by all the steroid use. The 'Stros are doing great this year, so maybe we can get you one from this season."

I point to what's left of my ball. "*This* is the only one I want! It was mine and I can't just replace it! Some things aren't replaceable, Dad!"

His face falls, and he whispers, "You're right, Sammy. Some things aren't replaceable. I know it's hard, but we have to accept things we can't change. We have to try."

Bialy whines again and lies down by my feet. He looks up at me with his big, sad brown eyes.

A sob escapes from deep in my chest.

My ball's not mine anymore. It's Bialy's new lovey now. At least it can help one of us feel okay.

I gulp the rest of my sobs down and toss him the ball. "Here you go, boy. It's all yours," I say, and I add to my mental list of things I've lost . . . one birthday ball signed by all my heroes, the Houston Astros greats.

Matty

I left my phone in my flooding room on purpose, but I'm not ever gonna tell anybody that. I put it on the floor under my bed with my baseball glove just to make sure they'd get good and wet.

I mean, I was never *that* into my phone anyhow, like Becky is. But Ethan's texts from all summer were there, and I just didn't know what to do with them. I didn't know what to text back.

I still don't.

And I couldn't delete them, either. I just needed a break from reading and rereading Ethan's texts to, you know, try to figure stuff out. Like all my new feelings and what to do about them. Like how to tell Sammy and my family.

His texts started right after I walked away from our play-off game.

Ethan: Matt, where are u?

Ethan: Matt, r u ok?

Ethan: Matt, I thought . . .

Me—zilch.

Then his texts came a few times a day.

Ethan: Can we talk?

Ethan: We need to talk.

Ethan: Please talk to me.

Me—zilch again.

Then they came about once a week and started spacing out: ten days, fifteen days, a month. And the whole time, I've felt terrible for not texting Ethan back. He's my best friend, and maybe my . . .

But I'm just not ready to figure all my new feelings out. I'm not.

Plus, figuring out my feelings was always Sammy's department.

And now who knows—Ethan's probably really mad at me, but I don't have a phone anymore, so I can't check.

Then suddenly I do.

Dad knocks on the door to the library. "Hey, Matt," he says, and tosses me a new cell-phone box.

I catch it 'cause, you know, baseball reflexes.

"Your new phone should be all set to activate, buddy. Bet you've been missing it like your sister has!"

I stare at the box, and nod.

He clears his throat. "Ready for the game?"

Ready for the game . . . ready for the game . . . ready for what game? Oh, that game—the first game in the 'Stros doubleheader against the Mets today. Our first home game since the hurricane. I never would've forgotten about one of my team's games . . . before.

But I don't wanna go. I wanna sit here and find a way to *not* turn this phone on and reread all Ethan's texts as they load from the cloud.

"Well, okay then. Great!" Dad says, like it's all settled. "We'll head out in thirty minutes. Go Astros!"

The door shuts, and I stare at the phone box. Then I get up real quick and stick it on the highest shelf with the Sandy Koufax book.

Pressure averted, again. At least for a little while.

I stare up at that shelf for twenty-nine minutes. Then I choose the lesser of two evils, and I'm in the kitchen to leave for Minute Maid Park. But I didn't rummage through Uncle Mike's closet to borrow any Astros gear like my dad and Sammy did.

The 'Stros have always been my team, but I said I hate baseball now, remember?

Uncle Mike jingles his keys and says, "Who's coming? We have eight seats in the Suburban and our eight season tickets!"

"I have this game getup on for a reason!" Papa grins.

Dad looks at my rumpled T-shirt, the one I might've worn yesterday, too, and gives me a nervous look. Then he nods. "Twins and I are in!"

Bubbe gestures to Mrs. Sokoloff. "If there's room, Esther and I would love to come cheer for that adorable Jewish rookie, Alex Bregman. If not, we'll watch the Astros whup the Mets here, and I'll win my ten dollars back from our last game of gin."

Mrs. Sokoloff says, "You can certainly try, Irene!" and her lips spread into a smile.

Right then, Becky flies down the stairs. "Go 'Stros!" she yells, in a Houston Astros cap and shirt, no less! She beams at me. "Are there any seats left? I wanna come!"

My uncle raises his eyebrows, then gives her a quick but emotional hug, like he's been waiting for this father-daughter fan moment his whole life.

Sammy glares at her, hard, and Becky flashes a giant grin . . . like Sammy's reaction is *exactly* what she was goin' for.

Our family's had eight partial-season tickets each year for as long as I can remember. Even though there are nine of us, it always works out fine, since somebody usually has a conflict and can't go. That somebody's usually Becky.

Sometimes I even get to bring Ethan, which is super cool. And sometimes Sammy brings Amanda, which isn't super cool.

My mom says, "You all go ahead . . . I have to supervise some things over at the house."

Aunt Deb hugs her. "I'll stick with Annie today."

Uncle Mike spins an enthusiastic one-fingered circle

over his head. "Okay, we've got our eight! Load up, troops!"

On our way to the ballpark, you can hardly tell that Hurricane Harvey happened. Sure, there are some piles of debris on the street corners and a few construction dumpsters in strip-mall parking lots, but most streets seem totally normal.

"Dad, why didn't everywhere flood . . . like our neighborhood?" I say from the wayback seat of the Suburban, where I'm stuck between Sammy and Becky, blocking the dagger glares they're throwing each other.

He shakes his head. "Houston is always under construction, Matt. When it rains, you never know where the water's going to go now. More than fifty inches had to go somewhere."

My voice goes lower. "So . . . it could happen again like this . . . to our house?"

He turns around and looks at me. "Yes, I'm afraid so."

Becky pipes up. "Maybe you should move somewhere high and dry like we did, Uncle Greggy."

Sammy leans over and snaps, "We don't want to move, Becky! Why are you even in this car? You don't like baseball!"

"Samantha!" Dad says.

Everybody shifts around in their seats. My uncle turns on pregame radio coverage. Sammy stares out one window, and Becky stares out the other.

Becky turns to me. "The barbecue-brisket-loaded baked potatoes at the ballpark are killer, right, Matty?"

"Umm, yeah, Becky," I say. Then Sammy throws daggers at me with her eyes, too.

We get to Minute Maid Park, and we're almost to our seats when a tall Black man laughs out loud and waves to us. It's Mack, our head-of-security friend. "Sammy-Matty!" he cries, then he calls to a few passersby, "Listen up, y'all! The Puttermans are IN THE HOUSE!"

Sammy and I laugh and give Mack high fives and fist bumps, like always. Dad, Uncle Mike, and Papa take turns pumping his hand, and Bubbe, Becky, and Mrs. Sokoloff are all smiles. Everybody loves Mack.

And for a minute, I feel just like I used to, before everything that happened *happened*. Before everything got so confusing. Being at our Home Away from Home makes everything better.

Mack turns to my dad, all serious. "Aren't y'all in Meyerland, Greg?"

Dad nods.

Mack raises his brows. "I sure am sorry about it," he says.

"Thanks, Mack. Your place stay dry?"

"Sure did," Mack says. "Was a miracle, and thank goodness the ballpark stayed dry, too!"

Dad nods.

We've known Mack since Sammy and I got lost at Minute Maid when we were eight. Actually, we knew where we were the whole time—but our parents didn't.

Sammy and I had been collecting change around the house, lots of it. So, after the second inning of the game, we asked if we could go to the bathroom.

"Okay," Mom said, giving us a suspicious stare. "But stay together and come back quick."

The first part was easy because back then, we always stayed together. But the second part, well . . . we kinda lost track of time since, you know, we were little kids.

We bought boxes of Cracker Jacks and bags of peanuts and walked around the ballpark munching them down. We snuck into the kids' Squeeze Play Club and ran the bases. We tried on hats and jerseys in the merchandise shop. We watched the game on the concourse TVs and jumped up and down.

Then we got more snacks. Ran more bases. Got a little tired. And remembered Mom and Dad.

But when we finally went back to our seats, our parents weren't there.

I might have started crying. I might have had a much-too-sudden urge to use the bathroom, since we had never actually gone. It might've been too late.

Sammy ran up the stairs straight into Mack, and he took us to the ballpark's security office. He sat me on a chair draped with a few Astros T-shirts since I was wet, and Sammy sat in the chair next to me.

I was still crying, so Mack gave us some Jolly Ranchers. They worked! I felt jollier and stopped crying.

Fifteen minutes later, Mom and Dad rushed through the office door. Mom alternated between raising her voice and telling us that we could never, ever, ever run off like that again or else, and kissing us all over our faces. Dad looked bleary-eyed and could barely speak.

Mack knew just how to calm our parents down. That's the part I remember most.

"This happens every week during the season," he said, and smiled reassuringly at my mom.

"Your kids are just kids," he said, and gave my dad a firm nod.

"It probably scared them more than it scared you," he said, and I glanced at Sammy.

Our twin telepathy was working perfectly: clearly, Mom and Dad were *way* more scared than us.

Back then, Mom always carried a spare pair of shorts and undies in her purse, just in case, so Dad took me to the bathroom to change. Mack let me keep the Astros T-shirts I was sitting on.

He's been our good friend ever since.

The whole Mets game, Becky sits on one side of me, and Sammy sits on the other. Every so often, they lean forward and glare at each other, then look at me for a reaction.

But I don't give them one. Sammy's hurt it's not us against Becky like always. But no way am I taking sides.

Becky and Sammy start this competition—who can heckle and cheer the loudest. Becky's doing it just to get Sammy riled, since we all know she doesn't really like baseball. It helps that she actually knows what's going on, even though Sammy and I were sure she didn't have a clue.

And it works. Sammy fumes. Her eyebrows dance around, her face flushes pink, and she gets super fidgety watching Becky.

A familiar feeling rises in me: I wanna cheer and heckle, too. I wanna be there for my team. I wanna root with my twin sister like we used to.

But I can't, since I hate baseball now, remember?

So I just sit there, trying not to care. Trying to stay out of the middle even though I'm stuck between them now for sure.

Sammy stares at me, eyes wide and searching, a hint of a hopeful smile. She's reading me like she always does. She knows that my mouth wants to open in cheers and sneers, that my arms want to fly up, that my heart *thump thumps* louder and louder each time my team makes a great play.

But I don't want her to read me, not anymore. It's too scary, since I have secrets now. Ones I'm not ready to share with anybody.

So what do I do?

I frown at her, deep and final, till her hint of a smile disappears. Then I turn to Becky. "Let's go get those barbecue-brisket-loaded baked potatoes," I say, and leave my twin sister in the stands.

Becky

The internet says that the social media accounts with the most followers have three very important features.

Number one: a meaningful, recognizable, and searchable handle, i.e., username. Easy—it'll be my name, my cat, and my mission!

@rebeccasdomesticcatfashions

Number two: a standout profile picture. That's super easy, too! I have lots of selfies of me and Jess. It's still summer, so I pick a seasonally appropriate selfie of us in floppy sun hats and round, rainbow sunglasses.

Number three: a delightful yet informative bio that tells my followers what we're all about. Hmm . . . that one's going to take some finesse. I've got it!

Rebecca N Jess // Fashionistas

A design-forward girl and her exceptional tabby cat redefine feline style.

New stories weekly! Follow us! Tag us! Like us!

I use lots of emojis like girl and cat faces, a high heel, and even a camera with a flash. It's a winning bio, I'm sure.

Next, I pick this week's story.

It's Monday, Labor Day, and people across the country are probably having holiday pool parties and backyard cookouts. But not us.

We can't swim, since the pool guy says we need to replaster. And my father's going to throw some burgers and hot dogs on the grill after we check on our family's flooded houses, but we'll probably sit around swatting mosquitos and staring at each other, since seeing the houses will be super sad.

I plump up my bed pillows, lean back, and scroll through the photos of Pool Party Jess on my phone. Just seeing them again makes me feel happier, and I want to share that feeling with my potential followers. I select a few to create my first post and list some hashtags in my niche for cat fashion enthusiasts.

#gorgeouscats #catsyoureye #catlovers

Then I upload the pictures and launch my page!

"Yay, Jess, we're live!" I call to her little cat bed.

She opens one green eye and yawns.

My door creaks, and Bartholomew darts over to her like he wants to eat her.

I hop up from my bed. "Bad cat!" I say and shoo him out. Then I plop back down and work on my page some more.

Sammy's on her bed with her knees tucked to her chest. She's holding her brand-new phone. "What are you *doing*, Becky?"

I wave my phone at her. "I'm setting up my new domestic cat fashions page!"

She looks at me like she doesn't know what I'm talking about, which is *super* annoying because my studio's right here and she's seen me shooting photos. "You know, for the work Jess and I do."

There's an awkward silence, so I search for more hashtags to add.

#catsrlove #catniprocks #purrbuddies

Sammy turns her phone on and starts scrolling. Her eyes get big and watery. "What are *you* doing?" I ask.

She rubs her nose with the heel of her palm and glances away. "I'm looking at some pictures of my house on the cloud . . . from before. My dad says it's not going to be like this anymore."

"Oh," I say. "God."

My mother pops her head in. "You two ready to go over?"

I wave my phone at her, too. "Can I stay home? I'm working on my new social media page!"

The question's not totally out of left field—I have *so* much to do!

I have hashtag research, I have outfits and story themes

to plan for Jess, I have to brush her coat out so it will be extra silky for our next photo session. And unlike Sammy and Matty, I have school tomorrow. Today's all I have!

My mom looks at me like she's terribly disappointed, again.

"And I still need to practice my prayers and write my bat mitzvah speech for when religious school reopens!"

"Becky, you told me you'd already written a lot of your d'var."

My cheeks burn. "I did, but it's not any good!"

It's *partially* true. I've started writing my speech, but I don't really know what to say. My bat mitzvah date corresponds to the part of the Torah where God tells Abram he's going to be great someday, renamed as Abraham, the father of nations, but then forces him to wander around the Canaan desert. I still haven't quite figured out what God's point is.

It would've been much easier if I'd gotten a date with a portion about, say, priestly garments.

Sammy flips through her pictures extra fast and big fat tears start to fall on her phone screen. My mother rushes over to her. "Oh, honey," she says, squeezing Sammy's shoulder in a way she hardly ever squeezes mine.

She turns to me. "Sammy could use your support, Becky."

I nod to my cousin. "Okay," I say. "I'll come."

"Thanks," Sammy says, and turns her phone facedown on the nightstand.

An hour later, every single person in our house heads out, a party of ten.

My mother takes Bubbe, Aunt Annie, and Mrs. Sokoloff in her car, and I ride in the Suburban with the rest of the family. The whole way there, my cousins stare out the window, silent.

We get to Meyerland, my old neighborhood. Usually, kids would be playing games in the yards and street.

But there's none of that now.

Debris lines all the curbs: furniture, carpets, and curtains; clothes and toys; Sheetrock, insulation, and appliances. It's littered up and down sidewalks leading to wide-open front doors. It overflows big dumpsters in the driveways.

Some people are walking house to house, sifting through the piles. I catch my father's eyes in the rearview mirror. "They lost everything, so . . ." he says without finishing his sentence.

We pass the house where I was born. The one we lived in until we moved to Bellaire.

I loved it there. I could play with my cousins and visit Bubbe and Papa whenever I wanted. It felt like home, way more than our new house.

It's gutted, too!

I catch my father in the mirror again. He takes a big breath and shakes his head. "This neighborhood was hit very hard, Becky."

Sammy glances at me. "But lucky for you, your new house is high and dry."

We pull up behind a huge pile of debris in front of my cousins' house.

Auntie Annie's already standing near the double front doors with my mother and grandmother. Mrs. Sokoloff sits on the edge of a low planter box in her yard, gazing at a giant magnolia tree that somehow still has big white blooms after the hurricane.

Matty refuses to get out of the Suburban.

Uncle Greggy says, "Come on, Matty. It's way better to see it firsthand than to sit around imagining it."

My cousins lock eyes, and even I know what they're saying, and I've never had telepathy with anyone. With all the huge soggy piles, anything they'd imagine is pretty close to what they'll find.

We join Auntie Annie and the others, but no one wants to be the first to step inside. A van pulls up behind our Suburban, and a contractor gets out and gives our group a small wave. "Mrs. Putterman?" he says.

Three women spin toward him at once.

"The Mrs. Putterman who lives . . . who lived here," he says, gesturing to my aunt. "Ma'am, the hallway near the bedrooms is the only one we haven't demoed yet, since we didn't know what to do with all those photos. We'd like to get to that today if it's okay."

My aunt's lips quiver, and she nods. "Of course. We'll go

122

ahead and take them down."

Bubbe sighs and shakes her head. "You all go in. Ira and I will wait outside. We've seen it all before. We don't need to see it again."

I put my arm around my grandmother protectively and say, "I'll wait here, too."

My cousins follow their parents inside, and a few seconds later, I hear a shrill, high-pitched, "Mom! Mom! Mom! My room!"

It's Sammy. I leave my grandparents and rush inside. It's been ages since I've been to her room, but I know the way by heart. I used to be here all the time.

"Where's my dresser, Mom? Where is it? Where is it?" she shrieks, standing on the damp concrete in her empty room—carpet and Sheetrock gone, clipped wires hanging everywhere, the stench of dirty floodwater thick in the air. "It had my photo in it! The one of me as a baby with Dad in the stands at Minute Maid! Mom, where did it go? I need it! I need it!"

Auntie Annie gathers Sammy into her arms and they both start sobbing.

I back into the hall. I feel like I'm rubbernecking at the scene of an accident. I feel like an intruder in someone else's tragedy. What am I even doing here?

I turn around in the long hallway and stop. A family photo montage covers the entire length of both walls. The tops of some of the photos look normal, above the water line, but the bottoms are wavy and blurry. Ruined.

There's one of Matty, Sammy, and me in saggy diaper-filled swimsuits, covered head to toe in sand on Galveston beach; there's one of us in front of our synagogue on our first day of religious school. There's a photo of us at the Jewish Community Center pool, hanging all over each other, and one of us grinning in front of three eighth-night lit menorahs.

Slip 'N Slides, bubble baths, Play-Doh spaghetti dinners. Twister competitions, pillow forts, sleepovers. Sparklers on the Fourth of July. Three musketeers on Halloween.

So many of the pictures have all of us in them, smiling, hugging, and laughing. All of us, together.

Oh, god.

A small gasp escapes my lips, and I run outside. I don't know if it's the wavy photos or the terrible smell or how dirty and sad everything is or what. I feel sick, like my lunch is going to spew everywhere.

When did everything in those photos change? Why did we stop liking each other? How come we don't remember that once we had something really special?

We weren't just family back then, we were friends. But now we aren't.

It feels like . . . it feels like . . . a total loss.

I sit down next to Mrs. Sokoloff and look up at the big magnolia. I sniffle, then start to tear up. She takes my hand and says, "Things will get better, dear, you'll see."

Sammy, Matty, and my aunt and uncle eventually come back outside, and we skip going to Bubbe and Papa's house. They say they don't want to go inside there, either.

When we get back to my house, Matty locks himself in the library. He doesn't even come out for dinner. The rest of us scrounge for leftovers and eat on the sectional in front of the game. The 'Stros win it against Seattle, 6–2, but no one cares.

Not when we've all just seen so much loss.

That night Sammy tries to muffle her crying with her pillow, but I still hear it. She cries buckets and buckets, like she'll never stop. "I'm so, so sorry about your house, Sammy," I whisper.

She croaks, "Thanks, Becky."

"And . . . I'm sorry about your special baseball, too."

Sammy

Each morning the next week, everyone leaves the house except for me, Matty, Bubbe, Papa, and Mrs. Sokoloff.

Becky heads to school. My dad goes to his clinic, and my mom goes to her part-time job at the pathology lab. My aunt and uncle go to their offices.

I text my friend Amanda to see if she can come over, but her parents signed her up for a weeklong tennis clinic since we don't have school and she's an athlete like me.

So it's just me and Matty.

My brother stays holed up in the library most of each day. He creeps out to get food from the kitchen, then he creeps back. He makes an appearance at dinnertime when our parents come home, but that's about it.

I eat breakfast with whoever is left each day without him.

I read through the sports section of the paper and talk to Papa about the Astros without him. I walk Bialy around the neighborhood without him. I wander around the house trying to find stuff to do until school starts next week, without him.

I text him a few times each day, but he doesn't respond. I call him, too, but his new phone goes straight to voice mail. I stand outside the library every so often, but it stays dark and quiet under the door.

I'm batting zero with Matty—I keep swinging and missing. And after seeing our house on Monday, I really need to talk to him.

At lunchtime on Friday, my grandmother sets two places with her famous homemade tomato soup and extra-crispy, extra-gooey grilled cheese sandwiches. "Go get your brother, doll," she says to me. "His moping has gone on long enough!"

Papa and Mrs. Sokoloff nod.

I head to the library, and poor Bialy's curled up in the hall with my baseball, waiting for my brother. I knock on the door, crack it open, and Bialy rushes in. "Matty?"

"Mmm?" he says, as Bialy's slurpy face-licking noises filter through the dark.

The library smells stale, like unwashed sheets and an unwashed person—Matty.

But *my* brother makes his bed without Mom asking, and *my* brother showers right after baseball games. I don't know what's wrong with *this* Matty, and I can't . . . read him.

My voice gets small. "Can I open your blinds?"

"Mmm," he says again, as Bialy settles down on his bed with a *humph.*

I take that *mmm* as a yes.

The library feels super depressing in the light. Empty cereal bowls pile on the desk, and dirty clothes are strewn across the chair back. The Jackie Robinson book, and some books about Jewish first baseman Hank Greenberg, and Jim Abbott, this amazing ballplayer who was born without a right hand, are on his bed amid the covers.

But I don't see the Sandy Koufax book anywhere.

I stare at this new version of my brother. His skin is pale and his hair is greasy; his lips are dry and cracked.

"Are you okay?" I whisper, but I already know the answer. It doesn't take telepathy to figure it out.

Matty sits up and blinks at the sun. "I'm kinda sad, but I don't want to talk about it, okay?"

A big lump fills my throat. I'm sad about our house, too, but I *want* to talk about it. I *need* to talk about it—with Matty.

He's the only person who'll understand, since every single big thing that's ever happened in my life has happened to both of us . . . together. We're twins.

We were born together, and we learned to walk and talk together. We've had every birthday, every holiday, and every first day of school, together. And since we've always, *always,* played on the same baseball team, we've had every single win and every single loss, together.

Matty was there when I lost my first tooth. He was there when I hit my first homer. He was there when Amanda and I had a terrible fight and I thought for sure we'd never make up.

And through every single thing, every first, we've always had each other to lean on . . . until now.

We've had this huge, sad, scary loss together—the hardest thing that's ever happened to us, the loss of *our home*—but apparently we're not going to lean on each other this time.

"Okay," I say looking away. "We don't have to talk, but can you please eat lunch with me? Bubbe made our favorite."

"I'm not really hungry, Sammy," he says. Then he lies back down and pulls his Little Mermaid sheets around him.

I stand there for a minute, watching my brother, then call, "Here, boy," and Bialy follows me back out.

When I get to the kitchen without Matty, Bubbe raises her eyebrows at Papa and Mrs. Sokoloff again. I sit down with them and try my soup and sandwich. But without my twin brother, my favorite lunch doesn't taste nearly as good.

By Shabbat dinner, I've fallen into a serious slump. The fact that the Astros have swept their last six games in a row against the Seattle Mariners and New York Mets, and now they're one game under their season high-water mark with eighty-six wins and fifty-three losses, can't even cheer me up.

I keep thinking about our flood-damaged house, with all our stuff piled on the street. I keep imagining my empty room, the photo of me and Dad in the stands gone now, forever. I keep seeing the look in my brother's eyes that no amount of telepathy can change; we're not a twin team anymore.

We're separate—I'm on my own.

I almost want to close Becky's heavy purple curtains and climb into her frilly sleepover bed and never get back out, just like my brother.

All dinner long, this is how it goes: Matty stares at his food, and I stare at Matty. Everyone else's eyes shift between us.

It's obvious that we're a twin team split down the middle.

Dad says, "The 'Stros played great this week!" and smiles at us.

Mom says, "We're going shopping tomorrow. You two need all-new clothes for school!" and claps her hands.

Uncle Mike says, "You'll need the Suburban for that kind of spree!" and reaches over and tussles Matty's hair.

Aunt Deb says, "Becky, can you clear out some more drawers and closet space for Sammy's new wardrobe?" and winks at me.

Becky looks between Matty and me and raises her eyebrows.

Then she starts rattling on and on about stuff—her studio and Jess, her new social media page, Rebecca's Domestic

Cat Fashions, and finding followers who believe in her—but I'm barely listening.

I'm trying to conjure up some twin telepathy.

How did this happen, Matty? Why won't you talk to me? What can I do? I miss you and need you so much.

Becky talks on and on for all of us; no one else says anything more.

Mrs. Sokoloff leans over and gives Bartholomew a sip of iced tea from her cup when she thinks no one's looking. And when Bubbe serves up extra-thick slices of her lemon cake, I'm not the only one who leaves it unfinished.

The next day, after the Astros lose the first game of their doubleheader in Oakland, my uncle flips the living room TV off. "They stink, Greg!"

Dad nods. "They double stink, Mike. They stunk last night, too."

Uncle Mike shakes his head. "Maybe our Houston Strong run is over."

I can't hear that. "No!" I say, a sudden loud, hard edge to my voice. "We can't abandon our team! They need us now more than ever! It doesn't matter how they got off their game, we need to put it behind us and root harder! We aren't fair-weather fans!"

Dad and Uncle Mike stare at me, and blink. Then Dad says, "That's right, Sammy baby. That's right!"

My mom stands up from the sectional. "Well, this seems

like a perfect time for some shopping."

I look down at Becky's floral tank top and trendy frayed jean shorts. I'm so sick of wearing her clothes. And I could never show up to school like this. Amanda would laugh so hard she'd pee in her pants.

I nod. "Thanks, Mom. That would be great."

My dad and uncle are sitting smushed together on the sectional now, scrolling through Astros game recaps on their phones, saying things like, "Well . . . we do have Verlander now . . . and so and so says . . . and if we just win the games against the Angels, Mariners, White Sox, Rangers, and Red Sox—"

Mom interrupts him. "Greg?"

He looks up, spacey-like. "What, Annie?"

She says, "Can you come with us and take Matty to the sports store? He can get most of his clothes there, and you could use some things, too."

"I need stuff from the sports store, Mom! My gear's all gone!" My voice sounds way too loud again, but I can't make it softer. My eyes shoot to my dad. "I'm playing fall ball, right?"

I've been worried that since Matty's not playing anymore, coaches won't want me since I'm a girl, even though I'm good. That without my brother sticking up for me on the team, my teammates won't want to play with me, either. I'm even worried that without Matty playing, Dad's going to tell me it's time to transition to girls' softball.

I mean, softball's a great game, but I've always wanted to play baseball. What does it matter if I'm a girl? I can hit with the best of them!

"Yes," he says. "You and your brother are all signed up for fall ball. You'll both move up to 14U since you have an April birthday, and I've already ordered your new jerseys and caps." He bites his lip and frowns.

Matty had told all of us he wasn't going to play this fall— *no way!* But I guess Dad hoped he would change his mind by now. So did I.

He hasn't.

But a wave of relief spreads through me: I'm going to keep playing. I'm still a ballplayer, even if my brother's not.

"Okay, honey," my mom says. "We'll start at the mall, then join Dad and Matty at the sports store when we're done." Her eyes meet my dad's, and they give each other a worried look. "Go get your brother out of bed, Sammy, will you please?"

I head down the hall to the library. I feel like I'm wearing a path in the hardwood floors. Bialy's outside the door asleep again, waiting for Matty to remember him.

I'm not the only one who's been shut out.

I knock, then I walk in without waiting. Bialy follows. "We're going shopping, Matty," I blurt. "Mom and Dad told me to come get you."

The blinds are open, and the lights are on now.

Matty's drawing in his sketchbook, his left hand moving a

pencil over paper fast, like it's on fire. I note a familiar scene from the hurricane news coverage—murky rising water and a lone car stuck on a bridge, a person standing on top of it, waving to the helicopter above him, a rescue ladder swaying out of his reach, whipped up in the hurricane winds.

But the person inside *this* drawing is Matty.

My brother doesn't even notice me. We're in different worlds again.

I stand there, watching. After a few minutes, I clear my throat. Matty pauses and looks up. "We're going shopping," I repeat. "Mom and Dad told me to get you."

"Shopping for what, Sammy?"

Shopping for what? All our stuff is gone! From the flood you're drawing!

Matty's room still smells stale, even though Mom swept through last night and hauled out the dirty bowls and clothes and changed his sheets. They're Beauty and the Beast now, complete with Belle, Gaston, the Beast, Lumière, Mrs. Potts, and Chip.

But my brother's shirt is rumpled like he slept in it, and he has terrible bedhead. I bet my eyes look just as worried as my parents' eyes do.

"It's back-to-school Monday," I say.

"So?"

"So what are you going to wear?"

He looks down. "This'll do. Tell Mom and Dad I'm good."

I stare at him. Again, it doesn't take telepathy to know that couldn't be further from the truth.

"What about when it gets cold outside?"

He looks out the window at the bright sun and stares back at me for a second.

I squeak, "Will you at least come help me pick out my new glove and bat for fall ball?"

My brother gives me a sad look and shakes his head, then he turns back to the world in his sketchbook.

Why am I even bothering? Why do I care what he wears, what he does, or what he says? Whether he plays baseball or not?

I don't even know this Matty.

I rush out of the room and slam the door, leaving Bialy inside. We go shopping without my brother, and Mom and Dad try to cheer me up. But it's no use.

Matty's nowhere I am—and he doesn't even want to be.

But I can't abandon my team with my twin brother. I just can't. So I need to find a way to root even harder.

Matty

After Sammy leaves, I sit on my bed drawing till I'm bleary-eyed and my hand cramps up. It's like I can't stop.

My drawings are all over the place . . . not in any order at all.

There's one of our flooded-out house with its tangle of cut wires hanging off the wood studs, and the mucky concrete floors. There's one of my family at Shabbat dinner, with Bubbe serving up big slices of lemon cake. There's another of the shelter with all the families sitting in their spots, waiting to see what comes next.

There's a drawing of Mack fist-bumping me and Sammy at our Home Away from Home, and there's one of my phone and glove on the floor of my room underwater. Then there's a drawing of the big pile of what used to be ours, sitting on the curb of our street: our couch and our beds, my mom's waterlogged, wavy-keyed antique piano, our sheets and clothes, buckets of swollen baseballs.

And among the faces in my drawings, sometimes there's a face that wasn't really there. Ethan's.

'Cause he *was* there with me, and I can't draw him out.

Most of my drawings come out the way I saw things, but some of them come out way different and super confusing.

In one, a house floats by our kayak while we're on the way to the shelter. In another, the shelter's half full of water and I'm asleep on a bobbing raft. In another, my uncle's Suburban becomes a speedboat on fire. In the one that my sister saw me drawing earlier . . . I know I'm not gonna be rescued from the top of that car.

Everything inside me is all jumbled up because I'm not used to figuring out how I feel about stuff. For the longest time I let Sammy decide all my feelings, and I let Ethan call every pitch. And now that it's my turn to sort stuff out, it's really, really hard.

I like Ethan so much, but us and baseball . . . how's that ever gonna work? It doesn't seem like it works for other ballplayers, so how would it work for us?

It's all way too much to figure out.

Finally I shut my sketchbook and lie down on the bed next to Bialy, exhausted. I run my fingers through his soft fur to stretch them out, then I take some big breaths and listen for a while.

I can't hear my family's voices, so they must still be shopping.

Bubbe yells to Papa, "It's our nap time, Ira!" and they clomp up the stairs.

Uncle Mike's Suburban revs, then the garage door screeches shut. Aunt Deb's talking on her phone in the kitchen. "Marcy, of course I need a break," she says. "But Greg and Annie's house won't be ready anytime soon, and Mike's parents, don't even get me started."

And Mrs. Sokoloff sings to her cat. "Bartholo . . . mew, mew, mew. Bartholo . . . mew, mew, mew. I love you, you, you."

Just about everybody's accounted for, except for Becky.

I get up on my tippy toes and reach for my phone box. Then I sit back down on the bed and think about opening it. I think about what it'll feel like to read all Ethan's old texts, and maybe some new ones.

I think about looking at photos of his face, instead of just the ones I draw.

Let's be honest. None of this started with the first kiss that wasn't the real one, or even the second kiss that was.

It all started way before that—with smiles. Really great smiles.

Not everybody has them, you know. Most people have regular smiles. But not Ethan.

If you ranked smiles from one to ten, his smiles are like a fifteen, that's how great they are. They're hall of fame great.

I remember this one smile in particular. It might have even been a sixteen or seventeen. We were playing in a game early last season, and we were on fire. My arm was hot, Ethan's target was perfect, and I knew his signs even before he made them.

'Cause Ethan and I—and I can never tell Sammy this—we have telepathy, too.

At least we used to.

Anyhow, when I struck the last kid out and our team won, Ethan threw his face mask off and there it was—that smile, all for me. And I knew then that his smiles weren't ordinary smiles, no way. Ethan's smiles are the kinda smiles I wanna kiss.

My door opens and Becky barges in. I drop my phone box in my lap.

"Oops, sorry! Why are *you* here?" she says, gawking at my rumpled, ratty T-shirt. "I thought you'd be shopping with Sammy."

I push the phone box under my Beauty and the Beast sheets. "Why don't you just come in, Becky?" I say, and she looks confused for a minute.

"Ha, ha, Matty, I'm already inside," she says, and sits on my bed next to my dog like she was invited. Bialy immediately hops down and slinks to the corner.

She sees my sheets, falls back on the bed, and starts shrieking. Like full-on hysteria, legs up, feet kicking at the ceiling, grabbing her stomach, snorting and laughing, tears running down the sides of her face like Niagara Falls.

"What?"

"Oh my god! I can't believe my mother kept my sheets from the old house and put them on your bed!" She sits up and wipes her eyes with the backs of her hands and looks at me.

I shrug. "Last week I had Little Mermaid ones."

She shrieks, wipes at her eyes again, and takes a big breath. "All this must really stink for you. Like big-time."

I give her a quick nod since there's no use pretending. I mean, if it's obvious to somebody like my cousin Becky, who's beyond self-absorbed, it's flat-out obvious.

And it's not like I've been putting on this brave things-are-going-to-be-okay face. I've mostly been holed up in the not-really-a-library/really-a-man-cave since we got here, and after we saw our house, well . . . let's just say my feelings are even more jumbled up.

"What do you do in here all day, anyway?" She points to Bialy. "Do you play with him? Does he do tricks? Why is he looking at me with his teeth showing?"

I get up to pet Bialy, who's cowering in the corner. His top lip is scrunched up by his nose, and he's grumbling low. Kinda what I'd be doing now if I could. "Dogs know when somebody doesn't like them, Becky. Everybody heard you yelling at him that time he went into your room."

"Well, he messed my studio up royally." She gets up off the bed and walks over. "Will he bite me if I touch him?"

Bialy's showing all his teeth now—not a great sign. I reach for some rawhide jerky on a shelf. He's a tough sell once he's judged somebody's character, but maybe it'll help. I hand it to her. "Give him the jerky, and maybe . . ."

Bialy nips Becky, and she starts shrieking again for real. He doesn't draw blood or anything; it's just a gimme-that-rawhide-and-back-off kinda nibble.

She sucks on her finger for a second, then wails, "I'm injured! So now you have to help me with Jess's photo shoot in my studio later!"

I stare at her and draw a complete blank. *Her cat? Her photo shoot? Her studio?*

"But you don't have to . . ." she blurts. "It's just that it's been hard corralling Jess for my sessions lately since she's distracted by wrinkly, hairless you-know-who." She wags her finger, which isn't really *that* red, on her way to the door. "I'm sure I'll manage all by myself like I always do . . . even though your dog maimed me."

I'm staring after her, still trying to figure out what the heck she's talking about, when she turns around and I catch a small tremble in her bottom lip.

I take a deep breath and say, "Okay, Becky, I'll be up in a little while."

My cousin looks kinda stunned for a second. Then she flashes me a big, silly grin and skips off.

I sure hope I made the right choice.

Becky

I head up to my room and shut the door behind me.

Quel désastre! What was I thinking? Why on Earth did I invite *Matty* to come up to my *studio*?

He's a guy! He's a star pitcher! He's an Astros fan! He's not going to like what I'm doing with Jess! He won't understand my new social media page!

And . . . he's my cousin. No one in my family likes what I do—they only like baseball!

I glance over at Jess, nuzzling Bartholomew on her miniature canopy bed, not giving me the time of day again. I've tried to keep them apart, really, I have. But nothing works! Along with Jenny and Rose . . . now my cat doesn't want to be with me either.

I collapse on my bed, feeling miserable and sorry for myself. I let myself wallow.

My family's never been a super-close-do-everything-together kind of family like Sammy and Matty's family. I mean, I've had a key to our house for after school since I could operate a microwave and dial 911!

But my workaholic parents are even busier with the Whole World here.

Especially my mother. We're *supposed* to get ready for my bat mitzvah. We're *supposed* to shop for dresses and pick out a theme for my party. We're *supposed* to finalize the guest list and mail invitations! We're supposed to finally bond!

There's hardly time for any of that, now.

And while I used to have a once-a-week reminder on Shabbat that my cousins don't want to hang out with me anymore, now I have an every-day reminder of that, too. Then to top it all off, my cat—the only one who's ever been just for me—has found someone new to love.

I really *am* all alone. I don't have anyone anymore!

There's a knock on my door, and I roll out of bed to answer it.

Matty stands in the hall with Bialy, who follows him around everywhere with Sammy's chewed-up ball. "I've changed my mind," I say, and a tear escapes out of the corner of my eye. "I don't need your help."

My cousin shifts from foot to foot and stares at my tear. I feel it running down my cheek now. "Are you sure, Becky? I feel bad about your finger."

Another tear escapes. God!

"Okay," I mumble, opening my door.

Bialy sees the cats, and his tail wags like a high-speed windshield wiper. "But *he* has to stay outside since he totally disrespected my studio. *And* my finger."

Matty nods, then he steps into my room for the very first time.

I sit down on my bed and watch him take it all in out of the corner of my teary eye. The wall-to-wall hot-pink-and-purple geometric carpet and matching curtains. The twin canopy beds and Jess's matching miniature one. The tacked-up white poster board that forms my studio. The shelves with the overflowing props.

"What *is* all this?" he asks, pointing to my poster board setup in the corner.

"Don't you listen during Shabbat dinners? I have a social media page now: Rebecca's Domestic Cat Fashions. I do themed photo sessions with Jess and post them."

He looks confused. "But why?"

I knew he wouldn't get it! I knew he'd think what everyone in the Whole World thinks about what I do with Jess—that it's just some silly little activity with my cat. But maybe it doesn't matter anyway because—I glance over at Jess and Bartholomew, staring into each other's eyes—maybe my sessions are all over anyway!

"I wanted to get followers," I squeak. "Who like what I like. Who think the photos of my sessions are really good."

"Do you have any yet?"

My face burns. I've had my page live for a whole week,

and so far I only have two followers: my mother and Bubbe!

"Not really," I mumble. "Maybe the photos aren't as great as I think they are."

He walks over and holds out his hand for my phone. "Can I see?"

I give it to him, and my stomach does a whole Simone Biles floor routine.

Matty takes forever, scrolling, examining, blowing the photos up with two fingers and looking closer. He finally hands my phone back. "Wow, they're great, Becky. You're an artist."

I sniffle and my face scrunches. I'm about to lose it. "*Me?* You think *I'm* an . . . artist?"

He nods. "It takes one to know one, Becky. And you've got a real eye."

I can't believe someone actually understands me! And that someone's not just anyone, it's Matty—and he's *family.*

I hiccup twice, then suddenly I can't stop.

"I can't believe—" *hiccup* "you think—" *hiccup* "they're great like I do but—" *hiccup.* I glance at Jess and Bartholomew. They're grooming each other now, their long, rough tongues taking turns, running chin to whiskers, chin to whiskers. *Ick.*

Matty comes and sits next to me. We stare at the cats, licking, licking, licking. We glance away.

He says, "What if you take pictures of both of them together, since you know, they kinda *like*-like each other?"

"Together?" I bounce on the mattress, and Matty startles. Oh. My. God!

"You're a genius! Together!" I say, throwing my arms around him, practically knocking him over. "Like in *Beauty and the Beast*! You are *so*, so creative, Matty!"

He smiles. "I'm an artist, too, Becky."

I say, "I know *that*. But still, this goes beyond. Beyond! It's going to be huge! Just look at their undeniable chemistry! The possibilities are ENDLESS!"

Matty gets excited, too. "And his name is Bartholomew, like from the ceiling of the Sistine Chapel where Michelangelo drew St. Bartholomew's skin, so he's destined for art!"

The Sistine Chapel? Michelangelo? Skin? That sounds kind of ick again, but like Matty says . . . Bartholomew the cat was destined for this!

I say, "Ha! I thought his name was like Bartholo . . . *mew*, get it?"

He laughs. "Maybe that's it, too!" he says. "I heard Mrs. Sokoloff singing, 'Barthlomew, mew, mew. I love you, you, you.'"

We both crack up.

I'm *so* excited. I walk over to Bartholomew and reach my hand out to pet him. I can't believe I'm actually doing it, since what am I going to pet—his wrinkly sphynx skin? But I want to get to know him since we're going to be working together now!

In a flash, Mrs. Sokoloff's cat bares his teeth fierce-like, hisses at me, extends his claws, and swipes my hand. "Ow!" I say, looking at four bright red scratches above my swollen Bialy-nipped finger. "Hey! I'm trying to be friends!" I say, but he just scoots closer to Jess, all protective.

"See, Matty?" I moan, collapsing back down on my bed. I start sniffling again. "It's the end of Rebecca's Domestic Cat Fashions! It's the end of my social media page! How am I ever going to get followers now?"

He gets up and paces the room. "We just need to figure out something *else* he likes, Becky. He's gotta be about more than just Jess."

"Wait here," I say, and sprint down to the kitchen.

I come back with the last cup of coffee from this morning's pot. It's cold and grainy, so I hope Bartholomew isn't picky.

He's not!

He laps it up and purrs, then wraps his skinny naked body around my legs and gazes up at me adoringly with those ginormous blue eyes. "Good kitty!" I say over and over, stroking his wrinkly skin.

It's not my style to be patient, but I will it. Success (beaucoup d'followers) lies where innovation (two cats are better than one) meets excellence (putting my best self forward).

After a while, I manage to strap a small black top hat on Bartholomew that he doesn't shake off. I throw a feathery boa on Jess and start a quick session—think Fred Astaire and Ginger Rogers, Bubbe and Papa's favorite old-time dancing duo. They're perfect for what I've decided is today's theme: Dancing Away the Blues.

Then I lure the cats to the studio and start snapping away.

Bartholomew looks dashing in all the photos, a real heartthrob! And the two of them together, *like*-liking each other . . . it's positively magnetic!

I post the photos to my page and say, "This calls for some Katy Perry dance music!"

Matty laughs when I blast her song, "Roar."

"It's our favorite, since Jess is a big cat at heart!" I gush, then I belt the lyrics at the top of my lungs.

Matty does, too. He starts singing right along with me. The cats go wild, chasing each other around the room, rolling in the props, jumping up on the beds.

"You know the words to this song!" I yell over the music.

Matty yells back, "Duh . . . it's Katy Perry!" Then he lets out a huge tiger roar.

I roar, too, and a feeling balloons inside me so big, I might just pop. I'm not alone in my family, not anymore.

The rest of the afternoon, we have a dance party in my room—Jess and Bartholomew, me and my cousin Matty.

Sammy

Monday morning, I rip the tags from my brand-new clothes and get dressed for my first day of school.

My eyes keep peeling to the glove I got for Matty on the shelf of the closet. I'd hoped that if he put it on . . . just smelled the leather . . . he'd remember our games together.

He'd remember he's still a ballplayer, too.

After we got home from shopping Saturday, I stood in the hallway outside Becky's room with the glove and listened to Becky and Matty for a good long while. They laughed as they jumped up and down on the beds. Becky cooed at Jess and Bartholomew, and Matty joined in.

Matty!

They talked about Becky's new social media page and her followers. They talked about setting up a dance scene in the studio. My brother even asked if he could draw a cool backdrop for the session and take a few pictures of the cats.

Matty.

Then Becky put on a Katy Perry song mix, and they jumped some more and sang and cracked up in between all the songs. And my brother Matty knew all the words.

Matty . . .

Maybe *I'd* like to sing Katy Perry songs, too. Maybe *I'd* like to laugh and dance and jump and take photos and feel what they're feeling. Maybe until then, I just didn't know it.

But with our twin telepathy broken, I'm on the outside now. I didn't know my brother liked cats and photo shoots and jumping on beds and dance music.

I never even asked. I just thought we liked all the same things, and we always would. I thought we'd figure out everything new along the way, together.

Because we were a team, the Putterman twins. We were Sammy-Matty, Sammy-Matty, Sammy-Matty.

But now we're not.

I head downstairs. During breakfast, Mom and Dad shift their eyes between us again. This time, I'm looking at Matty, but he's looking at Becky.

All of a sudden, they seem like they're the team now.

Becky says, "Matty, let's work on Beauty and the Beast after school! Can you make another backdrop? The last one was *beyond* fabulous!"

"Sure, Becks!" He smiles. "That sounds like fun!"

Becks? Smiles? Fun?

I push back from the kitchen table and mutter, "Mom, I'll be in the car when you and Matty are ready to go."

Our first day back to school is Monday, September 11, the anniversary of the day the planes crashed into the World Trade Center in New York.

During the moment of silence, I sit at my desk in first period language arts and think about how different that day was at the end than at the beginning. How you don't ever know when something that seems so permanent—like a skyscraper full of people, or your house, or a special connection you've always had with your brother—could suddenly be gone.

Just like that.

My new seventh-grade language arts teacher, Ms. Martinez, hands out crisp new journals toward the end of class.

She gives us a long look and says, "This isn't the writing project I had planned for our first six-week block, but I think it's what we all need after the hurricane. These are your feelings journals. Don't worry, no one's going to read them. Your words are just for you. But I'm going to walk around to check your page count totals at the end of each week."

There's a ripple of sighs and under-breath "ughs" around the room. But not from me: I'm ready to open my journal and write things down.

I have all these new feelings inside that need to find a way out.

Plus, other than baseball, writing is my absolute favorite thing to do. Sometimes I even dream I could write about baseball for a newspaper someday.

But I've never been brave enough to show anything I've written to anyone but Matty.

"I want you to fill up at least two full pages each week," Ms. Martinez says. "It's free writing, so you should put down anything that comes to mind. The more you write, the more you may find that your thoughts and feelings about the hurricane crystallize, and you start to feel better. Writing is cathartic, class, which means it helps your emotions release. So many of us have been through so much recently."

A boy across the room raises his hand. "Are you doing it, too, Ms. Martinez?"

"You bet I am," she says. "My house took on way more water than the last two floods, and because writing about how sad and angry I feel has helped so much, I had the idea for all of you."

I nod, but I'm not like Ms. Martinez, at least not yet. I'm only sad. I'm not angry.

"Some of you might still be out of your homes like me, and you'll be that way for a while," she continues. The room gets noisy: feet scuffle and desks shift, kids cough and clear their throats. "And it still may be hectic for your families in the evenings with all the changes, so we'll reserve journal time at the end of every class, rest assured. But if you find some time to write outside class as well, please do so. It will really help you."

After school, Matty and I ride home in silence while Mom frowns and looks between us in the rearview mirror, trying to figure us out.

"You have Ms. Martinez for language arts, too, Matty, right?" I finally say. "Did you get a feelings journal?"

Mom grins big in the mirror like, "Oh, what a relief, it's a normal car ride with my twins," but Matty only nods.

"Do you want to trade journals sometime, so we'll know each other's feelings? Matty, I'd share mine with you."

He shakes his head and looks out the window. I press my lips together the rest of the way to Becky's house.

We pull into the driveway, and I slam the car door and run upstairs to get ready for my first 14U fall ball practice. Along with Matty quitting our playoff game last season and our house flooding in the hurricane, I'm playing baseball without my twin brother today for the first time, too.

It all feels like so, so much.

I always knew that someday we wouldn't play together anymore. But I always thought we'd play together for as long as we could, and when it ended, it wouldn't be because of Matty—it would be because of me, since I'm a girl and girls don't get to play in the MLB.

Becky's already up in her room getting ready for her afternoon photo session with Jess and Bartholomew . . . and my twin brother. I try to ignore what's she's doing, but I can't.

My eyes drift to her studio corner where she's laying out a scene with a chipped teacup, a teapot, and a three-pronged candlestick. She's set out some new white poster board and some watercolors for Matty to make his backdrop.

I shrug on the uniform that replaces the one I lost in the flood: new knee-high socks, bright white pants without any stains, and a new team cap and jersey with PUTTER-MAN stitched across the back.

I gulp. Matty's identical jersey and cap still sit in Dad's trunk.

I stand at Becky's mirror and tuck in my jersey, then untuck it again. I pull on the fabric under my armpits. I pull and pull and pull.

"What are you doing, Sammy?" Becky says.

"This jersey doesn't feel like my old one," I say. "It's too tight." I point to my chest in the mirror. "Here."

Becky rolls her eyes. "Even though you play baseball, you're still a *girl*."

"But I don't want my teammates to see me as girl," I say. "I want them to see me as a ballplayer."

Becky shrugs and goes back to laying out her studio scene, screwing long tapered candles into the candlestick. I knew she wouldn't understand.

"Sammy?" she says, a few minutes later.

I growl, "What?"

"If *I* were *you*, I wouldn't worry about that jersey."

"And why is that?"

She gives me a little shrug. "Your teammates have seen you hit."

I turn away from the mirror and pick up my cleats so she won't see my face scrunch up. I wish hitting was all that mattered, but it seems like there's more to me being able to play baseball than just that. I sit down on my bed.

"Sammy!" Becky says, and I jump. "Don't even *think* about putting those cleats on in my room! They'll snag my new carpet!"

As I'm heading down the stairs, I bump into my brother on his way to Becky's room. "Have fun," I say, but I don't really mean it.

I don't want him to have fun in Becky's room talking and laughing and jumping and singing. I want him to have fun with me, playing baseball, like we used to.

Like we're supposed to!

Matty nods, and glances at my uniform for a second, *our uniform*, then he rushes up the stairs. But at the top, he calls down, "You too, Sammy. Have fun."

If we were still at our house in Meyerland, I could walk to the ball field, but now one of my parents will have to drive me for all my practices and games.

"It will be great for you to start playing again, honey," Mom says when I get in the car.

I nod. "Uh-huh."

We stop at a red light, and she says, "I saw in the new coach's email that a few of your teammates from last season, like Ethan Goldberg, are playing on your 14U team!"

I saw that email, too. "Uh-huh," I say again, but it's not what I'm thinking. I'm thinking, *But the* one *teammate from last season I care about playing with is* not *on my new 14U team! My twin brother, Matty!*

When we get there, I head straight to my position at first base and run through my fielding footwork drills: low athletic stance, right foot on the bag, stride to catch, stride to catch. Then I work on catching drills: short hop, long hop, backhand and forehand picks. The whole time, I watch the mound where my brother should be.

Matty!

Ethan's catching a tall skinny kid named Brandon— who's supposed to be our new team's best pitcher.

Brandon's totally wild, and Ethan's already getting a serious workout. He's up out of his crouch every few pitches when Brandon throws over his head or totally misses the strike zone. Brandon pitches ball after ball after ball.

Then when we finally line up for batting practice, he hits the first three batters in a row with the ball, and then it's walk, walk, walk.

Brandon doesn't nearly have the arm my brother has. None of our pitchers do.

Matty.

We go through practice, and I try to put on a brave face.

On any other first day, I'd be talking smack and laughing, giving each drill my all. But I'm not today.

I'm angry and frustrated, stomping out to cover first, hurling my bat when I strike out, overthrowing the bases, and scowling at my teammates when they look at me as they cover their mouths with their gloves and whisper to each other.

Sentences start with, "Sammy's not . . ." Then their voices get low. Someone says, "There's a reason there aren't any *girl* ballplayers in the MLB." And Brandon says, "*She doesn't belong on our team.*"

And nothing's right and nothing's the same. It can't be. The most important member of my team isn't here.

Matty . . .

Ethan runs up to me at the end of practice. "You okay, Sammy?"

I nod my head—*yes*—but it's a weak, puny yes.

"Doesn't look it," he says. "Don't let anything that jerk says get in your head. You're a ballplayer, Sammy, a great one."

I mumble, "Thanks."

Ethan kicks the clay. "Hey . . . does Matt ever say anything . . . about me? He . . . he's not texting me back."

I shake my head again. "He won't turn his new phone on. Says he doesn't need it anymore."

He nods. "Tell him I say hey, Sammy. Tell him . . ." He kicks at the dirt some more. "Tell him we need him out here. Tell him our pitchers don't have the right stuff. Remind him that he does." Then he bumps my glove with his mitt and heads to the dugout to pack up.

Later that afternoon at the kitchen table, the awful feeling I left practice with today, being the only girl on the team and playing without my brother, scoops out and hollows my insides.

It's a really empty feeling I've never had before.

I'm not part of a Sammy-Matty team anymore. I'm just Sammy. Without my twin brother, will I still be able to hold my own?

I stare at my journal. Ms. Martinez wants us to write down our feelings about Hurricane Harvey, but the storm wasn't really the beginning of everything falling apart.

For me and Matty . . . it had already started.

I pick up my pencil and write about the last baseball game I played with my brother during the 12U playoffs.

I write about how lonely it felt that day, left by myself on the field. I write about how lonely it's felt ever since, just being Sammy. I write about how lonely I felt today at the first baseball practice I've ever done without him.

Then I write about everything we were always about, together: great-smelling gloves and green, grassy ballparks; sand in our cleats and clay stains in all the right places; our friend Mack and our Home Away from Home at Minute Maid Park; our favorite Astros stars and cheering on our team like we'd never stop. And cheering for each other—always.

Two journal pages a week for all my feelings won't be nearly enough.

So much has changed. So much is gone. Our Sammy-Matty connection has been cut, and I don't understand how it happened or if we can string it back together.

Without my brother, everything feels like a total loss.

Matty

During Ms. Martinez's language arts class on Friday, everybody's scribbling in their new feelings journals like they've been doing all week.

I listen to the *scratch, scratch, scratch* of pencils on paper and know that words are being made from feelings for just about every one of my classmates.

But they're not for me.

'Cause my feelings don't make words: they make pictures.

I glance over at Amanda and she's flipping pages, filling them up like she's Stephen King. She looks right at me, and grins.

I glance down quick, press my pencil into the paper, and try to think of words to write. But I can't help it . . . another image appears instead.

This time, it's my mom, Bialy, and me in our kayak.

Ms. Martinez walks around to check our progress. She raises her eyebrows at me when she sees my drawing and whispers, "No doodling, Matthew. This isn't art class."

I nod and shut my journal. I really wish it was.

After the first day of school, I helped Becky in her studio with the cats while my mom took Sammy to fall ball practice. Mom had asked me if I wanted to ride along to say hi to Ethan, since I hadn't seen him all summer, and wouldn't that be great.

I said, "No!" way louder than I meant to, and felt really bad.

Then Sammy got home from practice and slammed the door to the rental car. She stomped up the stairs to Becky's room to change, and when I raised my eyebrows at her, she snapped, "What? It was terrible! What did you expect? The kid who's supposed to be our best pitcher, Brandon, can't hit the broad side of a barn and . . . and he hates me!"

I wanted to talk to my sister about her practice right then. I really did. I wanted to help her feel better, but I just couldn't find my words.

Nothing's changed Sammy's mood all week, not even the Astros.

After they'd stunk in the Oakland A's series with four losses in a row, things started to look up. They'd won against the Angels at Anaheim two out of three. With only eighteen games to go, they have a comfortable lead now, and a favorable schedule down the stretch. Playoffs, here we come!

Not that I'm paying attention. Not that I'm still rooting

for them or anything. I hate baseball now, remember? At least that's what I'm letting my family think.

The important thing is, I'm not playing fall ball, so I'm not seeing Ethan and his amazing, anything-but-regular smile. 'Cause if I do . . . then what?

But it sounds like Sammy and Ethan's team, with their lousy pitching, doesn't stand a chance without me.

At the end of class, when Ms. Martinez checks our page counts, I still have zilch. Nothing but a few erased words and some partly finished pictures.

She raises her brows and whispers, "You're still doodling, Matthew. Let's talk after class."

I stand in front of her desk once everybody's gone. "I wasn't doodling." It comes out defensive, even though that's not how I meant to say it.

"You're not?" She smiles with the question, and my guard comes down.

I thought maybe I didn't like her, but she's kinda nice, so maybe I do. She waits for my answer.

"I like to draw," I say. "Drawing what I feel is way easier for me than words 'cause words sometimes stick in my . . ." My face screws up all of a sudden and then it starts—the chicken thing in my throat again.

Ms. Martinez nods. "Take a breath, Matthew. I want to understand what your drawings mean to you."

I do as she says, then I swallow and look around. It's still just us.

"Umm." I test my voice. No defense, no chicken noise.

"So . . . I was thinking that my journal could be in pictures. Since pictures can show feelings just like words. And they can tell a story, too, right?"

"Pictures?"

I nod. That's what I said.

She nods back. "Yes, they can, Matthew, but like I said, this isn't *art* class. It's *language arts*. It's my job to help you learn how to write."

"But what if I draw pictures of the hurricane instead to, you know, talk about my feelings and stuff? Like maybe a graphic novel."

"A graphic novel?"

She looks skeptical, so I dig in my backpack and pull out one I love, *Mighty Jack*. The pictures are so sick! And sure, there are some words, just not as many. Then I pull out my sketchbook from home and flip to one of the pages I drew in the shelter. "I can't write my feelings in words very well, Ms. Martinez, but I can still show them . . . like this."

I point to my drawing of our first night in the shelter: with the line of computers playing the Astros getaway game in Anaheim; with the gathering crowd, muddy and dripping wet; with people's stuff, maybe all they had left, piled in wet heaps along the walls. With my dad's arm around Papa, their teary but smiling eyes staring at the screens. With Sammy drawn at the center, her hands raised high to the ceiling in a cheer—her superfan energy radiating, big and loud and bright, filling up the whole place.

It kinda felt like hope, and it was just what we all needed.

Ms. Martinez leans across her desk and looks close. She gets really still, except for her chin. It quivers, then she starts blinking fast. Finally she takes a deep breath and says with that same smile from before, "Well, Matthew, a picture journal it is. But it's not a graphic novel, it's a graphic memoir. You're telling the story of what you saw in the hurricane, the story of what happened to *you*, right?"

I nod and smile back. She totally gets it—I'm telling *my* story. "Ms. Martinez?" I say as I walk out the door. "You can call me Matty or Matt for short. That's what people who know me pretty well call me, okay?"

"That sounds great, Matty," she says with another smile.

After school, I help Becky out in her studio, then I get to work on my journal. I start at the beginning, August 27, the morning of our evacuation, the last time our house was . . . *a home.*

My pencil flies, since all the pictures of what I saw are stored in my mind. And now that I'm telling the story of what happened to me in pictures, not words, it's easy for me to put everything in order.

Some of the pictures are hard to draw. I might be crying a little. But I draw them, I do, and they turn out great. 'Cause my feelings are in them, you know?

I fill up page after page of my graphic memoir, and pretty soon, just like Ms. Martinez said, I start to feel better.

Becky

Sunday afternoon after our first day back at religious school, Bartholomew claws up my purple velvet curtains like he's scaling Houston's near-highest building, Williams Tower in the Uptown District.

Not a single thing can be easy today!

This morning I finally ran through all my bat mitzvah prayers and pitched my speech to our rabbi. Suffice it to say, I have *lots* of work to do on both fronts. I kept messing up my prayers and Torah reading, and my speech, to quote him, ". . . might benefit from some *earnest* reflection."

Jess's pupils widen, dark and saucerlike, watching Bartholomew—her hero. She stretches one paw out and digs her sharp claws into the bottom of the curtains. She's about to follow him up.

"Not even, Jess!" I say, and she swivels her head in my direction and flicks her long tongue. Bartholomew hisses at me from above. "I think we might've given him too much coffee."

Matty nods. "How do we undo that?"

Sammy looks up from the journal she's writing in on her bed and rolls her eyes. "Maybe you should ask Mrs. Sokoloff. Bartholomew is *her* cat."

"I don't know . . . maybe we should Google it instead," I say, shaking the curtains, hoping Bartholomew will drop into my arms and I can stroke his skin until he calms down. "He's positively maniacal and my mother's going to kill me . . . cat-claw snags run all the way up!"

I finally get him down by threatening to leave the room with Jess. Then the cats start chasing each other and tumbling through all the props we'd set up in the studio.

"How's anyone supposed to get anything done in here?" Sammy says, shutting her journal and storming downstairs.

I shrug at Matty. She has a point.

But that's okay—since Matty and I started photographing the cats together, we've gotten almost a hundred followers, and we're adding new ones each day! And everyone, and I mean *everyone*, has been super complimentary.

One follower said, "This feline duo has irresistible je ne sais quoi type charm!"

Another one said, "Bartholomew breaks stereotypes with his unconventional beauty!"

And another said, "Look no further, it's cat couture at its greatest! Rebecca's line is cutting-edge in this burgeoning, booming market!"

Jenny and Rose have even signed up as my followers and are responding with things like "Bartholomew's hairless, so I won't be allergic!" and "Insiders' studio tour soon, pleez!" but they're a little too late to the party, if you ask me.

Bartholomew and Jess keep flying around my room. I actually think his coffee high hasn't even peaked yet. "Let's skip today," I tell Matty, and start placing props back on the shelves so they won't get trampled in the mayhem.

Matty eyes a tiny baseball glove on one of the shelves, right next to the mini felt Torah I made in first-grade religious school that I plan on using in early October for my bat mitzvah lead-up post with Jess. The post will be amazing, and my bat mitzvah will be, too, if I can just get my prayers right and figure out how to revise my speech.

Matty picks up the tiny glove, brings it to his nose, and sniffs the leather.

It's a toddler's mitt, the smallest one I could find. I also got two baby Astros T-shirts from the merchandise store in Minute Maid Park. I figured I'd do a celebratory post for my followers when the Astros win the World Series this year.

I mean, I'm not saying they'll win for sure, but like I said, they're flippin' amazing. It only makes sense to be ready for a timely post!

"Do you miss playing baseball?" I raise an eyebrow at the glove.

"Maybe a little," he mumbles.

I give him a long look. I wasn't sure before my cousins got here, but I am now. No one knows why Matty quit playing. No one! Especially not Sammy, since it doesn't take the kind of telepathy they *used* to have to know that between them . . . something big is broken.

Matty's still staring at the mitt.

"I mean, you played forever, then you just up and quit all of a sudden." I raise the other eyebrow.

He takes a deep breath. "Becks? Maybe I miss playing a lot."

My cousin starts tightening the leather straps on the glove. He seems like he wants to talk about it all, finally. My heart flips around . . . and he wants to talk with *me*!

I mean, we *have* gotten close doing our studio sessions. Things have been so fun, and we never run out of stuff to talk about. Liking each other again has turned out to be so—easy.

I take a deep breath, too, and try not to act overly excited. "Then . . . why? Why aren't you playing?"

Matty glances away. "Because of the kiss."

"With Amanda?" I say. "Sammy spilled about *that*. It was ages ago!"

"Not that kiss . . . another one."

Another kiss?

I feel a quick spark of jealousy. I've been waiting for my first kiss from Yale for two whole years, but nada. And Matty's already had two kisses!

"Who did you kiss, Matty?"

He looks back at me, and a smile spreads over his lips. "Ethan. At my 12U playoff game."

I say, "OH. MY. GOD," and grab the corner of his T-shirt and drag him over to my bed. We sit, facing each other, and I say, "We have SO MUCH to discuss!"

"Becky, I'm not sure I'm ready to—"

"Well, how *was* it?"

He gets quiet.

In my mind, what's there to think about? You either like a kiss, or you don't. You either want another one, or you don't. But I'm trying to be patient. Matty talking about this is a really big deal.

Finally I say, "Well, was it good?"

"Maybe it was more than good."

"Well, do you *like* him now?"

"Maybe I more than like him."

"Well, he *is* your best friend."

Matty looks at me. "Becky, maybe we're more than best friends."

"Well," I say, trying to be nonchalant. "What did he say when you talked to him about it?"

"We haven't talked about it."

"At all?"

"No."

"Not even texting?"

"No. I haven't even turned my new phone on."

Wow, I'm overwhelmed. Matty and Ethan kissed, and they haven't talked about it.

All. This. Time.

My heart aches in places I've never felt before. My eyes water up.

I reach out and squeeze Matty's hand. "I think you should turn your phone on. I think you should talk to him."

"And say what?"

"And say, 'I like you, a lot.' Since it's obvious you do!"

Matty squeezes my hand back. "Becky? Thanks for talking about . . . my new feelings." He gets quiet for a moment again. "I haven't felt ready to talk to Ethan or my family. Things are kinda wrapped up with me playing baseball. I'm still figuring out how me and Ethan . . . are gonna be *us*."

I nod, and a couple big tears dribble down my cheeks. "Well, your secret's safe with me," I say, reaching for a tissue.

"Thanks a lot, Becky."

"And I have a secret, too."

"Want to share it?"

A hot blush spreads up my neck. "I like Yale from religious school!"

Matty grins. "That's not exactly a secret, Becks."

I flop around and bury my face in my pillows and muffle, "Oh my god! It's not?"

He laughs. "It's kinda obvious, you know?"

We talk about our feelings for a while more. Then, after Matty leaves, I can't sit still.

I fumble around with a few of my new cat patterns, I brush Jess out and paint our nails, I pluck my eyebrows and straighten my hair with my flat iron, I scroll through my social media page and respond to a few of my new followers. I put my face in my pillow and scream. I even laugh a little.

My cousin Matty *like*-likes his best friend Ethan. How cool! I totally get what he sees in him. Even though I've haven't talked to Ethan much at school, he seems super nice.

But more than all that . . . my cousin Matty trusted *me* with his feelings.

It's almost like it used to be in the hallway photos when we did everything together. When we were more than just family, more than just cousins. When we were friends.

Now that's *really* cool.

Sammy

The Houston Astros have been on a serious hot streak, finishing strong at Minute Maid Park!

In between my 14U practices, my games, and checking on our house, my family's rotated our eight season ticket seats at our Home Away from Home, rooting for our team. Becky and Mrs. Sokoloff have even caught a few more games.

I got to be there when the 'Stros swept the Mariners and clinched the American League West title! I got to see José Altuve hit his twenty-fourth homer in the first winning game against the Chicago White Sox, and George Springer practically steal home on a routine out at first! I got to see my team win the next game against the White Sox, too, before cratering to them on the first day of Rosh Hashanah.

But they made up for it. Justin Verlander threw seven shutout innings against the Los Angeles Angels in the first game of the next series. And the Astros even took a second win on Saturday before they lost their home finale Sunday, even though Springer hit another home-run dinger.

But none of it was the same since Matty's still not cheering with me. And no matter how hard I've tried to read him and figure out why, I just can't.

Without twin telepathy, I don't know what he's thinking or feeling anymore.

But it sure seems like Becky does.

When I'm not at baseball practice after school, I sit on my bed in her room filling up my feelings journal while she and Matty do photo sessions with Jess and Bartholomew.

They plan out themes and outfits. They set up the props and position the nightstand lamp to shine on Matty's backdrops just right. They give Bartholomew a big dose of coffee, and somehow manage to get him dressed. Then they place the cats in the studio and snap away.

The whole time, Becky drops silly French phrases like "Oh là là!" and "C'est magnifique!" and "Très bon!"

Matty doesn't roll his eyes like I do, even though Becky's fake French is one of the things that's always annoyed us the most about her.

And even after all the snapping away and all Becky's oh là làs, they're still not done. They pick filters and hashtags. They post and respond. They plan what they'll need for the next session, and the one after that.

It's a bit over the top, if you ask me. But no one ever does.

No one asks me if I want to lend a hand. No one asks me if the cats look great. No one asks me anything.

And the whole time Matty's with Becky, he seems happy. And somehow that makes me feel miserable.

It doesn't help that I struck out every at-bat for my last two games, and now, along with the slump I'm in over my brother and our house getting flooded, I'm in a hitting slump, too.

Coach has even moved me down in the lineup, from batting third to batting seventh!

Maybe my hitting slump's happening because my brother isn't playing with me. Maybe I'm only good when he's around. Maybe it's happening because Matty isn't even in the stands during my games . . . *and he's stopped cheering me on.*

I'm not used to being in a slump. I've been writing a lot about it in my journal, trying to figure it out. I sure hope that what Ms. Martinez says about writing your feelings down and catharsis comes quick, because if it doesn't, I'm going to burst and catch on fire like an overfull hot air balloon.

Before my slump, people were always surprised I was such a great hitter since I'm a girl. But I had great teachers: Dad and Papa. And there's a little thing called physics.

Hitting is all about energy transfer and timing, the exact

moment when a ball strikes a bat, and a bat strikes the ball. If you transfer the energy through your hips to your swing and keep your bat flat in the hitting zone, it's almost like you're not hitting anything at all. It's almost more of a catch.

I can feel a perfect hit in my fingers right when it happens. They get tingly, but not like when I'm upset or nervous. They get tingly in a good way—it's definitely *oh là là!*—and my ball sails through the air. See ya!

Or at least, that's the way it used to be, before my hitting slump.

Before everything changed and I stopped being part of Sammy-Matty, an invincible twin team, and started being just Sammy, a girl who probably won't be able to play baseball much longer if she can't turn her terrible slump around.

I need my brother on my team now more than ever.

Tuesday, the week of Yom Kippur, I tag along with my parents to meet the contractor again at our flooded-out house since Matty and Becky started another cat couture session right after school. You know it's bad when going over to your empty, ruined house seems like a better activity than hanging out with your brother and cousin.

We take Bialy with us, too, so he can run around his old backyard. Dad says that things are cleaned up and our fence is secure, so he's not worried Bialy will get into something dangerous.

All three of us stay quiet in the rental car the whole way home.

It's been almost five weeks since Hurricane Harvey, and some Meyerland streets are cleared of debris now. Kids play in the front yards again, and mailmen deliver like usual. But some streets are still like ours—they're empty-housed ghost streets lined with stinky piles and FOR SALE signs popping up.

When we get there, the contractor is waiting on the porch. Our house's dark inside since the sun is dropping low. Our neighbors' houses are dark, too.

Bialy makes a sprint for the backyard gate as soon as we open the car doors. "Have at it," Dad says, laughing and letting him in.

We walk to the front porch and both my parents shake the contractor's hand.

"We've demoed everything, Dr. and Mrs. Putterman," he says. Then his eyes shift up and down our street. "But I've gotta be honest with you, and I'm not trying to talk myself out of a job, but some of the folks on your street bailed on me this week. Their repairs are so big, they're selling their lots and leaving the neighborhood."

My dad looks at my mom, and they nod.

Wait! What? Are my parents thinking about us leaving, too? My fingers start tingling, the bad way.

"You sustained a lot of damage," the contractor says. "If you want to stay, we could elevate the existing house and try to repair what's left." He shakes his head. "But I'd recommend building a new house altogether on a higher foundation."

My mom gasps and looks at my dad. "With the other floods, we just fixed the water damage."

The contractor shakes his head. "This time it's . . . different."

Dad tells him, "Thanks. We'll need some time to think on it, if that's okay," and the contractor shakes my parents' hands again and drives off in his van.

Right then, we hear Bialy's loud happy barks, like maybe he's cornered a squirrel. We walk through the gate into the backyard to see what's up. He's running in circles near a big tree, his tongue hanging out to the side, a sloppy grin on his face. I walk closer. "What, boy? What's got you so excited?" He stops and looks at me, his tail wagging so hard it's smacking into his sides.

I lift his lip and something's tucked into his cheek. It's gross and brownish, but little neon-green fibers peek through.

Bialy's found his favorite tennis ball! So much has been lost, but this one thing—Bialy's lovey—somehow hasn't been.

I run my tingly fingers through his fur. "Can he keep it, Mom, please?" I ask, bracing myself for a no since the ball's super disgusting.

She rubs his head and sighs. "Yes, Samantha. I'll run it through the washing machine on hot a few times."

That night after dinner, we all settle in on the sectional to watch the Astros second away game against the Rangers, and Becky starts in about the cats again. She's speaking lots of fake French, and she's going on and on about her followers and how great her sessions with Matty are.

Bubbe, Mom, Aunt Deb, and Mrs. Sokoloff nod and smile, like hearing about my cousin and brother's fun project is just what they needed tonight and if we weren't all living in the same house they never, ever would've worked as a team and isn't that a silver lining to this whole sad natural disaster.

Then even Dad and Papa and Uncle Mike are smiling, too.

And none of it's like my hitting slump games, where the only ones who are coming to cheer for me now are Mom and Dad and he's checking his phone and she's finishing paperwork from the lab.

And I'm the only one not smiling right now because it's all . . . just too much. The swirling hurt inside me heats up hot and expands to my edges, threatening to burst open wide.

"How long do we have to stay here?" I ask my dad before I can stop myself. "It's already been over a month!"

Everyone turns and looks at me. Dad clears his throat. "That's a big question, Sammy, and to be honest, we haven't quite figured it all out."

But I need to figure it out—I need my brother back. Maybe if Becky weren't around all the time, we'd already be Sammy-Matty again! We'd be a twin team like we used to be!

Uncle Mike nods to Aunt Deb. "We're, uhh, committed to having everyone for a while longer until you all can, uhh, sort things out."

Dad reaches over and grabs his shoulder. "Thanks, Mikey. We had a tough meeting with the contractor today, and now we're just not sure what to do."

Mom clears her throat. "Sammy-Matty?"

We both look up. We haven't heard anyone call us that in a while. I close my eyes and steady my breath. Just hearing our names together makes me feel a teensy bit better.

But the feeling doesn't last. Dad says, "We were thinking about what the contractor said. We've taken on water three times in three years. Maybe we should think about selling our lot and moving to an area that doesn't flood. Get a fresh start."

Bubbe, Papa, and Mrs. Sokoloff all nod.

"No!" I scream. "I don't want to live in a different house or a different neighborhood! I want things to be the way they used to be! You said our house wasn't a total loss, Dad!" I stare at Matty. "That means there's something to save!"

Mom says, "Calm down, honey. Nothing's been decided yet."

Dad shakes his head, and his voice gets quiet. "Honey, you were there with the contractor. Our house *is* pretty much a total loss this time. There's so much to fix. We're not sure if we should go back."

I finally burst. "We have to fix it! We have to go back!" I scream. "We have to! We have to, Dad!"

Everyone shifts on the sectional, quiet. My dad gives me a long, steady look.

It's a look I've seen a million times from his seat in the stands during my games. I can almost hear the words that go with the look, soft in my ear, like the very first time I heard them. I'd struck out on the last pitch of a game when I was nine. My team lost, and I threw my bat, completely out of control. Luckily, it didn't hit anyone. I was so embarrassed that I couldn't hold it together and I'd been a bad sport, I ran off the field.

It felt kind of like how I feel now.

He'd caught up to me and held me tight, then crouched down low and whispered, "Sammy baby, you've got to stay strong for the long game. You're going to be playing for a while, and sometimes you or your team will hit a slump. You'll feel like giving up right then, but things will get better, I promise."

I'm crying now, big gulping sobs, and everyone's still quiet. I'm in a serious slump, that's for sure—with the epic hurricane and our house destroyed, with being split down the middle from my twin brother, with being the only girl on an all-boys baseball team without Matty to back me up.

I rub my eyes and look at the TV. The Astros are winning, up 6–1 in the fifth inning. Aunt Deb hands me a tissue, and we all start watching the game again. I dry my tears, honk my hose, and start cheering—super small *way-to-go*s and *that's-it*s.

Dad's the first to start cheering with me. Our eyes meet and he nods, strong.

I steal a glance at Matty petting the cats on Becky's lap.

Someday, I hope, he'll start cheering with me again. Someday, I'll find a way out of this slump. But for now, I've got to stay strong for the long game.

Matty

At Shabbat dinner, Sammy stares at me hard, like she's trying to read my mind.

I don't let her.

But if our twin telepathy were working, she'd find out that I feel better than I have in a really long time.

Turns out it's a lot to carry around a big secret. It's a lot to have a bunch of new feelings and keep them to yourself.

And when you finally let somebody in, you feel a whole lot lighter.

But here's the thing: deciding to let somebody in is way different than somebody—I'm not saying who—reading your mind all the time and telling you what you think.

I'm starting to say what I think on my own. I'm starting to get my feelings out. I guess that's what Ms. Martinez's feelings journal is all about.

Earlier today when she checked my page counts, I'm sure she got the gist of what I've been feeling, since you know that saying—a picture's worth a thousand words.

Well, I drew six.

She leafed through them fast and businesslike, but I could tell she wanted a closer look. So after class I went up to her desk and slid my feelings journal across to her. I said, "I want to share my drawings with you since you lost your home in the hurricane, too."

She covered her heart with her hands and smiled, then she opened my journal. "I'd be honored, Matty."

Mrs. Martinez lingered at each picture, taking it in. When she finished, she closed my journal and ran her fingers over the cover. Gave it a little pat. "Thank you, Matty. I've never seen anything like this," she said. "It's like I'm there with you since you captured all your feelings so strongly. Keep telling your story. It's a great one."

I smiled. That's what I was goin' for! That was why winning the Bayou City Art Contest with my drawing of Bialy meant so much to me: I had wanted to share my feelings all along, but I needed to figure out how.

And now that I've practiced sharing my feelings with Becky and Ms. Martinez, sharing them with Sammy, Mom, and Dad will be a whole lot easier.

In addition to being Shabbat, Yom Kippur starts tonight. We're going to Kol Nidre services at our synagogue after a big early dinner, and then we'll go back to services tomorrow. It's not like we're super religious or anything, but in my Jewish family, it's just what you do, okay?

As Bubbe says, "Religion every single week? Ehh. Holidays and celebrations? Of course. But we Puttermans are mostly about food and family!"

She's made all our favorites for dinner: a round raisin challah, roast chicken with crispy potato medallions, sweet glazed carrots, and sautéed green beans. And she's substituted her lemon cake with a honey cake tonight. We're stuffing our faces before sunset, and then most of us will fast all tomorrow.

Becky's fasting this year since she just turned thirteen, and even though Sammy and I don't technically have to since we're twelve, I've decided to fast with my cousin. It'll help keep me focused on figuring stuff out, even though I've gotten a head start.

Yom Kippur's the day when Jews across the world turn inward to think about how they've treated their friends and family, then figure out how they're gonna atone, or ask for forgiveness for anything hurtful.

In fact, it's a day so sacred that Sandy Koufax, not that I've taken that book about him down from the highest shelf of the not-really-a-library/really-a-man-cave a few times and started reading it or anything, decided *not* to pitch in Game One of the 1965 World Series, since it was on Yom Kippur!

It kinda makes him my hero, since doing something like

that means that he's a guy who knows what he's about.

Tomorrow during services, I'm gonna think about Sammy and Ethan the most. I've kinda kept to myself while I've figured stuff out, and Sammy's really upset. I bet Ethan is, too. But I'm not sure how I'm gonna make it up to them yet.

Sammy's phone starts vibrating in her pocket during dinner. I hear it since I'm sitting right next to her.

She peeks under the dining room table, and her eyes go big.

"Matty," she super-loud whispers. "Ethan says you're *still* not texting him back. What do you want me to tell him?"

Bubbe hears her. It's like she's got this sixth sense about things that are *supposed* to be private. "Ethan Goldberg, Matty's ballplayer friend who goes to Becky's school?"

The hairs on my arms bristle, and Becky's back gets stiff. Sammy instantly looks sorry she said anything. We all start shoveling big bites of food into our mouths, like we haven't eaten in days.

For once, the three of us are on the same page—none of us like where this conversation is headed.

"Matty, why don't you bring him around anymore?" Bubbe asks. "He's such a nice boy, and he has such a nice mother!"

I shovel another big bite into my mouth.

She grins at Becky. "Like I said, you and Ethan would be adorable!" She winks. "And he might make a nice date to your bat mitzvah party."

Becky's face flushes deep red and her brow furrows. She looks more ornery than Bartholomew coming off coffee.

Uncle Mike jumps in to help her. "Mom . . . *please*. Becky doesn't even *think* about boys yet!"

"We're just talking, Michael. What's the harm? Right, Becky?"

Becky snorts. "Ethan Goldberg is *taken*, Bubbe! You're going to have to think of someone else!"

She spins to Uncle Mike. "And I *do* think about boys, Dad! Just not *that* one!"

My grandmother raises an eyebrow. "*Taken?* Ethan's taken?"

Becky stuffs her mouth with a big bite of challah, like that'll stop her from talking. I chew the food in my mouth over and over, but I can't seem to swallow.

My grandmother raises the other brow. "Are you *sure*, Becky? We could invite him over and . . ."

"I'm sure, Bubbe!" Becky snaps through her mouthful. "He's *taken*, but not like you *think*! He and Matty *like-like* . . ." She claps both her hands over her mouth.

My fork scrapes across my plate and my throat makes a sudden loud chicken noise. I start choking on the food I'm chewing on—the bite gets stuck for a second until I reach for my water and gulp it down.

Everybody watches me and gets quiet.

Becky's hands drop away from her mouth and soggy, mushed-up challah falls onto the table. Her eyes well up and she sinks into her chair. "I mean . . . what I really meant to say . . . about Ethan, but not about Matty and Ethan . . . my god . . . ," she stammers.

Bubbe's instincts take over and she says, "Oh!" My aunt and uncle freeze with their silverware in the air, and my parents lock eyes. And Sammy—she's probably reading me perfectly for the first time in a while.

I picture my face. I'm sure me *like*-liking Ethan's written all over it.

Big heavy tears form on Becky's lashes and spill over. She starts to whimper. "I'm so, so sorry, Matty! I'm so, so sorry! I didn't mean to tell anybody. I promise I didn't!"

And I have to get out of here. I have to get away from them all!

I push my chair back from the table with a screech and yell, "Bathroom!" Then I sprint to the library. As I dart down the hall, more chairs in the dining room screech back, too. "Bathroom!" Sammy and Becky yell at the exact same time.

Then they're right behind me.

Becky

Sammy and I run down the hall, together. We pound on Matty's shut library door, together. We yell, "We're so, so sorry!" to him, together. And when his door doesn't open, we both melt to the floor and start sobbing, together.

But that's the extent of our togetherness.

We argue about whose fault it is that Matty's holed up in the library again. I lose! We argue about who Matty needs more. I lose again! Then somehow we start arguing about which Houston Astro is a better hitter—José Altuve or George Springer. I'm not about to lose on that one!

Sammy tells *me* to go up to my room, then I tell *her* to go up to my room.

Finally Aunt Annie and Uncle Greggy walk up and tell us *both* to go up to my room and get ready for Kol Nidre services.

"Greg, I'll stay home with Matty and maybe he'll talk with me," Auntie Annie says as Sammy and I shuffle down the hall.

Then at synagogue, no one in the rest of my family, and I mean *no one*—not even my parents—says a word to me all evening!

By the next day, three things have become crystal clear.

Number one: I'm a terrible person.

Number two: the Whole World hates me.

Number three: I can't say I blame them.

The fact that today is Yom Kippur, the Jewish day of atonement, seems like some kind of cosmic message. *Listen up, Becky Putterman, you have a lot to think about! You have so much to work on! You haven't been nearly your best self!*

Today's all-day marathon at our synagogue begins with a morning service, moves through an afternoon service, and ends after the closing service when a shofar, a long ram's horn, is blown.

So I'll have lots of time to sit and think about how to get back on track to being my best self, after my awful setback last night. And since I'm fasting today for the first time ever, I won't even have food as a distraction.

I really blew it! And I'm not even sure how it happened.

One minute, one of my two cousins was already back to being my friend. Then the next minute, our friendship evaporated like the Astros' chances against the White Sox in their only World Series.

189

But truly, talking about Matty and Ethan together had started to seem like a regular thing, at least in my studio.

Or in *our* studio—mine and Matty's—as I'd begun to think of it.

While Sammy was at baseball practice, Matty talked and talked during our photo sessions, and finally got his words out. I felt honored to be a part of it, so I just listened and listened. It's another one of my talents, when I put my mind to it. And after a while, *Matty-Ethan* didn't seem like a secret anymore.

But it was, outside of my room.

And somehow I let that secret slip. To our entire family!

Sammy sits on one end of our family's pew during services, and I sit on the other. Matty's smack in the middle. The three of us are separated by our parents, grandparents, and Mrs. Sokoloff.

We're so far apart.

And everyone in my family's still mad at me. Uncle Greggy and Auntie Annie frown at me every so often. Sammy leans over and glares at me each time she rises for a standing prayer. Matty's eyes throw fastballs at my head over and over. Bubbe glances my way, takes deep breaths, and sighs. And my mom nods to my dad and hisses down the row to me, "I hope you're paying attention, young lady!"

The only people who seem unfazed about last night are Papa and Mrs. Sokoloff.

The rabbi gives his Yom Kippur spiel, and I think about

the bat mitzvah speech I'm supposed to be revising. It's just another thing for me to mess up.

My speech is my chance to shine and show everyone that I can be my best self, so I need it to be really good.

I've tried rewriting it so many times, but it's still not coming together. Unlike Sammy, who fills up her journal like it's no big deal, writing does *not* appear to be one of my talents.

Now we're on to the afternoon service. I know, I know! Yom Kippur sounds like a drag of a holiday, because who likes sitting all day thinking about what they've done wrong and how they're going to fix it?

But it's not really a drag, if you need it. Because it's all about hope.

That even if you haven't been your best self and you didn't get close to it, you can look inside your heart to see where you've messed up and hurt yourself or someone else, and you can make amends.

Say sorry. Be forgiven. Be better next time. Nothing has to stay the way it was.

I don't want things to go back to exactly the way they used to be, like Sammy does. I was on the outside for so, so long. I want to be on the inside again.

All during services, I try to figure out why I was in all the hallway photos at Sammy and Matty's house for all those years, and then I wasn't.

Sure, I had absolutely no interest in playing baseball.

Sweating outside in the Houston humidity? Endless bad hair days? A definite no.

But still, it can't be all about baseball . . . or can it?

I was dragged to so many of my cousins' games over the years, even before they became star athletes. I guess going to those games wasn't just because my father and Uncle Greggy and Papa were baseball players once, and nothing seemed better than an afternoon at a ballpark. I guess we went to show our Putterman team spirit, too.

To say I was not on board with being at those games would be an understatement.

I didn't want to go. I didn't want to cheer. I didn't want to sit in the stands and watch my cousins shine and get all the attention when I wasn't getting any.

But the more I sulked, the more I whined, the more under-breath nasty comments that escaped my lips maybe on purpose, the more I felt alone.

Like everyone was doing this happy thing I couldn't be a part of. Like everyone expected me to join in the family cheer.

But I just couldn't. I just wouldn't. I was so jealous of them, and all the attention they were getting.

It felt so, *so* good to have Matty on my side with my social media page because . . . he was cheering me on. That's what family does—they cheer for each other.

I haven't been a very good cheerleader at all.

Maybe I can be a Putterman team player someday, if

Matty forgives me for accidentally blurting his secret, if Sammy forgives me for being so self-centered and mean. Maybe we could all be friends again, and new photos of the three of us could hang on the walls. Maybe somehow, I can become my very best self.

Sammy

All during Yom Kippur services, I think about how much I need to talk to my brother.

About what happened the day he walked away from our 12U playoff game at the start of it all. About our broken twin connection that's getting worse and worse. About what Becky said, that Ethan was *taken*.

I've tried to fix things with Matty so many times, but nothing's worked.

And it doesn't take telepathy to see how upset he still is after last night. He hasn't said a single word to anyone all day. It's in his eyes that stare away. It's in his mouth that turns down at the edges. It's in his body that hugs into itself.

When the shofar blasts at the end of services, loud and long and strong, I know I have to keep trying with Matty.

He's my twin brother, and fixing our connection means so much. We need each other now more than ever.

So I'll never give up!

We listen to Astros away game coverage on the Suburban's car radio on the way back to my cousin's house.

Last night, they won their hundredth regular season game against the Red Sox after demolishing the Rangers. And today, the 'Stros lost 6–3 against the Sox, but there's one more game tomorrow before our team heads into the postseason. We'll get to play the Red Sox again in the Division Series playoffs next week, with a home field advantage, while the New York Yankees play the Cleveland Indians.

Uncle Mike flips the radio off and says, "Doesn't matter we lost! Our position's solidified as AL West champs! We'll just shake this one off!"

I nod from the back seat. It's just the reminder I need right now. We're still solid. We have to shake it off and get back to playing. It almost seems simple.

It's what you tell yourself every time you strike out or lose a game, or at the end of a season if it doesn't go your way. Athletes go on after their setbacks. They keep playing.

It's true on the field, and I want it to be true off the field, too—for me and Matty. The two of us have had a setback—a big one—but we have to keep playing. We're still a team. I just need to remind him!

But his spacey eyes out the window tell me he didn't even hear what Uncle Mike said.

Becky tries to get his attention. "I have a great idea!" she says, and grins at him. "Let's do a session in our studio right after break fast, Astros versus Red Sox!"

She waits a beat, but Matty doesn't respond. "I'll bet my dad has a Red Sox cap in his collection for Bartholomew, and Jess is an Astro, of course! It'll be adorable! It'll be fun, right, Matty?"

He stares out the window, quiet.

Becky squeaks, "Right, Matty?" one more time, then she stares out the window, too.

My mom, grandmother, and Mrs. Sokoloff rush inside the house to brew a pot of coffee and put out the big breakfast spread they prepared in advance: bagels and lox, tuna salad, sweet noodle kugel, quiche, and chopped green and fruit salads. Mrs. Sokoloff has made her amazing chocolate rugelach, too.

The adults break their fast with sips of coffee and massage their sore temples from caffeine withdrawal. Then everyone piles food on their plates.

I gulp down a few big glasses of water before eating. But even though I fasted for the first time, I'm not as hungry as I should be.

Matty's space at our dining room table is empty. He's nowhere in sight.

My mom and dad notice, too. Mom takes a quick bite of kugel and heads down the hall toward the library. A few minutes later, she comes back into the dining room and sits down.

"Well, Annie?" Dad says.

"He still doesn't want to talk, Greg. We can try again later."

I'll try! I finish up quick and make a break-fast plate for Matty. He must be hungry!

I smear a thick layer of cream cheese on a bagel and pile on lox, a tomato slice, a little onion, and some capers, just how we like it. I scoop some fruit salad onto his plate and grab a few rugelach.

When I get to the library, the door's locked tight like it was when Becky and I followed him last night.

I start knocking again. "Matty? It's just me this time, and I brought you some food. Aren't you hungry?"

"Yeah, I guess I am. Thanks, Sammy," he mutters. "Can you leave it on the floor?"

Bialy's lying at the end of the hall, his nose wiggling after the smells from the plate. I lean close to the door. "Bialy's nearby, and he loves fish!"

There's a long sigh, then Matty's hand pokes out. "Thanks," he says, taking the plate.

I put my foot against the door so he can't shut it. "Why don't you want to hang out with me anymore? Why won't you talk to me? Why have you been talking to Becky instead?" My words run together. There are so, so many.

I've been writing them in my feelings journal, and it's helped just like Ms. Martinez said it would, but my words need to reach my brother, too.

197

His eyes catch mine for a second, then turn to the floor. He doesn't say anything.

"You can tell me anything, Matty. We're twins. We're a team."

He bites his upper lip. "We're only a team sometimes, Sammy," he says. "Sometimes we've gotta do stuff on our own."

Somehow it feels like a slap.

I step back and the door shuts. Then I stand in the hallway. My fingers that just held his break-fast plate tingle the bad way, and suddenly every single part of my body feels achy and tired.

I head up to Becky's room to lie down. My cousin's still downstairs, thank goodness. Jess and Bartholomew are curled up together on their little cat bed, nuzzling whiskery faces. They look so happy, just being together.

My over-full emotions whip around inside me like a mini hurricane. Just like Brays Bayou, they need somewhere to overflow. I reach under my mattress, pull out my feelings journal, flip to a fresh page, and write.

Once I was part of a twin team called Sammy-Matty. It was the greatest team, ever.

We were even better than the Astros this season, and that's hard to be. We were better than the Big Red Machine or the Miracle Mets. Our team was even better than the 1927 Yankees.

Because it was ours, all ours. It was Sammy-Matty, Sammy-Matty, Sammy-Matty, all the time.

And when you're on a team like that, you know that someone's always there to root for you. You know that someone's there to help you when your swing's off, or you make a bad play, or when you're a girl trying to keep her spot on an all-boys baseball team.

You're never alone. You've got a brother there to vouch for you each season, each game, to tell anyone who gives you the side-eye, "Kiss off! Just watch my sister swing!"

When we were Sammy-Matty, there were so many smiles that only we understood the secret meanings of. There were so many laughs, where we were the only ones who knew the inside jokes. And even when there were tears, we dried them faster together.

Every big thing that happened to us, happened together, and that seemed like the perfect story. At least it was for me.

But now we're just Sammy, and just Matty. We're not a team anymore.

By this part of the story of us, big fat tears fall on my journal and blur my shaky writing, but I can't stop them. I don't want to. I'm so, so sad.

I let myself cry, and when I'm done, I shut my journal and hide it under the mattress again. I splash my face with cold water, then I head downstairs to get some rugelach of my own. Maybe that will cheer me up.

But on the way, I can't help peeking down the library hall.

My parents stand in front of Matty's door, and my dad's fist is raised like he's going to start knocking. But he hasn't yet. It's like his arm is frozen that way.

"What are you doing, standing there?" I ask.

They give me a long look. "We need to talk to your brother."

I walk over to them and say, "So do I." I'm so tired and upset from all the feelings swirling around my family that we don't have words for. Keeping them in is destructive, just like Hurricane Harvey.

Dad clears his throat. "Sammy, this conversation's going to have to be just between me, Mom, and Matty."

My voice gets small. "I should know what's going on, too, so I can help. Matty and I are twins and we . . . need to be there for each other."

My brother opens the door, and our parents head into the library with Bialy. I try to follow them, but Matty steps in front of me and blocks the way.

He looks sad. "Please, Sammy. Please," he says, then he shuts me out.

I stumble back up to Becky's room. She's sitting on her

bed hugging Jess, looking just as sad as Matty, but I don't care. As many words as I have trapped inside for my brother, I don't have any for her.

We get ready for bed without talking, without even looking at each other. We brush our teeth, throw on our pajamas, get in our twin beds, and turn off the nightstand light.

Becky cries into her pillow, and I remember the day a few weeks ago when I was standing outside her room, crying, too.

Left out of the laughs and jokes, feeling jealous.

It's hard to admit, but it felt like it did sometimes at my baseball games, when Matty and Ethan were completely in sync with calls and pitches, smiling ear to ear at each other after every strikeout.

Then I smushed that bad feeling down because I'm a team player who cheers her teammates on and I knew shouldn't be jealous that Matty and Ethan . . . had some kind of telepathy, too. Their connection seemed so, so strong.

Ethan is taken by my brother. They're a team of their own. Maybe a part of me always knew that they *like*-liked each other.

It was there all along.

I reach for my feelings journal again and turn on my phone's flashlight. I write a note for Matty and tear out the page. Then I sneak downstairs to the library.

My parents are long gone, and Matty's room is dark. I

slip the note under his door so he'll find it in the morning. It says:

> Wish you had felt like you could've told me. Wish I'd just known. Love you so much and I'll always have your back. Someday. . . I hope we can be a twin team again.

That night I toss and turn, running through the mental list of all I've lost this year. At the end of my list, I add my brother Matty. Game over.

Matty

Sammy knows just how I like my bagel. After she leaves, I practically inhale it. It's gone in two minutes, flat.

I didn't feel hungry until I smelled the cream cheese and lox, and bit into the perfectly toasty crust and chewy inside. I *knew* I was hungry from fasting, since my stomach cramped during services and made these loud, obnoxious gurgling noises.

But my brain's been too busy for hunger to register.

It's been busy working out what I've been feeling since Becky blurted about me and Ethan last night.

First I was pissed, really pissed. I'd stormed from the dining room to the library and slammed the door. I had to be alone to calm down. I ignored Sammy and Becky's knocking and all their apologies. I was kinda mad at Sammy since she started it all with Ethan's texts, but I was mostly mad at Becky.

'Cause telling everybody about Ethan was *mine* to tell, and she stole it before I was good and ready! I was trying to get there. I was trying to figure stuff out.

But I needed to take it slow.

Then I was disappointed, super disappointed. I'd seen a whole new side of my cousin working with her in her studio. I thought I'd misread Becky, you know, unfairly judged her as self-absorbed and ridiculously whiny. I thought we were making this great new connection, that we had an understanding, that I could trust her with my new feelings.

Guess I was wrong.

Finally I was sad, really sad. I mean, my parents and Sammy like Ethan, and the rest of my family does, too, so I think they're gonna be cool with us *like*-liking each other. But here's the thing: I *still* don't know what to do about baseball.

I walked away from it. Said I hated it. Said I was done playing.

But it wasn't true. It wasn't! So nothing's changed: I'm still stuck wondering if two ballplayers like me and Ethan could ever stand a chance.

I reach up to the highest shelf in the not-really-a-library/really-a-man-cave and feel for my phone, then I lie down on the pullout and turn it on. All of Ethan's texts load—the ones I've read and the ones I haven't. They're all still there.

How many times can somebody ask you the same questions, over and over, without getting an answer, and not give up?

But as I read through Ethan's texts, he hasn't. He hasn't given up on us. So I shouldn't either.

I take a deep breath, Google out ballplayers in the Major Leagues again, and wait. I scroll through the articles that pop up and my insides feel punched.

Zilch. There's still nobody playing who's out.

There are just some articles about two former Los Angeles Dodgers, Glenn Burke and Billy Bean. And Glenn Burke never came out while he was playing, and Bean only let people know after he retired.

So what am I supposed to do? Hide how I feel about Ethan? Never play baseball again?

They're both a big part of what I'm about.

I turn my phone off, then I put it back on the high shelf. Just as I crawl onto the pullout, there's a knock at the door.

"Go away, Sammy," I mumble. "I still don't wanna talk."

My dad clears his throat. "Matt, can Mom and I please come in?"

I've been avoiding them, but I can't forever. I open the door, and Bialy rushes in. Sammy's out there again, too.

My parents walk inside, and I start shutting the door.

Sammy seems hurt and confused and scared all at once. And even though it's Yom Kippur, and I'm gonna have to figure out how to say sorry for shutting her out, I can't do that right now.

I've shared almost everything important with my twin sister up till now. But I can't share this. Right now, I need Mom and Dad without her.

So I close the door on Sammy, again.

My parents are quiet, shuffling around near Uncle Mike's framed jersey wall. I sit down on the pullout and nod my mom to the space next to me. She rushes over.

Dad stays standing, his hands deep in his pockets in front of the Jeff Bagwell jersey.

He clears his throat and tries to put on his a-bit-higher-than-usual happy and calming pediatrician voice, but it cracks wide. "Matt, Mom and I think we know what Becky was talking about last night. About Ethan."

I keep my eyes down, and nod.

"And it's okay, Matt. We want to tell you it's all okay."

I can't help it. The chicken throat thing starts right up again. And it's bad, really bad, this time. My mom squeezes my hand.

"Matty, I want you . . . to look at me. I want you . . . to hear me," Dad says. He's got the chicken thing going now, too. "I don't want there to be any misreading . . . any misunderstanding . . . of what I'm about to say."

My mom squeezes my hand harder and says, "It's all right, Matty."

I still can't look up. My eyes water and my throat's a

swollen knot and I try to suck in some air so I can breathe, but I can't.

"You like who you like, do you understand?" Dad says. "You love who you love. Don't *ever* let anyone tell you it's not okay."

"I thought maybe . . ." My voice totally gives out, and it takes me a minute to get it back. "Me and Ethan showing we *like*-like each other . . . wouldn't be okay. That maybe we'd have to hide . . . what we're about."

"No, honey, no! Why would you think that?" Mom says. "Our whole family stands with the Pride movement—me and Dad, Bubbe and Papa, and Aunt Deb and Uncle Mike, too."

My dad walks over and puts his hand under my chin. He repeats slowly, gently, "Matty, please look at me."

My eyes become a leaky faucet. Tears plunk all over my feet. I raise my face.

"You and Ethan are perfect. You're perfect. Always remember that."

When he says it, I see the strong, certain look that I've seen so many times before: when I knocked my front teeth loose at the playground and ran home with a bloody face; when Sammy broke her leg sliding home and I cried harder on the way to the hospital than she did; when Bubbe got cancer and lost all her hair two years ago and I was so, so scared.

When he loaded our family into two fishing kayaks as

hurricane floodwater poured into our house.

It's the look that tells me everything's gonna be okay. That I'm gonna be okay. That all my new feelings about Ethan, they're okay, too.

I trust my dad. I trust my mom. They love me more than anything.

I nod and stand, then both my parents rush around me, almost winning the World Series pileup style. Dad kisses my hair and Mom rubs circles on my back as they pull me into a big hug.

We stay like that for a long time, the three of us together. We finally pull away, and Dad says, "Matty . . . do you really hate baseball?"

I shake my head. "No, Dad. I love baseball. I'm a Putterman. But I've looked online . . ." My voice almost gives out again. "And there aren't any players in the MLB who are . . ."

He looks at me hard. "Gay? Sure there are, Matt. Sure there are. The world is changing all the time. Maybe someday they'll feel comfortable speaking up."

"So I can still play?"

"Of course you can still play, if you want to." My dad smiles. "With that southpaw arm, can you ever play baseball, if you want to!"

When they finally leave, I sit back down on the pullout next to sleeping Bialy and take another big breath. I put one hand on his chest to feel his steady heartbeat; I put the other hand on mine. My heart beats steady now, too, perfect.

But then I feel a surge of Yom Kippur guilt. The whole time my parents and Bialy were here with me, there was a big gaping hole, since one member of our team, my twin sister Sammy, wasn't here with us.

And that doesn't feel perfect at all.

Becky

The next few days when I'm not at school, I stay holed up in my room, since the situation in the rest of the house is . . . well, unbearable.

The Whole World still hates me.

It's all my fault, since I messed up, big. Epic! I've wreaked Hurricane Harvey levels of destruction on my family. I've strayed so far from best selfhood that there's no obvious path back.

Every time I pop out of my room, I feel worse about myself.

My parents' faces have frozen Medusa-like in total disappointment. Auntie Annie and Uncle Greggy get extra quiet in my presence. Bubbe serves me paper-thin slices of leftover honey cake. And when Matty comes out of the library, which isn't very often, he looks at me pained, like I've scraped off his skin Michelangelo-St. Bartholomew-style.

I've tried to apologize twice, but he pretends I'm not even there.

But Sammy's worst of all. She sits on her bed in my room, glaring at me in between scribbling feelings into her journal. I can only imagine the awful things she's writing about me—but they're probably true.

And my bat mitzvah speech, which should be a similar outlet for all my feelings, only stresses me out. Even though I've been reflecting like the rabbi told me to, my Torah portion still doesn't make much sense. I've figured out that God's testing Abram, but I'm not sure why.

Meanwhile, Rebecca's Domestic Cat Fashions has gone positively viral.

Everyone adores Jess and Bartholomew's cat couture. My notifications for new followers ding over and over on my social media page—five hundred people and counting think my studio sessions are amazing. That I'm amazing: Rebecca, not Becky.

I'm finally known for something that's just *me*.

But really, my new followers aren't the people I care most about. They're not the Whole World. And they're not the one person in my family who cheered me on from the very beginning: my cousin Matty.

Because what I blurted about him *like*-liking Ethan was private, and if he wanted to share that private part of him when he was ready . . . that was up to him.

I've really hurt him since it wasn't my story to tell.

Wednesday afternoon, I walk around my room gathering props and assembling them in my studio corner for today's session, which is all about tragedy.

Jess is Jane Eyre, this terribly lonely girl from a movie I watched one night while my parents were out again. I told my teacher at school that the story really resonated with me, for obvious reasons, and she said *Jane Eyre* is a literary classic that I'll get to read in high school. Yay!

Bartholomew is Mr. Rochester, Jane's love interest, who's bristly on the outside but soft on the inside. I have to say— this cat was meant for this role!

Jane and Mr. Rochester find each other, and for a while, they're not as lonely anymore. Until everything falls apart.

Nothing comes together in my session today. The braided bun I made out of yarn for Jess's hair keeps coming undone every time she shakes her head, and she furiously scratches at the lace collar around her neck. The black over-coat I pieced together for Bartholomew comes completely unglued, and I have to stop and heat my glue gun up and start over.

Then, just as I finally put everything back together and get them settled, the nightstand lamp I'd positioned for shadowy ambiance falls over with a crash, and the cats bolt back to Jess's canopy bed and glower. Bartholomew starts chewing Jess's lacy collar for her, trying to get it off.

Sammy sits on her twin bed after baseball practice in her grimy uniform, sneaking glances at the mayhem while watching loud Houston Astros replays on her phone.

I always wanted to share my room with someone, like a sister. But since my cousin's been here, things haven't been sisterly at all. All we do is trade insults. We haven't tried to do a single fun thing together.

Maybe we're both to blame for that.

And we've been fighting over Matty. But that doesn't matter now, since he doesn't want to hang out with either of us.

It's truly tragic, and I can't help it, I start tearing up again. I really can't control my waterworks anymore—*drip drop, drip drop, drip drop.*

"Okay, that . . . that's it," I blubber to no one. "I give up."

Then I sit down cross-legged in the studio and start dismantling the session.

Sammy's bed creaks, and she sits down cross-legged next to me. "What's wrong?"

I shrug. "It's not going that well today. Usually the cats will do anything if they're together. Since it's . . . way better than being apart."

Sammy nods.

A feed on my page pops up, one of the last sessions I did with Matty where we transformed Jess and Bartholomew into Katy Perry tigers for our Big at Heart empowerment theme. It was flippin' amazing, and my followers found it super supportive, so they're tagging and sharing it.

I smile for a second, remembering how easy it was for me and Matty to transform Jess with tiger-orange hairspray since she has her own black tabby stripes, but how the hairspray and marker stripes we drew all over Bartholomew were tough to get off his wrinkly skin when we were done.

But it was a super-great session, because, because . . .

Then I feel it again—a cold shiver running through me, like in my cousins' flooded-out house with everything stripped bare and raw, needing to be built up again, somehow.

The feeling of total loss.

Sammy notices. She holds out her hand for my phone. "Can I see your photos?" she asks.

"Sure," I say, handing it over. "You can follow me on social media, too, if you want."

She nods, then she smiles as she scrolls through the pictures. "The cats are kind of . . . cute. You're super creative."

I shake my head. "Matty's the real artist; he helped a lot. I feel so terrible!"

Sammy nods, then bites her lip. "How long did you know about . . . Matty and Ethan?"

I glance away. "Maybe two weeks?"

Sammy's quiet for a minute, then mumbles, "It's great they like each other. I just thought . . . I thought I would always know if something big was happening with my brother, since we're twins. But I didn't, and I guess he didn't feel like he could tell me, either."

I don't know what I say, so I scoot over so our knees touch. I know what it feels like to have a strong connection with someone and then lose it. It really stinks. And my cousins' connection was super strong once.

Sammy leaves our knees that way. Her eyes run over the cat props in the studio: the half-unglued black overcoat, the yarn bun, the glossy manor house photos I'd printed out on my mother's emergency-use-only fancy printer, the rocks and the tufts of grass I'd hauled in from the backyard to fashion some English moors. It's a complete mess.

"What were you going for in today's session?" she asks.

"Have you seen the movie *Jane Eyre*? It's a tragedy . . . but in the end, the characters get back together and triumph over their loneliness."

Sammy bites her lip again and looks at me. "That sounds really nice."

Sammy

Friday morning when Ms. Martinez walks around to check our feelings journal page counts, her eyes grow big. Unlike the other students in my class, mine's already completely filled up and I need a new one.

She whispers, "Samantha, would you like to stay after and talk for a minute?"

I glance around to see if anyone's watching, and nod. I've been pouring out my feelings on paper, but it's not enough. They're growing stronger each day and pushing at my edges. I'm about to burst again.

After class, I stand at her desk. She hands me a new journal and says, "You've been doing a lot of writing about your feelings. Is it helping?"

"A little . . . ," I say. "But as fast as I write my feelings down in my journal, new ones crop up."

She smiles. "That's the way it is sometimes when we're going through big changes. It's hard for us to keep up. I've filled up two whole journals since my house flooded."

It sounds like Ms. Martinez has just as many feelings swirling around inside as I do!

"Samantha, you don't have to share anything with me if you don't want to, but I'm here if you'd like to talk."

I take a deep breath. Ms. Martinez is still new to me, but I really like her. I think I can trust her with my feelings.

"I'm really upset about the hurricane and our house. I mean, we lost about everything."

She nods.

"But even more than that, things aren't right with my twin brother, Matty. See, we used to be really close," I say. "We had a special connection, kind of like telepathy, since we're twins . . . but we don't anymore."

She nods again, so I keep talking.

"And going through everything without him . . ." I gulp. "Is so hard and lonely."

She's quiet for a minute. "Without saying much, I'm pretty sure Matty thinks a lot about you, too. Have you told him about your feelings?"

I thumb through my journal. I've written about how much better it felt, us being Sammy-Matty; how I wish we were still playing baseball together like we always did; how I miss us being a team, in so many ways. Especially now.

I hope my teacher's right, that he thinks about me as much as I think about him. But it doesn't seem that way since he's been shutting me out.

I shake my head. "We're not talking, and I hoped things would go back to the way they used to be, and our connection would glue back together, somehow. But it hasn't."

She smiles. "Sometimes we have to make new connections with people we love as we change and grow. The old ways might not work well anymore, but when you're close like you and your brother, you'll find a new way. I bet if you reread everything you've written, you'll get some ideas."

"Thanks, Ms. Martinez," I say, waving goodbye.

On my way to my next class, the big bursty feeling inside deflates just a little with the hope she's given me: that Matty and I can find a new way.

I hug my feelings journal to my chest. Maybe the answers can be found inside.

But at fall ball practice the next day without my brother, that bit of hope dries up when my hitting slump only gets worse.

Unlike José Altuve, who hit three homers in the first American League Division Series game against the Red Sox on Thursday and got the MVP, the Most Valuable Player Award, the physics of my swing are totally off.

I've lost the catch and release energy transfer that always gave me my power. And since the 14U fence is so much farther away than the 12U fence was, even when I manage to connect with the ball, my old dingers turn into easy-out pop fly balls!

I need my brother Matty here, to tell me how I can fix it.

Ethan comes up to me after practice as I'm throwing all my gear into my bag. "Hey, Sammy."

"Hey." I squint up at him, a little uncomfortable since I know things now that maybe he doesn't.

But he smiles this really great, easy smile, and without thinking much about it, I smile right back. And just like with Ms. Martinez, that bursty feeling calms down.

I totally get it, why Matty *like*-likes him.

Ethan reaches over and gives my shoulder a tiny push. "Cheer up, Sammy! Your hitting will get better."

I nod, a bit longer than I need to, like I'm trying to convince myself. Yeah, I've still got what it takes to be a ballplayer in 14U, even if I'm a girl, even if I'm short. Even if the person who always stuck up for me and rooted for me isn't here anymore. Don't I?

But maybe not. Maybe I'm not meant to play baseball much longer. Maybe I'm done . . . like Matty.

Across the field, I see Brandon smirk at me. He's been saying things under his breath all practice that I can actually hear, like, "What do we need a girl on this team for, anyway? She can't even hit!"

"I need Matty here," I tell Ethan before I can help myself. "I need him on my team."

He shuffles his cleats in the clay. "I do, too, Sammy."

I keep going. "He's not talking to me. I miss him."

His eyebrows lift. "Same."

Now I'm shuffling my cleats. "What are we going to do about it?"

He shakes his head. "I'm not sure we can do anything. Sometimes people need time to figure stuff out, at least that's what my mom says."

Now my eyebrows lift. "Did you tell your mom . . . about you and Matty?"

He smiles wide, like he's relieved that I know, that I said something. "Yeah, I had to tell someone. I felt like a shook soda can, all bottled up with nowhere to go."

I nod. That's exactly how I feel, everything building up inside and fizzing.

Ethan picks up a ball and nods to my bat. "Well, I know one thing. The only way to fix a swing is to practice."

I text my dad that I'm staying late with Ethan. And an hour later, my swing's a bit better; my hits make it a little closer to the 14U fence.

But I still don't have it, not like before. Maybe it'll never go back to the way it was before Matty quit our team. Without him, nothing's going to be right.

That afternoon, my mom comes to get me from Becky's room, and my dad goes to get Matty and Bialy from the library.

We meet at the rental car outside. "Where are we going?"

I ask them as they slide into the front seats.

Dad says, "Hop in. We're going home."

I shudder. I haven't heard my dad call our house "home" since we evacuated.

Matty says, "Why? And is anybody else coming, like Mrs. Sokoloff?"

My mom looks back over her shoulder as she buckles up. "No, it's just us. We have some big decisions to make, and we thought our family should be at the house alone together to make them."

My eyes lock with Matty's for a few seconds, but we say so much: *We're going home, alone! . . . What are the big decisions? . . . They sound so serious!*

We get there and walk up to our front porch. Our house is even more of a shell this time than it was last time—it's wide open.

The double front doors are off their hinges. All the windows are out of their frames, stacked against the side of the house. Two-by-four studs where our walls used to be show through the gaping holes. Exterior bricks pile up in the yard.

I look at my mom, panicked. "Mold set in, Sammy, so we took everything down as far as we could," she says.

I nod.

Dad puts Bialy in the backyard to run around again and walks back to the porch. He pops his knuckles. "We have a few options, since Mom and I have decided that we don't want to elevate the existing house. We could tear down what's left and build a new—"

Mom interrupts, "But Bubbe and Papa aren't coming back here, and Mrs. Sokoloff is selling her lot, too, and moving to Florida with her daughter. This flood's been so hard on them." She raises her eyebrows to my dad. "And it's been really hard on us, too."

"So . . ." Dad says. "That leaves us. There are going to be more storms because of climate change, and while there are plans to widen Brays Bayou to help with future flooding, there's no guarantee our neighborhood will fare better next time. Maybe we should sell our lot as well, and move. . . ."

Suddenly it feels like everyone's giving up. First Matty . . . now Mom and Dad. I can't make things right again without them. I can't do it alone!

"No!" I scream. "No! No! No! Puttermans aren't quitters!"

"Sammy! Baby!" Dad says. "That's enough!"

But I'm not done. I yell at Matty, "At least *I'm* not!"

His head jerks back like I punched him. His face turns red. "What?" he yells, deeper and louder than I've heard before.

Then I'm a mess—face steaming hot, breath raggedy. No amount of writing feelings on paper was going to help with this. I have to say my feelings out loud—to Matty. "You're . . . you're a quitter!"

He turns his back to me, but that's nothing new.

"Things are hard, Sammy," he mumbles. "I'm trying to sort them out. I didn't feel like I could just walk back onto a team because . . ."

I ignore my dad clearing his throat and my mom covering her mouth with her hand. "Because you like Ethan? You think that's what this is about? It's great that you like him, he's awesome!" I yell. "That's not what I'm talking about at all!"

He whips around. "Then what, Sammy? What else did I quit? You've been dying to tell me, just like you always do, so tell me! Tell me!"

One giant sob funnels from my chest, a feeling so huge it could fill a whole journal.

Then I say the deep hurt that I've been bottling up ever since Matty left me at our playoff game, even before an epic hurricane created the shell of a home we're standing in front of.

"You're a quitter, Matty! Because you quit *us*!"

My mom gasps. My dad runs his hands through his hair. Matty's face bunches up and he hangs his head.

Dad steps forward and holds my shaking shoulders. "No one's quitting here, Sammy . . . not me, or Mom, or Matty. But things can't be the way they used to, not now, not anymore. You and Matty will be different, now that you're growing older and discovering new things about yourselves. This house, our home, has changed forever, too. Things change, people change, and we have to change with them."

I nod my head up and down, up and down, trying to convince myself.

Mom wraps her arms around me, and Dad wraps his arms around Matty. We both calm down, and they lead us inside what's left of our house and open the back door for Bialy. Then our family walks from room to room along all our old pathways, remembering the times before everything changed.

The time Matty and I put socks on our hands and feet and slid down the hall. The time Bialy fell asleep in his water bowl when he was a puppy. The times Becky . . . *Becky!* . . . would spend the night and we'd turn our whole living room into a gigantic fort. And the first time Matty and I put on our matching baseball uniforms with jerseys that said PUTTERMAN across the back.

And I know it's our last time in this house together, that we won't ever walk through it again.

We sit on the concrete floor in our living room and stare out at our quiet street, without kids running through all the yards and families watching from their porches. It's lonely now, it's changed.

The afternoon wind picks up and breezes in through our window frames, carrying the familiar scent of Houston rain. And even though it's not going to be a Category 4 storm, and it will pass as suddenly as it comes, my whole body tenses up.

I start crying soft raindrops of my own, falling, falling,

falling. My mom, my dad, and Matty cry, too.

The storm reaches my family through our gaping walls. But this time, we don't leave. We huddle together, letting tears and rain wash over us.

Matty

I excuse myself to the bathroom during dinner Saturday night and sneak up to Becky's room.

I haven't been up here in a week, and Jess and Bartholomew clearly miss me. They wrap themselves around my legs and purr like little tigers, then get up and saunter to the studio corner. They blink at me and wait, like I'm here to do a photo session.

I'm not.

I reach under Sammy's mattress and find it—her feelings journal.

It's right there at the edge where she can pull it out when she wants to, barely hidden, almost waiting for somebody to take it out and read it. And I know reading my sister's journal without asking is the wrong choice, I do.

But after our blowout fight yesterday at our house—I need to understand her feelings better.

'Cause what do you do when you used to know the person closest to you, but you don't anymore? When your connection's cut, and there's so much misunderstanding? When you were hurting so much you made that person hurt, too? When they think you quit them forever?

You gotta fix it, right? Right.

And she'd offered to let me read her journal that one time, so I guess it's still okay.

I flip her journal open to the first page. But it's blank!

I've seen her writing and writing, carrying this thing around the house and at school. It should be chock-full of her feelings by now.

I crouch down and stick my arm under the mattress, barely breathing, till I feel the hard edge of the second journal I'm betting is there. It is!

So I pull it out, put the blank one at the edge of the mattress like I found it, and sneak back downstairs to the library. I stash Sammy's filled journal on the high shelf with mine and hope she won't miss it. Back at dinner, I can barely look at her as I finish eating.

After everybody goes to bed, I stay up all night reading Sammy's words.

I push every bit of doubt out about what I'm doing from my mind and tell myself that once, I would've known her feelings anyhow, before our twin telepathy broke.

I'm just catching up.

The parts she's written about me and how lonely she's felt are really hard to read. It's not easy knowing you've hurt somebody you love, even when you didn't mean to. I have to stop reading sometimes when the chicken thing starts up in my throat, when I need to take a break and hug on Bialy.

But something happens as I read Sammy's journal entries about the hurricane: I remember it just like I saw it, even though she's telling it. And we're back there together.

I pull my journal off the shelf and set it beside Sammy's. I flip her pages and mine one by one. It's all there.

The story of when the water rose in our yard while we were sleeping, and our parents decided to evacuate. The moment in the living room when our dad loaded us into the kayaks. When we paddled to the shelter with all the other families, escaping our flooded homes. The getaway game in Anaheim that played on the line of laptops and gave us some Houston Strong hope.

And you know what?

Even though my feelings are changing in some ways, with *like*-liking Ethan and wanting to focus on my art . . . in so many ways, our feelings still line right up.

And the best part? Her words are great, and my drawings are great—but they're even better together, side by side.

The next morning, Papa and I sit at the kitchen table. He reads the Sunday newspaper and sips his coffee while I munch down a bowl of cereal. Bialy lies at my feet, happily mouthing the remnants of his two balls—his old tennis ball, and Sammy's used-to-be signed birthday baseball.

I smile, feeling a bit teenage-movie gushy: Bialy has more than one lovey, just like me.

My grandfather points to the paper. "This picture's a heartbreaker . . . just look at these people sitting in their gutted-out house."

I shake my head. I don't need to look, since we were those people at our house last night.

"Says here you can submit your Hurricane Harvey story to the paper. Each week, I check for a more hopeful story, Matthew, but there's nothing yet!"

"Hey, Papa?" I say. "Actually, can I have that section of the paper when you're done?"

Sammy, Becky, and I head to religious school, and when we get back, Dad calls me from the library. "Hey, Matty! We're breaking into watch parties for the third Astros-Red Sox Division Series game! Come on!"

We pass the living room, and Mom motions Sammy and Becky to the sectional. Bubbe's serving game-day egg salad tea sandwiches, which I love.

I start to sit down, but Mom says, "Honey, it would mean so much to Dad if you could watch this game with him."

I groan and walk to the library, where Papa's serving some brisket sandwiches that make me forget all about Bubbe's egg salad. I have a sneaking feeling that these parties are my mom and dad's way of giving Sammy and me a breather after last night.

All during the game, I think about teams, for obvious reasons.

Cheering the Astros on after Hurricane Harvey made our city Houston Strong again. The big family team I'm on, the Puttermans, has pulled together in one house for the last six weeks. And all the teams Sammy and I have played on helped us both become great ballplayers.

Teams are important. They're there for you when you need them.

But it takes everybody on a team—sticking it out, rooting for each other when things get hard—to make them great. I know that now. It really hurt Sammy when I wasn't there for her.

I have to show her we still have a connection. I have to show her that we're still a twin team.

The Houston Astros lose big, 10–3 to the Red Sox, but they still have a series lead since they won the first two games. Verlander's pitching tomorrow, so hopefully with a win it'll be on to the championship series!

I look around the room at all the sports memorabilia my uncle has hung on the walls: jerseys and glossy signed pictures and loads and loads of framed newspaper stories from all the winning seasons.

Then I know how to show Sammy we're still a team. The answer's there in our journals.

Everybody stretches and gets up to go, and I catch Uncle Mike. "Do you have a big envelope and some stamps in your library?" I ask.

He nods and pushes a panel behind a row of jerseys, and it spins around to show all kinds of office supplies: printers and shredders, and even a cabinet filled with more books. I guess this really *is* a library/man cave!

After he leaves, I take out our journals and my hands start sweating. I wipe them on my shorts, then rip a page out of each journal. I want to show Sammy that even though things are changing, so many of our feelings are still the same.

And her words are so awesome. She shouldn't have any doubts. They belong in a newspaper!

I stick our pages in the envelope and plaster it with stamps. Then I address it to the Houston newspaper's community section regarding Hurricane Harvey. I'm gonna put it in Monday's mail.

'Cause my drawing and Sammy's words—together— make some great story. It's one we can both hope on.

Becky

I'm coming down the stairs the next Friday afternoon, and I hear my mother on her phone in the kitchen.

"Yes, Amy," she says. "Absolutely! I'll tell her as soon as I hang up. It's been quite a long stretch, but Esther's been no trouble at all! How wonderful you've fully recovered!"

I'm suddenly wobbly. I grab the stair handrail to steady myself and inch the rest of the way down.

In the kitchen, I immediately start spritzing the countertops.

"Well, she's settled in nicely . . . like family . . . and Bartholomew has, too! Oh, your dog doesn't get along with cats?" she says, glancing to the kitchen floor, where Bialy's in a front-paw crouch, his tail-wagging tuchus high in the air while the cats dance around him. "That's a shame, since

232

Esther's cat has really taken to Annie and Greg's golden retriever."

I see my stricken face in the countertop. I've polished the whole kitchen island in record speed. I start in on the cabinet fronts next.

My mother finally notices me.

She points to the phone and mouths, "Mrs. Sokoloff's daughter!" then smiles like she's just won the Texas Lottery.

I listen to a series of *uh-huh*s and *of course*s, and with each one, my heart squeezes harder. Mrs. Sokoloff and Bartholomew are going to leave soon.

How could that be? It seems like everyone just got here!

Finally my mother says, "Thank you, Amy! We'll see you next weekend when you get here from Florida!" and hangs up. She turns to me, still smiling.

I give a cabinet one last swipe and run back up to my room.

When I get there, I throw myself on my bed, fully intending to have a serious cryfest. But one look at Sammy's face, and I can't. *She's* already crying.

"What's wrong?" I say.

"What do you care?"

I stare at my lap. I guess that's fair. I haven't exactly been very supportive since she got here.

"You wouldn't understand, since you live *here*, Becky," she says, gesturing to my recently redecorated room. "Our house is a total loss. We have to tear it down! We might even sell our lot and move out of our neighborhood!"

My heart squeezes tight again. *A total loss?* I do understand.

She turns away from me, and I want to do something to help her. But what?

Think, Becky, think!

Then I figure it out, I really figure it out. How I can be my very best self.

I grab my laptop and rush around the house, looking for Auntie Annie. I find her reading on the sectional in the living room.

I stand next to her, breathing hard. "Do you have it . . . on a cloud somewhere?"

She looks up at me. "Have what, Rebecca?"

Normally, I'd appreciate someone in the family using my proper name, but my aunt sounds a bit snippy when she says it.

Considering recent events, I guess that's fair, again.

I shake it off. I'm trying to be my very best self here, now that I've figured out what that actually means. It's not just about doing my thing in my room, holding what's bright and sparkly together with hot glue, for me alone. What made my sessions so special these past few weeks is that they helped Matty feel better.

Being my best self is all about doing my part to help my family when they need it! Because the Whole World are the followers I really want!

"The photo of Sammy and Uncle Greggy in the stands at Minute Maid when she was a baby. The one from her nightstand . . . that means so much to her . . . that she lost in the flood."

My aunt blinks at me for a second and her eyes pool. "I'm not sure if I have that one anymore, Becky. It's not on my phone, and my laptop was lost in the flood. We did upload some of our old photos to the cloud along the way, but I planned on consolidating them next year for your cousins' b'nai mitzvah video."

I shift my weight between my feet. I hand her my laptop and sit down next to her. "Sammy needs that photo, Auntie Annie."

She nods and logs on to her Amazon account. It's not there.

She logs on to her Google account. It's not there either.

Then she logs on to her old Shutterfly account.

The first photos we find are some of the ones that had been framed in their hallway. "Oh! Oh. Oh . . . I thought we'd lost all these," she says. "Just look at the three of you!"

I tear up seeing them again. "We were really good friends."

"Yes, Becky, you were." She smiles at me. "You can be that way again."

I nod, and we scroll through hundreds of pictures. We're just about to stop when suddenly I spot it. "There it is, Auntie Annie!"

We both throw our hands to the air, then she hugs me tight. Then I download Sammy's most important photo. "Thank you so much for helping me find a bit of what we'd lost, Becky," she says. "What are you going to do with it, honey?"

I smile. "I'm going to remake a friend."

I photoshop the picture real nice, like I do with my session photos, and I print it out on glossy photo paper using my mother's emergency-use-only fancy printer.

Later, I gobble down Shabbat dinner, and while my family's glued to the first Astros-Yankees American League Championship Series game on TV, cheering their hearts out, I head up to my room.

I have some other important cheering to do.

I remove a photo of Jenny and me from a nice glass frame on my dresser and replace it with the photo of Sammy and her dad. Then I position it on the nightstand between our twin beds, so she'll see it when she walks in after watching the game.

Just for good measure, I put Itty Kitty on Sammy's pillow—she needs her now way more than I do.

Then I run back downstairs and wait.

When we head back to my room after the Astros beat the Yankees, Sammy's eyes pop big when she sees her photo.

She says, "Oh my gosh! Oh, gosh!" and sits down real slow. She stares at the photo and picks up Itty Kitty and strokes her. "Did *you* do this, Becky?"

I nod, playing it cool.

I know finding the photo for Sammy and lending her Itty Kitty won't erase how awful and unsupportive I've been since she got here after the hurricane—like presto—and we'll be instant friends again like in the old hallway photos.

But maybe this little bit of cheer will help.

Sammy's face screws up tight, and she clings to Itty Kitty. She pinches her lips together, but they tremble anyway. "Where did you get it?"

"Your mom and I found it on the cloud with a bunch of your old family photos."

She nods, then picks up the photo and puts in her lap.

"Does it make things feel any better?"

A few tears fall from Sammy's eyes to the glass. "Yes."

Sammy

Early Sunday morning, the day after the 'Stros win game two of the ALCS against the Yanks as well, Papa yells from the kitchen, "Hallelujah, Irene! Everyone! Everyone! Come see!"

Becky and I bolt out of bed. "Come on!" I say, and we scramble downstairs.

We join Matty, Mom and Dad, Uncle Mike and Aunt Deb, and Mrs. Sokoloff on our way to the kitchen to see what my grandfather's yelling is all about.

He points to the Sunday newspaper, and accidentally overturns his coffee cup. "Just look at what our TWINS did!"

Bubbe's holding her cup midair with an open-mouthed smile. Bartholomew starts lapping the coffee that's dripping onto the floor, and Jess joins in.

My dad rubs his eyes. "What's going on, Mom and Dad? Is everything okay?"

Papa grins from Matty to me and back again. He thrusts my dad the paper. "Is it okay? *Is it OKAY?* It's stupendous! Hooray, Sammy-Matty!" He pulls Bubbe up from the kitchen table by her hands, and they start dancing around the kitchen—this jig that resembles their moves at bar and bat mitzvahs when we dance the hora.

My dad holds the paper, and his hand starts to shake. He rubs his eyes again with his free hand. "Matt? Did you make this drawing of your sister? It . . . it's so amazing. You're such an artist!"

Uncle Mike peers over Dad's shoulder, then he's grinning, too. "Made good use of that envelope and those stamps, I see!" he says, mussing Matty's hair.

"Don't be mad at me, Sammy," Matty says. "You always wanted to be in the paper."

I walk over to see what everyone's gushing about. I have to fight my way in at this point, because my mom, aunt, and even Mrs. Sokoloff are huddled around my dad, all trying to catch a glimpse.

The first thing I notice is a big, bold title.

ASTROS SUPERFAN SAMMY PUTTERMAN'S SHELTER CHEERING INSPIRED HOPE ON THE DARKEST DAY OF HURRICANE HARVEY

What in the world?

The next thing I see is a picture of me in the church shelter the day of the Astros getaway game, in a style of drawing I could recognize anywhere, because it's so, so good. It belongs to my twin brother Matty, and below it are *my* words.

On August 27, our city got covered in water. My family left our flooded home and paddled to safety, like so many families. At first, looking around the shelter at everyone who'd lost everything, I didn't feel very lucky, and I didn't feel very strong. But when my team, the Houston Astros, played the Los Angeles Angels that day, they gave me something to cheer for when I needed it most. Because cheering for each other matters. It makes us Houston Strong.

I gulp and look at my brother. It's what I wrote in my feelings journal . . . that Ms. Martinez said *no one* would ever look at. But here it is, in the black-and-white newspaper.

I gulp again . . . in a city of over four million people. *But how?*

I whip past Becky and bolt up the stairs to her room. I ignore Matty calling behind me, "Sammy, wait!"

When I get there, I slam the door behind me and feel under my mattress. There's only one journal there now— the empty one. *That's how.*

Matty knocks. "Sammy, can I please come in? I'm so, so sorry! I was trying to fix things!"

My feelings spin and swirl like a Category 4 storm.

I told my brother I'd share my journal with him some-time, but he still needed to *ask*. And I *never* told him he could send my words to the Houston paper. I would've done it someday, when I was *ready*!

Matty finally wants to talk, but now I don't know what to say to him. This time he has to wait for me.

My brother knocks on the door for a few long minutes, and I let him. Then I hear him pad back down the stairs.

Amanda starts texting me. Things like *Way to go, super-fan!* and *OMG you're gonna be famous!*

I turn off my phone and ignore her, too.

An hour later, Matty, Becky, and I ride to religious school in the Suburban in complete silence.

Matty stares at me like he's trying to will our twin telepathy to kick into hyperdrive, Becky looks between us, wide-eyed and starstruck, and I'm closed up tight like a Galveston beach clam, with a jumble of sloppy insides.

On the one hand, I'm furious that Matty took my jour-nal, since it was private. But on the other hand, my brother's heart was in a good place, however misguided.

So, I'm back to feeling happy-sad again.

But when we get there, everyone's seen the article, all the kids and teachers and even our rabbi. They pat us on the back, fist bump us, and congratulate us in the hall.

Some kids tell me they felt the exact same way watching that game, and Matty gets lots of "You're such an amazing artist!" comments.

It's all a bit overwhelming.

On our way back to Becky's, I can tell even Matty's wondering if sharing our journal pages was the right call.

When we walk into the kitchen, Bubbe and Papa are sitting at the table cutting the article out of a tall stack of newspapers. Our grandmother smiles and knocks a finger to her head. "Papa and I had the best idea! We went door-to-door and asked the neighbors for their copies, and we're sending them to all the out-of-town relatives!"

I escape to Becky's room to try to get my swirling, confused feelings under control. Maybe then the big bursty feeling that's pushing on my insides again will deflate back down.

Becky follows me up and sits on her bed. She gives me a long look and pulls a newspaper from under her shirt and lays it next to me.

"You barely looked at Matty's drawing, Sammy. It's *such* an amazing picture of you!"

I turn away. I don't want to examine it up close. Since Matty and I fought at our house the other night, I've started to accept that some things are final: our home is gone, and so is my twin team with my brother.

Like Dad said, "Things change, people change, and we have to change with them." So, wishing that things will go back to the way they used to be is a big waste of time.

Becky says, "I'm really sorry I never asked you what it was like for you in the shelter. Were you scared?"

I nod. "A little, but I was mostly just sad. But then some people set up laptops for the game and we all started cheering and the Astros won, and it felt . . ."

"Hopeful?"

"Yeah, like things were going to be okay."

"Maybe your words and Matty's picture will make other people feel that, too, Sammy. . . . All the people who are still sad."

I look down at Matty's drawing. It looks so, so real, just like his winning drawing of Bialy for the Bayou City Art Contest.

It's just like I remember it.

Me in my Astros baseball cap, watching the laptop screens with my hands raised high in the air. Papa, rocking up on his toes to kiss Dad. The man with his head tipped to the ceiling in thanks, and the woman with the little girl dancing on her toes. My mom, my grandmother, and Mrs. Sokoloff close by. Everyone cheering their hearts out because we still had something to cheer for. Superfans who'd never give up.

It's like Matty caught the moment and he's giving it back—to me, and to everyone.

That day, I thought for sure my brother didn't see what I saw. I thought he was nowhere I was, but I was wrong.

Matty was right there with me, all along.

Becky nods to her doorway. My brother's standing there with our feelings journals tucked under his arm.

There are a few awkward seconds, all of us glancing at each other, not knowing what to say or do, but then Becky says with a tiny voice, "I guess I'll go back down and help my mother unload the dishwasher."

I can tell she wants it to be the three of us, together: Sammy-Matty-Becky. I can tell she wants me to ask her to stay.

And a part of me wants that now, too.

Becky's been trying hard to help me feel better—by finding the photo of me and Dad, by lending me Itty Kitty, and by talking with me about the newspaper article, too.

She's changing, and we had so much fun together when we were little. Maybe we can have that again.

But not right now. I need to work things out with my brother.

Becky shuffles past Matty, and he sits down on the bed next to me. "Want to see my journal since I've seen yours? It's only fair."

I nod. I've been trying to figure out my brother's feelings since our connection got shaky.

He puts it in my hands, and I slowly leaf through it.

There's a picture of me standing in the open doorway of our house with my signed birthday baseball and Astros cap, watching floodwater from Brays Bayou rise in our yard. There's a picture of me in my Houston-grade yellow raincoat in our living room next to Dad's packed kayaks. There's a picture of Dad and me paddling to get some speed onto the asphalt parking lot of the church.

I stop and take a deep breath. "I'm in almost every picture, Matty."

He nods. "I'm sorry I was so wrapped up in figuring out my stuff that I wasn't there for you when you needed me. But I'd never quit us, Sammy."

I croak, "Then why couldn't you tell me about Ethan? Why didn't I know first? Our firsts have always been together: baseball wins and losses and family holidays and every single birthday. We're twins, Matty, so I always thought I'd know about your important firsts . . . *first*."

My brother scoots closer and puts his arm around my shoulders.

His arm's bigger than it used to be, and all the hairs are thicker and darker. The lines of his cheekbones sweep stronger and his jaw's set wider, too. I didn't notice before now—how much he's changing.

I glance down at my chest, which isn't quite as flat as it used to be, and at the way my hands look more like Mom's than they used to. Maybe I'm changing, too. Maybe we're all changing.

But I didn't want Matty and me to be different. I thought us being different would break us apart.

"Will we both change so much someday that we won't

stay connected?" I whisper. "That we won't know each other?"

"We'll always be twins and it'll always be special, Sammy. And maybe sometimes our telepathy will work like it used to, and sometimes it won't, but talking like this is okay, too."

I nod, and something inside me squeezes and flips and finally settles because we're not going to be Sammy-Matty exactly the way we used to be. Nothing will be the way it used to be.

Things change, people change, and we have to change with them.

Gigantic tears run down my cheeks, then we're hugging. Matty's throat makes choked-up noises for a few seconds, then he recovers and says, "You've known me longer than anyone else, Sammy. We've been together from the very start. Nothing can ever change that."

We'll always be connected. Matty will always be my brother, and we'll always be twins. And we'll never quit each other.

We catch up all afternoon.

Matty tells me all about his kiss with Ethan, which sounds wonderful and amazing and real and exactly how I want my first kiss to be someday. He tells me that he still hasn't responded to Ethan's texts.

I ask him if he's figured everything out.

"Almost, Sammy," he says. "What about you? I mean . . .

you've written a ton in your journal. Are you still figuring stuff out?"

I nod my head. I guess I am—I'm changing, too.

I'm a ballplayer, and I root for the Astros and my family, and I love writing in my journal. I say, "Maybe . . . I'll be a sportswriter someday, Matty."

He picks up our newspaper article and hands it to me. "You already are, Sammy . . . a really good one!"

I grin. Seeing my words in print *is* kind of awesome. "Thanks, Matty. But right now, I need to focus on my serious hitting slump!"

I tell my brother about my broken swing and how the 14U fence seems farther and farther away. I tell him about my team's terrible record this season and how Brandon has made it clear he wants me off the team.

Matty's left fist clenches like he's gripping a baseball.

And I can't help it, this little thing inside me blooms. Maybe my brother's baseball-playing days aren't over.

"Hey, Matty? One more thing, and it's kind of a big ask. Even though you're not sure you want to play baseball anymore, could you pitch to me sometime? It'd really help me with my swing."

He hesitates a moment, then says, "I'll think on it, Sammy . . . promise."

Later that afternoon, I take a chance like Matty did when he sent my feelings to the paper. I put the new glove I got for him in a bag with some other baseball supplies and hang it on the doorknob of the library.

Just like Matty knows me—I know him, too. He's about lots of stuff, all together.

I leave him another note, a small cheer that says:

Just in case. Love, Sammy.

And it feels like hope again.

Matty

After dinner when I get to the library, there's a bag with a brand-new infield glove hanging on the door.

Before I can stop myself, I take it out and bring it to my nose. The leather smell takes me back to the mound for a second, left foot planted in the clay, right foot raised, hands at my chest right before my windup.

Before I throw another perfect pitch.

I blink the image away and read the note. The glove's from Sammy, not like I couldn't guess *that*.

There's a bunch of other stuff in the bag you need for a new glove, too: some shaving cream and a soft rag to rub it in with, an old baseball that looks like it's from Uncle Mike's bucket in the garage, and a bunch of rubber bands.

And even though I'm not gonna try the glove on—*I'm*

not—it's stiff and dry. The best way to break it in is by using it, of course, but that's not gonna happen.

But you can't just ignore a stiff new glove.

I almost leave the bag in the hall, 'cause I'm not ready to say I'm gonna play yet, but then I can't. I'm on autopilot like when we kayaked to the shelter during the flood.

I carry everything into the library and sit down on the bed. I take the cloth and work the shaving cream into the leather in nice, small circles. When the whole thing is worked over twice, every single bit of great-smelling cowhide, I take my uncle's baseball and rubber band it inside the glove, tight.

Not that it'll ever get used by anybody, but it's just what you do with any new glove.

Knee-jerk, I slide it under my mattress. But then I reconsider and stick it up on the highest shelf with my phone and the Koufax book.

When I get to school the next morning, it's a repeat of religious school. Everybody's seen my picture of Sammy in the paper, the principal and teachers and students and lunch ladies and even Mr. Evans, the school janitor.

When I walk by him, he says, "Putterman?"

I nod.

He holds up his fist for a bump and says, "Houston Strong."

I hold up mine. It feels really good cheering us on.

Ms. Martinez beams at me during language arts, till I

almost dart for the bathroom. Then she catches me as I walk out past her desk. "Matty, you did such a brave thing, sharing your drawing of Sammy with our city."

I beam back. I feel brave, putting my feelings out there. It feels way better than when they were stuck inside.

"I think I'm done with my Hurricane Harvey memoir, Ms. Martinez. My feelings journal's almost filled up."

"That's great, Matty," she says. "Did it help you?"

I nod. "Wanna see it?"

She covers her heart with her hands again, and I slide it across to her. She turns the pages careful and slow, examining each of my drawings like they're important. Like my feelings matter.

The feelings on her face change with each page, and I smile huge the whole time. That's exactly what artists go for when they make their art—they go for feelings.

When she's done, she slides my journal back and whispers, "Thank you." Then she hands me a fresh journal.

"What's this for?" I ask.

She winks. "Your next great story, Matty."

When I get home, Bubbe and Papa are in the kitchen. Their mailing operation has expanded: they have even more newspapers and stacks of envelopes and stamps. They've enlisted Mrs. Sokoloff's help, too.

The cordless rings, and I hear, "Puttermans! No, KHOU Houston, this is the grandmother. The father and mother are out, and any questions for our amazing twins should be directed to drgregoryputtermanMD at . . ."

OMG, I can't believe a news station wants to talk to me and Sammy!

I grab a banana and escape to the library. But when I open the door, something's off. It's the gosh-darn great-smelling glove calling to me from the highest shelf.

Okay, okay!

I take it down, untie it, rub some more shaving cream into it, and retie it. Then I stick it under my mattress before I can talk myself out of it.

'Cause it's a new baseball glove, and that's what you do to break it in. You stick it under your mattress. You've gotta do it right.

The Astros lose the next three ALCS away games against the Yankees, so we're trailing two games to three. If we lose one more time, we're done!

Our team's bats have been asleep, and George Springer's barely hitting. In game five, we didn't even score a single run. The highs and lows around the house this week have been like a Six Flags roller coaster!

Dad and Uncle Mike pooled our season ticket rights for the playoffs so we can all go to game six on Friday night.

Everybody's excited—my parents, aunt, and uncle take off work early, so we can get to our Home Away from Home when doors open around five o'clock. "We'll say a few Shabbat blessings at the game!" Bubbe says on the way.

"God knows our team needs them!"

We settle into our seats to watch the teams warm up. After a while, I excuse myself to go to the bathroom. But that's not where I'm going.

I hear Mack on the phone behind his office door, and knock.

When he sees my head peek in, he waves me inside and ends his call. Then he cups his hand to his face and says what he always says when he sees me or anybody in my family at Minute Maid Park. "Listen up, y'all! The Putter-mans are IN THE HOUSE!"

He starts laughing, a funny soundless laugh where his big belly jiggles. I start laughing, too.

"Matty, my man! I sure did like that drawing of your sister in the newspaper. You're some artist!" he says. "What brings you my way?"

"I just wanted to say hi, Mack," I say, my eyes settling on the photos in his office that I remembered.

It's been years since Sammy and I got lost in the park, and even though Mack's the head of security now, his office is nearly the same. There are a bunch of photos on his walls that I could swear . . . yup, I'm right.

I point to the first one. "That's you as a boy with Jackie Robinson! He was the first Black ballplayer in the MLB!"

He smiles. "Sure is. I was in elementary school, and Jackie ran a baseball clinic I was lucky enough to be a part of."

I point to another. "And that's you and Bob Watson!"

His belly jiggles again. "Yeah, me 'n Bob go way back! To the Astrodome back, when I started here in security."

I smile. "My grandfather talks about Watson's one-millionth run as an Astro all the time! Hey, wasn't he also the first Black general manager of an MLB team, right here for the Houston Astros, then with the Yankees?"

Mack grins. "You got it, Matty. Funny the Yanks are playing here tonight!"

I nod. "Both of their stories are so amazing. And I read some books about some other amazing ballplayers, Hank Greenberg and Jim Abbott." I look away. "It must've been really hard for all of them, being the first to do something, being a little different."

Mack gives me a long look. "Sometimes, Matty, a person has to play by their own rules. They have to make the future they know is right. Just like those players did."

Big feelings well up, and I nod. "Thanks, Mack. I'd better go back to my family."

We fist-bump. "Go Astros!"

The 'Stros win it, 7–1. Justin Verlander dominates with seven shutout innings. It'll be a winner-take-all game tomorrow.

All night back in the library, the glove under my mattress calls to me.

To check on it. To see how it's doing. To make sure that I've rubbed enough shaving cream into it. To see if I tied the ball in the right spot, real tight.

It doesn't help that I can still smell the leather under the mattress.

By 2 a.m., I can't take it anymore. You can't argue with baseball truths.

'Cause while the shaving cream, the ball tied inside, and the mattress are all helping break the glove in—they won't be enough.

A new glove's gotta be used by somebody.

So I take it out and untie it. Then slide my hand in to see if . . . it fits me perfectly, like I knew it would.

Of course it does—my twin sister, Sammy, picked it out for me.

Becky

Sunday during religious school, I try to put my very best self forward.

I'm happy for my cousins, really, I am.

The fame . . . the recognition . . . the pats on the back. They're special, just like they always were. Once a star, always a star.

They're Sammy-Matty: they're a twin team again.

I run through my entire bat mitzvah service beginning to end with our rabbi, including my speech, which I've entitled, "A Jewish Teen's Thoughts on Facing Great Challenges," which I feel uniquely qualified to elaborate on, since clearly I've faced a lot of them.

My prayers and my Torah reading go great, but my speech, again—not so much!

I've reflected a bunch and worked really hard. My speech has a relevant title, a great opener, and some well-developed points, but the rabbi tells me it's still lacking the most important part—the takeaway lesson. Why God was testing Abram.

He tells me to go home and work on my d'var some more.

After religious school, I sit in the kitchen playing gin rummy with Mrs. Sokoloff, about to face another great challenge. Her daughter, Amy, is coming today to take her and Bartholomew to Florida.

I'm losing big, and I'm not just referring to this game.

I reorder my cards and stare at my hand, surprised. "Oh my god! Gin!"

Mrs. Sokoloff grins and tallies my score: twenty-five points for gin, plus another twenty-eight for her unconnected cards, for a total of fifty-three.

I raise an eyebrow and examine the one-sided curl of her smile. "Did you let me win that hand?"

"Maybe."

That figures.

While she shuffles and redeals, I read all about the Astros' big win last night on the front page of the Sunday paper. Our team won game seven of the ALCS, and they're going to the World Series again!

But though the Astros are thriving, my favorite player, George Springer, is not.

He went without any hits two games in a row, and now

he's in a serious slump. Just watching him struggle so made my heart crack open. We have so much in common!

So going into the World Series, I'll be cheering for him, hard. I believe that a person can work out of some seriously tough spots if they have the unwavering confidence of those who love them.

At least I hope so.

The cats have fallen asleep together on the kitchen window seat in the sun's warm rays, while Bialy snoozes on the floor below them. They're nuzzled close, whiskers flicking in time to dreams and smells. Every so often, Jess opens a green eye and Bartholomew, just knowing, opens a blue one at the very same time.

It's so, so sad they're losing each other. It's another tragedy . . . a total loss.

I mean, they didn't know they wanted to be close, or that they needed each other to shine, until they were thrown together all of a sudden.

But now that they do, now that they know how much better it is to be together, how are they going to live apart? It's pure devastation.

How can I ever console my cat, my followers, or myself?

I lose two more hands to Mrs. Sokoloff while we're waiting. It's enough to make my eyes water.

She nods to the cats. "They're quite dashing together, don't you think, Rebecca?"

"Hmm?" I stare at my next lousy gin hand. She's going to

win again. "What was that?"

"They're a match . . . like Beauty and the Beast, like—"

"Like Jane Eyre and Mr. Rochester!"

"Precisely."

"They . . . really like each other," I mutter.

"They most certainly do," Mrs. Sokoloff says, then she gets quiet for a minute. "You know, my daughter has a dog that absolutely hates cats, unlike sweet Bialy. I'm terribly concerned for Bartholomew's safety."

I lock eyes with her.

"I love him so, but I need to do what's best for him," she continues. "And he's so happy here with you and Jess."

OH. MY. GOD! Is this conversation going in the direction I think it is? Because if it is . . . I'm going to lose it!

"I will surely miss him, Rebecca, but do you think you could keep him for me?"

I bolt up from the kitchen table, and my cards flutter to the floor. "Yes!" I cry and rush over to hug her. "I don't even have to ask my parents since they've already acknowledged Jess's need for some feline companionship!"

She laughs and hugs me back.

"I'll take good care of Bartholomew, I promise," I say, burying my face in Mrs. Sokoloff's purplish-gray hair. "I'll send you lots of photos, and you can follow me on my social media page and see him all the time!"

"Well, this hurricane has been the *best thing* for his love life," she says after I sit back down. Then she raises her eyebrows and smiles.

Mrs. Sokoloff leaves, and there are hugs and tears all around. Bubbe bakes two lemon cakes for tonight's dessert, to bolster our spirits.

I'm inspired to craft a new studio theme with the cats this afternoon: Unexpected Happy Endings.

Just like Westley and Buttercup from *The Princess Bride*—which is my absolute favorite book *and* movie because the story is so, so romantic—forces beyond Jess and Bartholomew's control conspired to keep them apart.

But in the end, the undeniable power of true love kept them together.

I've just put a long, flowing yellow hairpiece on Jess and secured a Dread Pirate Roberts mask on Bartholomew's slippery face when Sammy walks in. "*The Princess Bride?*" she asks, nodding to the miniature sword I've fashioned from a chopstick.

"You guessed it!" I say, glancing up at her. "The cats' outfits are pretty good, right?"

She nods. "You're some kind of genius with a hot glue gun!"

Her compliment fills me up.

"Becky? How do you get Jess to sit still like that and keep those clothes on?"

I glance at my cousin. "It's easy. I make her feel special. Everyone likes to feel special, you know?"

She nods again. "And what about Bartholomew? How do

you get him to do all this?"

I smile. "He'll do anything for love . . . and coffee."

Sammy's eyes crinkle at their edges, and she starts laughing.

"I could sure use a hand with this session," I say, taking a big breath. "My fire swamp looks like a joke, and the cats keep playing with the rodents of unusual size since the only stuffed mice I could find have catnip inside them."

Sammy sits down on the floor next to me again. "*The Princess Bride* is the best story, ever. I can help . . . if you want."

"That would be great," I say, handing her the stuffed mice. "Maybe we should glue them down."

We work on the fire swamp until it's close to dinnertime. Sammy goes outside to gather big sticks and moss for the swamp trees, and I cut flames out of red, orange, and yellow crepe paper. The scene looks fabulous.

We get the cats in their outfits and shoot away.

Sammy smiles at me when we're done. "This was really fun, Becky."

I smile back. "No duh!" I say, and start dismantling the scene, shoving the sticks and moss out my cracked open window. "Hey, Sammy . . . do you think Matty will stay mad at me forever, after what I did . . . accidentally blurting about him and Ethan to the whole family?"

She shakes her head. "Probably not."

I'm overcome with emotion, fire swamp flushed. I open

the window wider to cool off.

"I want it to be like when we were little," I blurt. "Like all those photos of the three of us that used to hang in your hall . . . when we were friends."

She nods, remembering them. "We had fun then, didn't we?"

I bite my lip, then ask, "How do you know . . . that Matty won't stay mad at me?"

Sammy wiggles Jess's wig off and smiles. "Because, Becky, Matty and I are twins."

Sammy

The cordless phone in the kitchen rings while we're polishing off our lemon cakes. Aunt Deb pushes her chair back and starts to stand up.

"You rest, doll. I'll get it," Bubbe says with a smile. She loves answering the phone ever since Matty's picture got in the paper.

She rushes into the kitchen, and we hear, "Puttermans!" Then she rushes back to the dining-room table with her hand over the receiver, eyes popped out wide. "Oh my god, oh my god, oh my god! It's the Astros manager!"

Dad and Uncle Mike shoot up from their chairs, and Papa's so flustered he spills his iced tea down the front of his shirt.

My mom and aunt stare at my grandmother in complete shock.

Matty high-fives me, and I high-five Becky. She holds a hand up to Matty, and before he can even think about it, my brother high-fives her, too.

Within minutes, everyone's standing around my grandmother, but she won't give up the phone!

"You see, from a very young age, our twins threw baseballs, swung bats, ran bases, and rooted for our favorite team, the Houston Astros," she says. "Matthew's drawing? Oh, yes, he's multitalented in both athletics and art. And Samantha is playing fall ball right now. She's an amazing hitter, just like Alex Bregman! Would you like to come to a game? The family would be honored!"

Dad grabs the phone from her. "Uh-huh . . . uh-huh . . . uh-huh," he says in answer to the manager's questions, but no actual words come out.

I grab the phone from him. "Hi, sir, it's Samantha . . . Sammy," I say breathlessly.

"Our superfan! You're just the person I want to talk to!" he says back. "Is your brother Matthew there with you?"

"Yes!" I say, and nod to Matty so he'll scoot closer. I angle the cordless so we can both hear the manager of our most favorite team, the Houston Astros, who *knows our names* and *has called us at home.*

I can't even believe it!

"Well, I wanted to tell you both how much your superfan sentiment means to all of us—to the other Astros fans, to the players, and to me personally," he says. "That drawing and those words really touched the heart of this city. Even with the cleanup that's left ahead, we're still Houston Strong!"

I catch Matty's eyes. We're both beaming, inside and out.

He says into the phone, "Thanks so much, sir!"

And I say, "Go Astros! Houston Strong!"

The manager says, "Well, kids, I'm calling because we need you here at Minute Maid Park to cheer us on during the World Series. So how about some tickets for your family for one of the games? Which one would work for y'all?"

Our mouths hang open. Our family's going to cheer our team on at the World Series against the Los Angeles Dodgers in our Home Away from Home! It's a Putterman dream come true!

I glance at Becky. She's frowning at our beyond-excited family. Maybe going to the World Series is our dream right now, but it's not really hers.

She's dreaming about her bat mitzvah this Saturday.

And her special day doesn't seem to be on almost anyone's mind right now, except somehow . . . mine.

But we can't pass up these tickets! We can't pass up the World Series! How can we do both?

I cover the phone's receiver, and whisper to everyone, "He's giving us tickets to one of the World Series games!"

"Oh my god!" Bubbe swoons, and Papa has to sit back down.

My dad and uncle are wordless, goggly eyed, and grinning.

Aunt Deb's eyes fix on Becky, and she plasters on a thin, nervous smile.

I glance at my cousin. She's clinging to Jess, burying her face deep into her stripy fur. Jess hisses, but Becky ignores her.

And I know: even though going to the World Series is such a *big* deal, Becky's bat mitzvah is an even *bigger* deal.

I uncover the receiver. "Tickets would be amazing, sir! Thank you so much. We'll take game . . ."

I run through the likely timeline in my mind real quick: the Dodgers have a better record, so they'll be home field; it'll be Tuesday and Wednesday away, then home games at least Friday and Saturday.

But that's when we'll be celebrating Becky's bat mitzvah, so we can't go then!

I clear my throat, "Umm, can we please have tickets to game five?"

"Are you sure?" he says. "That would be on Sunday."

Matty elbows me and whispers, "What if the Astros don't make it to Sunday?"

I elbow him back. "Yes, sir . . . Sunday's best." I beam at Becky, and she loosens her hold on Jess and smiles. "And we'll need nine tickets so our whole family can come. Thank you so much!"

Monday after school, my hitting slump gets even worse. My balls barely make it out of the infield during batting practice.

Weak contact to the pitcher, weak contact to the short stop, weak contact to the second baseman. Weak, period.

Everyone's making under-breath comments about how much my hitting stinks—all my teammates and even Coach. Ethan doesn't have any encouraging advice for me after practice either.

I throw all my stuff into my baseball bag, and Brandon comes up to me and mouths, "Girls play softball," so Coach won't hear, and all my teammates crack up.

I look around the dugout. I always felt like I belonged here, but I don't right now. A terrible and sad thought pops into my head: maybe it's time for me to quit baseball, too.

Then my dad's late coming to get me.

I text him.

Me: Where r u? My team left!

Dad: Almost there! Sorry, baby!

Great. Just great.

I plop down on the dugout bench. For the first time in a while, there's nothing to do—no cat fashion sessions to watch, no homework or journal entry to write, no family to talk to, no baseball game on TV.

So I stare out at the blue sky, and think about what my mom always says: with the bad, comes good. After today, I sure hope she's right.

I run through my mental list of all I've lost again, the bad: my flooded house and chewed-up birthday baseball, my twin telepathy with Matty, and my baseball swing.

267

It's a dark feeling that even a bright Texas day and the Houston Astros going to the World Series can't push away.

Then I get up and walk the bases, like I used to do after games when I was little. It was Dad's idea to calm me down if I didn't get any runs, and it totally works.

"Sammy, you make it to first, then you make it to second. You make it to third, then you come on home. One step at a time, honey."

While I walk, I make a list of all I've gained, the good: becoming friends again with my cousin Becky, spending lots of time with Bubbe and Papa, sorting out my feelings in my journal, learning how to talk to my brother.

And it's like that for my city, Houston, too. With the bad, came the good. Hurricane Harvey, the most damaging American hurricane on record, brought all sorts of people together to become Houston Strong.

Would any of us have known how strong we could become, without the bad?

When my dad pulls up, I forget all about him being late, since Matty's in the car with him!

My brother wears new cleats and has brought the glove I gave him, all conditioned up. He unloads the trunk with Dad—there's a brand-new hitting tee and Uncle Mike's old bucket of baseballs.

"What's all that for?" I ask.

Matty grins at me. "Ready to turn that slump around?"

I smile, and a huge burst of hope surges inside. "Am I ever!"

Dad looks at us, barely holding it together. He's smiling big, but his eyes go soft and moist. "Is that everything you need to help your sister?" he asks Matty.

My brother nods.

"Umm, because I could stay and catch for you or field balls or something."

"Thanks, Dad," Matty says. "But Sammy and I need some twin time."

Dad gets in the car and backs out of the parking lot real slow like he's prying himself away, and we laugh.

I glance at Matty's new glove. "Does it fit?"

He grins again. "What do you think?"

I nod. I knew it would when I picked it out, but it never hurts to ask.

"I hope you're not too tired out after practice. Turning things around takes a lot of work."

"Nope," I say, and it's true. My brother's here, and it's just how it's supposed to be. I'm all fired up since I've been waiting for him to play ball with me again for so long.

Matty has it all planned out.

First he sets up the tee in the cage and watches my swing. After a while he says, "It looks smooth, but you're not swinging as hard as you used to, Sammy."

I shake my head, and the bad takes over again. "What's the point?" I say, gauging the three hundred feet from home plate to the 14U fence line. "I'm just going for line drives, since there's no way I'm ever going to hit it out again."

"That attitude stinks! You think just because you're small, you can't hit it out? Lemme see your phone."

Then he shows me a bunch of replays of José Altuve's swing. "He's about your height, and he's strong like you, Sammy," Matty says. "He's small, but he's a power hitter. He swings as hard as he can, every single time. He's not just trying for line drives."

"Do you really think I can hit like him . . . even though I'm a girl?"

He rolls his eyes and nods. "So what if you're a girl, Sammy? You did last year; you gave it everything you had. But you're holding back now. You're a little like me . . . something big has changed, and you're not sure how to handle it."

I raise my eyebrows. "You mean, like you quit playing baseball, and I've had to play all by myself, and you weren't even here to cheer me on?"

He gives me a long look. "Big changes are scary, but that doesn't mean you can't handle them, Sammy."

I nod and shuffle my cleats in the clay. Maybe I am scared.

Before, when we were a twin team, I always had Matty to stick up for me. And then when I didn't . . . all the whispers I'd heard from the time I was little, about how girls can't play baseball, got louder and louder.

I started to think being a ballplayer couldn't be part of what I'm about anymore.

"Mack says that sometimes a person has to play by their own rules. They have to make the future they know is right," Matty says. "We can play our game, Sammy, no matter what anybody else says."

I say, "I'm a baseball player who happens to be a girl."

"I'm a baseball player who happens to have a serious crush on his best friend," he says back.

I grin. Maybe we're both a bit different, playing this game, but so what? We can handle it. We can be everything we are.

We play catch for a long while to warm Matty's arm up. And even though I'm not an artist like my brother, I imagine the picture of us sure looks nice.

"Whoa," he says when he stands on the mound for the first time. Home plate in this league is about eight feet farther away.

"You've got this, Matty," I say, while my brother throws some warm-up pitches.

And he does. Even with the all the new space between him and the plate, he's bigger and stronger now. His ball whistles as it comes on in. And since pickoffs are allowed in this league, runners better watch out if they ever get on. Matty's got a southpaw advantage!

I put my glove down and pick up my bat. "Give me everything you've got."

He smiles. "You sure?"

I nod. I am sure. If I can hit Matty's pitches, I can hit anything.

And even though I can't know how much longer I'm going to play baseball, I can sure swing my hardest while I'm playing. I can give it everything I've got.

It takes me awhile to adjust my timing, since Matty throws harder and faster than the other kids. I swing and miss, swing and miss. I foul a few off.

But I don't give up. Puttermans aren't quitters.

Finally I hit one straight at my brother.

His new glove flies up to catch it, and he smiles. "You hit that one really hard, Sammy."

"Yup!" I say, a smile spreading clear through me.

Then we're both ready, my twin brother and me. We can play this game if we want. The good takes over.

On the next pitch, Matty throws to the heart of the plate, and *bam!* My ball sails over the 14U fence. I drop my bat like we're playing a game for real and jog the bases: first, second, third, and when I come on home, my brother's there waiting for me with a big hug.

I've hit a lot of balls and I've gotten lots of homers. Lots of them were easy-peasy lemon squeezy. All of them felt great.

But the bad with the good made this one feel so much better. And it doesn't hurt to have my brother cheering me on again!

We text our dad to come get us as the sun dips to the edge of the field.

When Dad pulls up, Matty turns to me and says, "Next time we do this, we're gonna need a catcher."

I say back, "Next time, Matty, we're going to need a whole team."

And my twin brother doesn't disagree.

Matty

Sometimes, a picture's worth a thousand words, but sometimes, it's not.

See, if I drew a picture of me pitching, you'd notice a lot of things.

You'd notice my left arm cocked way back and you'd think it was gonna be a hard throw. You'd notice my grip on the ball, and maybe you'd be able to tell if I was throwing a fastball or a curve. You'd notice my right leg stride, and where my toes point, and maybe you'd think the ball was heading in the right direction.

And the picture would tell you a lot, really it would.

But it wouldn't tell you the whole story.

For instance, it wouldn't tell you that I've dreamed about pitching almost every single night since I quit last season.

And it wouldn't tell you that the glove I'm breaking in on my right hand is my new good-luck charm, way better than any rabbit's foot ever was, since my sister picked it out for me.

And it wouldn't tell you that someday, I wanna be a Jewish southpaw pitcher in the MLB, just like Sandy Koufax.

And it wouldn't tell you that if there still aren't any openly gay ballplayers in the MLB when I get there, I'll be the first.

For some things, you've gotta find words.

That night after I pitch to Sammy and she hits her big dinger, I clean off the stuff on the highest shelf of the library.

I prop the Koufax book on a lower shelf, with the other books I've been reading. I face it forward so you can see the cover, like they do in bookstores when great books are featured on displays. And yeah, I finished reading it. Twice, maybe three times. Who knows?

I take my phone out of its box and charge it. When it's all powered up, Ethan's texts load.

He's still there, waiting for me to be ready, like I probably knew he'd be.

And I am ready. It's time to write my next great story.

I open the fresh journal Ms. Martinez gave me and draw the picture of us. Of our smiles and starry kiss. And it's a really, really great picture. But now, even though it's still so hard, I've gotta find the words that go with it. My own words.

Before I chicken out, I write them down, real quick.

I'm a Putterman, and I love my family.
I'm an Astros fan, and I love my team.
I'm a twin brother, and I love my sister.
I'm a pitcher, and I love playing baseball.
I'm an artist, and I love turning feelings into pictures.
I'm Ethan Goldberg's best friend, and I might love him, too.

I know what I'm about, and sometimes a person's got to make the future they know is right. So I pick up my phone and text Ethan back.

Me: Hey.

Ethan: Finally.

Me: Sorry it took so long.

Ethan: I wasn't worried.

Me: Really?

Ethan: Really.

Just like Ethan's always sure when he calls my pitches, he's sure now. I just needed some time to be just as sure, too.

'Cause I don't wanna hide what we're about.

Then I call him, and we pick up right where we left off, since best friends can do that, especially best friends who *like*-like each other, even if they haven't talked in a while.

Later that night, I take Bialy out to do his business one

last time and head to the kitchen for a snack.

Faint music floats down the staircase from Becky's room. I can't believe Sammy's still up, since she's usually no night owl like me. Plus, she had two hard practices today!

I head up and whisper through the crack in the door, "Sammy? Can I come in?"

She doesn't answer, but Becky says, "Suit yourself, Matty."

Sure enough, Sammy's out cold in her bed with her mouth wide open. Bartholomew and Jess are curled up on their bed, fast asleep, too.

The only night owls are me and Becky.

She's sitting on the floor near her studio with her chin on her knees, playing Katy Perry's song "Rise" on her phone. When it ends, she immediately starts it over. I wonder how many times she's listened to it tonight.

It's this great song about overcoming tough stuff, which seems like a perfect anthem for today for so many reasons.

I sit down on Becky's bed. "What are you doing?"

She doesn't look at me. "Nothing, can't you see that?"

Every other time I've been in Becky's room, she's got something in the works. But now her studio's completely empty and all the props are up on the shelves. "How are your cat couture sessions going?" I ask.

She glances to some dresses hanging outside her closet with the tags still on. "It's my bat mitzvah week. I don't really have time for any sessions, since my Torah speech still isn't right. So I told my followers the cats are on holiday."

I look at the dresses and nod. I knew it was Becky's bat mitzvah week. Aunt Deb's been a total wreck.

She's been harping on Uncle Mike to finish Becky's bat mitzvah video. She's been talking to the caterer and the DJ on her cell phone. She's been shuttling Becky to run-through sessions with the rabbi. She's been making surprise table arrangements for Becky, and now my library's full of them.

Aunt Deb likes themes, just like her daughter. If I had to guess from the centerpieces, I'd say the theme of Becky's bat mitzvah party is gonna be Domestic Cats.

But with my parents trying to decide what to do with our total loss house and the Houston paper picking up my drawing of Sammy and the Astros heading to the World Series and the manager calling and Sammy and me trying to put our twin team back together and me trying to find my words for Ethan . . . Becky's bat mitzvah has kinda been on my back burner.

Plus, we haven't spoken to each other since she blurted out my secret to our entire family.

She presses play again, and the song starts over. She hugs her knees and rocks.

I guess it's time for us to find some words, too.

"Look, Becky—"

She interrupts, "I really messed up!"

"You did."

"I tried to apologize a bunch of times!"

"You did."

"You didn't let me!"

"I didn't. I'm sorry."

She whips her head around. "Wait, so we're both sorry?"

"I guess."

Becky gets up from the floor and sits next to me. "So . . ."

"So . . ."

She bites her lip and leans her head on my shoulder. "Wanna help me with my bat mitzvah party playlist?"

I lean mine back and smile. "Sure, Becks . . . let's start with Katy Perry."

Becky

There are three things I did not think would happen during my bat mitzvah year.

Number one: my cat Jess would get a boyfriend before me.

Number two: my cousin Matty would get a boyfriend before me.

Number three: my cousin Sammy would move into my room, and I'd really like it.

Oh, how could I forget? There's one more thing. . . .

Number four: I'd be rooting for the Houston Astros in the World Series, even though they're ruining my bat mitzvah!

World Series fever takes the city of Houston—and the Putterman family—by storm.

Tuesday morning during breakfast before school, Papa

folds up the paper and runs through the week's schedule. "Game one away, tonight. Game two away, tomorrow. Rest a day. Game three at home, Friday. Game four at home, Saturday. Game five at home Sunday . . . *unless we sweep*," he says with a wink. "Rest a day. A possible game six next Tuesday, and a possible game seven next Wednesday."

That schedule doesn't include my bat mitzvah!

I look around the kitchen table at my family's glowing faces. A World Series win would mean so much to them. After watching our city get covered in floodwater from Hurricane Harvey. After the total loss of their homes. After the Astros helped our city keep Houston Strong hope.

Except . . . it's my bat mitzvah, too!

I've been looking forward to it for as long as I can remember, and I hoped that everyone in my family—my grandparents, my aunt and uncle, my cousins, and my parents—would be able to put everything else aside and finally focus on me. Because for just one special day and one special night, I want to shine bright, like a star. I want to show everyone my very best self. And to do that, I need the Whole World firmly behind me. I need them to cheer for me the loudest.

Is that too much to ask?

Plus, I'm facing a moral dilemma of epic proportions that I'm ill-equipped to handle.

I know I should root for my team to clinch every game, no matter what. When you're on a team, that's just what you do: you never give up on them. But unless both World Series contenders lose *at least one* of the first three games, it'll force a must-see elimination game during my bat mitzvah party, and that would be très, très terrible!

So I have no choice—I have to root against the Astros, for at least one game, to save my bat mitzvah.

On Tuesday, I spend the whole day at school weighing my dilemma, feeling like a traitor. Root for my team, root for myself? Root for my team, root for myself? Root for my team, root for myself? God!

When I get home, it only gets worse. Let me set the scene I walk into.

My family has their navy-and-orange fan gear on, all of it, and someone, I'm guessing one of my cousins, has put my baby Astros T-shirts on the cats. Bialy's even carrying around the remnants of Sammy's baseball, signed by all the Astros greats.

Every TV in the house is turned on to the game station.

If you're in the kitchen, you're covered. If you're in the living room, you're covered. If you're in the library, you're covered. If you're in any one of our bedrooms, covered! Even if you're in Papa and Bubbe's bathroom, you're covered!

My mother, grandmother, and aunt have cooked up all our game-day favorites: kosher hot dogs with yellow mustard, relish, and ketchup; cheesy ballpark nachos; grilled chicken sliders and french fries; barbecue-brisket-loaded baked potatoes. They even have Cracker Jacks and peanuts in their shells!

Everyone's already laid out on the sectional, eyes glued to the TV, anticipating this all-important first game.

They're discussing whether the Astros manager is going to bench George Springer because of his slump. They're discussing who'll be the reliever after Dallas Keuchel pitches. They're discussing each player's stats and speculating about who might get the World Series MVP.

For the whole game, I'm on pins and needles, pacing the room.

Rooting for my team, then not rooting for my team. Knowing I need a loss, then hoping my team won't lose. Feeling needy and selfish, then resolving to put my bat mitzvah dreams aside for the greater good.

It's all super confusing and completely exhausting!

My cousins, in between their unwavering cheers for the Astros, register my internal conflict. I can see it in their twin telepathy.

It would be hard not to, since I'm a wild Becky Six Flags ride: come on down, y'all, and take a spin on our newest roller coaster! Climb to the very top, then plummet to the depths below, then do it again!

And then there's George Springer, my kindred spirit, who needs me right now.

But I'm not there for him in my inner turmoil, not nearly enough. With my on-again, off-again, half-hearted cheers, he goes zero for four with four strikeouts. It's his worst game, *ever.*

It's beyond tragic for both of us.

Because you work so hard for something so you can shine on your most important day, so you can be your very best self. Then when the moment comes—it all falls apart.

The Astros end up losing the first game in only two and a half hours, breaking a twenty-five-year World Series loss-time record, and I feel awful.

Even though I'm not sure it's what I wanted, one thing's for certain—it feels like my fault. I didn't give my team my complete support and cheer them on when they needed me the most.

Story. Of. My. Life.

It's a vicious cycle. Sammy needed a friend when she moved into my room, and I let her down. Matty needed to confide in someone about Ethan, and I let him down. George Springer needed a real superfan to help him out of his slump, so he won't get benched for game two, and I let him down.

Because, well, I'm anything but super. I'm anything but a star. I can't even figure out what my Torah portion's about.

And worst of all . . . I feel relieved because I'm one game closer to my bat mitzvah not being completely ruined, as long as the 'Stros win at least one of the next two games! Ugh!

I sit on the sectional with my sad and quiet family.

Bubbe rubs Papa's shoulders. Auntie Annie smushes against Uncle Greggy while he searches his laptop for game one commentary. Sammy and Matty's eyes cloud over like their big game got rained out. My mother and father watch them all, shaking their heads.

My family looks like they did when they got here from the shelter—defeated. A first Houston Strong winning game would have meant so much!

I have a little heart-to-heart with myself: even though it's my bat mitzvah week, and I wanted everyone to focus on just me, I need to get behind my family and root for them, no matter what. It's another great challenge.

It's time for me, Rebecca Putterman, to take one for the team.

Sammy

The last and only other time the Houston Astros went to the World Series, Matty and I were babies, only six months old.

My parents tell this story all the time.

Houston had just survived another epic hurricane that September, Hurricane Rita. It was the most intense tropical cyclone in the Gulf of Mexico on record.

Three million people evacuated our city in advance of the storm, including the Puttermans, in two barely moving, caravanning cars.

Our family only made it to the small town of Fayetteville, halfway between Houston and Austin, before running out of gas on the side of the highway. We walked into town, my dad pushing me and Matty in our double stroller and my uncle pushing Becky in hers.

All the hotels and motels in Fayetteville were full. All the gas stations in Fayetteville ran dry.

Bubbe sweet-talked the owner of a bed-and-breakfast into renting us her college daughter's room, and we crammed in, all of us, for the three days it took for gas to arrive so we could make our way back to Houston.

When we got home, our houses were without electricity for more than a week.

My mom and dad, aunt and uncle, and both of my grandparents all agreed: our city did not feel very strong.

Then the very next month, the Chicago White Sox swept the Astros in that first World Series in four consecutive games, easy-peasy lemon squeezy.

The Puttermans decided one thing unanimously after that most difficult fall—they were never abandoning their city again.

And so, in Hurricane Harvey, we didn't. We stayed in Houston in our homes and battled the rising floodwater until we were forced to evacuate. We moved into our one surviving house and became Houston Strong.

Our city shakes off Tuesday's game one loss and gets behind our team for their second game on Wednesday.

I wear my new Altuve jersey to school, and Matty wears his new Verlander jersey. And when we get there—I'm not surprised—lots of kids are wearing Astros jerseys, not just the kids who are ballplayers! Between classes, a flood of

Springers, Bregmans, Altuves, and Verlanders pour down the hall. A bunch of the teachers and Mr. Evans, our school janitor, are wearing jerseys, too.

So is Amanda! She just happens to be wearing a Verlander jersey like Matty.

The Astros are all anyone can talk about. But no one, and I mean no one, wants to ask the question we're all thinking: will the Dodgers sweep the World Series just like the White Sox did?

The Dodgers did have the better season record . . . the Dodgers do have Clayton Kershaw, one of the greatest lefty pitchers ever, maybe even better than Sandy Koufax . . . and the Dodgers also have some of the best young batters in the MLB!

But the Astros have Altuve and Springer, even though Springer slumped in game one . . . and the Astros have Verlander, who'll be a future Hall of Famer for sure . . . and the Astros have a city behind them that lost almost everything, except their team spirit.

Ms. Martinez comes up with another unplanned writing assignment in language arts: fan letters to the Astros players that she'll hand-deliver to Minute Maid Park in advance of the home games this weekend.

I figure the more cheering the better, so I write letters to José Altuve, George Springer, and Alex Bregman.

On the way back to Becky's house after school, Matty tells me he wrote a short letter to Dallas Keuchel and a long letter to Justin Verlander. "The Astros became a different team when they signed Verlander," my brother says. "He made all the difference."

When we get there, it's a repeat of yesterday, but *more*. My family's preparing more ballpark food, they're wearing more Astros gear, and there's more speculating and pre-game cheering.

But after our game one loss, there's more worrying, too.

Matty, Becky, and I sit at the kitchen table before the game starts. Becky shows me an article about George Springer.

That she's read *three* times.

"They said such awful things about him! That he's lost his swing, that he should be benched, that he's not worthy of playing in the World Series. People are so fickle! Don't they remember all the good things he's done? How could they lose confidence in him . . . after a few mistakes?"

I nod. I've seen the articles, too. Some of the fans are being pretty ruthless. "Don't worry, Becky," I say. "I know a thing or two about slumps. They don't last forever."

"But what if George can't redeem himself?" she says. "What if he doesn't get a chance to show everyone what he's capable of and be his very best? What if he doesn't get to shine?"

Matty raises his eyebrows, and I raise mine back. It doesn't seem like Becky's talking about George Springer anymore.

"The Astros manager won't give up on him. He knows how amazing George can be." I bite my lip and glance at Matty. "He just needs his biggest fans to keep cheering him on."

Game two starts and we get an early lead, but by the sixth inning, the Dodgers are ahead 3–1 and they have a great bullpen. Their relievers haven't given up a run in twenty-eight innings!

I run and get my glove for good luck during the seventh-inning stretch. It's not like I'm going to catch anything, of course, but just wearing it, just smelling the leather, makes me feel better, closer to the ballpark.

I'm out of my seat permanently now, jumping up and down, crouching and covering my head with my glove during bad plays, cheering like there's no tomorrow. "Come on, Astros! Come back! Come back!"

Matty is, too, and so is our family . . . except for Becky.

She sits in the corner of the sectional, hugging her knees and giving little cheers now and again. She wrings her hands and watches George Springer.

The rest of us high five and low five and heckle and boo calls. We cheer like our city depends on it. We have to stay Houston Strong.

So many people like us are living somewhere that's not home. So many people like us are trying to find a way to put their lives back together. So many people like us need some hope.

The teams are tied up in the ninth, then José Altuve puts

us ahead at the top of the tenth with his sixth postseason homer. But then the Dodgers tie the game up again!

George Springer's coming up, top of the eleventh inning, and we have to focus our cheers on him! I turn to tell Becky—but she's not there anymore.

"Where did Becky go?" I ask Matty, and he shrugs.

I run upstairs to find my cousin. She's sitting on the bed in her room, furiously writing.

"George Springer needs you to come back and cheer for him!" I say.

"What does it matter, Sammy?" she mumbles. "I'm not a superfan like you. I'm not very . . . super at all."

I try to tell her that's not true, and that our team really needs her, but she stays in a funk. Then I have to get back to the game!

I race back downstairs just in time to root for Springer.

Even on TV, his hit sounds right. It's a catch and release . . . almost effortless. It's going . . . going . . . going . . . and see ya! The mostly Dodger crowd goes silent while a few sprinkled Astros fans go wild! His homer's just what we needed: it puts the Astros ahead by two. I wish Becky had seen it!

By the bottom of the eleventh, it's a one-run game again. Then the Dodgers strike out, and the Astros win it! We win our first-ever World Series game! We all cheer our hearts out!

The win took eleven innings in four hours and nineteen minutes, the precise amount of time it took me to realize that though this win feels great, it really does, it would feel way better if my cousin had been cheering her heart out with us.

We were missing one Putterman—and that's not okay at all.

After the excitement dies down, I head back upstairs to check on Becky.

She's surrounded by crumpled papers, and Aunt Deb's sitting next to her, saying, "Honey, maybe you could just sum up . . ."

Becky shakes her head and sniffles. "Thanks for trying, Mom, but . . . I think I might have to wing it."

Aunt Deb takes a deep breath and heads back downstairs.

I walk over and uncrumple one of the papers. "Becky . . . what's going on?"

She bursts into tears and flops down on her wall-to-wall hot-pink-and-purple geometric carpet.

"My . . . my bat mitzvah's in *shambles*!" she sputters. "Why . . . why did it have to be World Series *this* week? I . . . I wanted this week to be *special*! And . . . and I still have *no clue* what the point of my Torah portion is! My . . . my speech is going to be *terrible*! I-I'm not a good writer . . . like you."

I hand her a tissue and sit down next to her. "Gosh, Becky, I'm so sorry about your speech," I say. I can't do anything about my cousin's bat mitzvah being the same week as the World Series, but maybe I can help her with her d'var. "What's your Torah portion about?"

She blows her nose. "So God tells Abram that he's going to be great, really great. But then he makes him leave everything he knows and wander around, first to the Canaan desert, where there's famine, then to Egypt, where his wife is kidnapped by the Pharaoh! I know God's testing him, *big*, but it doesn't really make any sense why. . . . It's hopeless!"

"Hmm," I say. "Matty and I don't have our b'nai mitzvah till next spring, so I haven't started my d'var, but I've noticed . . . when our rabbi gives his d'var Torahs at synagogue, it seems like they're all about making connections."

She sniffles. "Exactly, Sammy! He says I need to figure out what my portion's *takeaway lesson* is!"

"Well," I say, glancing at her studio setup and overflowing prop shelf. "Isn't that kind of like picking a theme? You're really great at that."

"I thought I was . . . before," she mumbles. "But maybe I'm not anymore."

That night, I can't fall asleep even though it's so, so late.

I stare at the picture of me and Dad in the stands when I was a baby by moonlight, while Becky snores in her bed next to me. The picture I thought I lost in the hurricane. The picture my cousin found for me again.

It's the picture that started it all.

It destined me to become a die-hard Houston Astros

superfan. It destined me to want to be a first baseman and a great hitter like Jeff Bagwell. It destined me to be a girl ballplayer and a part of a stellar twin team.

But tonight, looking at my cousin's sad face, I knew.

I'm not just an Astros superfan anymore. I'm not just a superfan of my twin team. I'm a superfan of another team, too: my family, the Puttermans.

So please forgive me, Houston Astros, but my cheers are needed elsewhere. You have a whole family of Houstonians rooting for you this week, and my cousin Becky needs her whole family rooting for her, too.

I head downstairs and pass my mom and aunt in the kitchen, still cleaning up the kitchen from tonight's game. Light filters under the door of the library, so I knock.

"Becky's so sad," I say, lying down on the pullout next to Matty.

He nods and makes some room for me. "Is she ever!"

"Well, our whole city's caught up in the World Series!"

"Yeah, the Astros are all anybody talks about."

"The week of her bat mitzvah!"

"The week of her bat mitzvah."

"Even *our family*."

"Even *her parents*."

"Poor Becky!"

"Poor Becky!"

"What are we going to do, Matty?" I ask.

He shakes his head. "We need to do something!"

"We need to root for her, hard."

"Agreed! We need to be Becky's superfans."

Then our twin telepathy kicks in perfectly.

We grin at each other, then head to the kitchen to see if Aunt Deb and Mom are still there. We have a lot to do, and there's not much time!

Becky's bat mitzvah is in just two days.

Thankfully, they're still there. My aunt gives us a tired smile. "Kitchen's closed, twins. Come back for breakfast."

"We're not here for food, Aunt Deb," Matty says, eyeing a lone hot dog on a platter.

I elbow him, and he shifts his gaze to our aunt.

"We're here about Becky's bat mitzvah."

"Her bat mitzvah?" She shakes her head again. "What a week . . . I sure hope we can pull it all together and she won't be . . . disappointed."

My brother nods. "That's why we're here. Sammy and I want to help."

She raises an eyebrow and perks up. "What did you have in mind?"

Matty says, "For starters, we'll need Becky's bat mitzvah video on a zip drive and the DJ's phone number, please."

I turn to my mom. "And we'll need access to our old family photos on the cloud."

Maybe it's the way we say it, like we know what we're doing and we're going to make Becky's bat mitzvah so much better, but they both grin. Aunt Deb throws up her hands and says, "All right! Here we go!"

Maybe it feels like cheering.

Matty

Thursday is a World Series rest day, and our whole family needs it. We're seriously beat after staying up late watching games the last two nights.

Papa reads through the newspaper at breakfast, nearly nodding off.

My mom says Sammy sounds like her chain-smoking great-aunt Martha from all her over-the-top rooting.

Bubbe puts out boxes of cereal and a jug of milk for breakfast and says she's all cooked out.

And my dad and uncle turn the sports radio station they like to listen to in the kitchen down a bit lower.

And me? I'm tired like everybody, sure. But I'm also super excited, 'cause last night, I cheered my heart out. And it felt great, really great.

I cheered for so many things. I cheered for the Astros, of course, and their first winning World Series game. I cheered for Sammy getting her swing back. I cheered for me and Ethan since we decided we're gonna start hanging out again.

And I cheered for Becky, 'cause even though she doesn't know it yet, she's gonna have an amazing bat mitzvah.

After school, Becky and Aunt Deb head out to take care of last-minute party details.

Sammy hands me a piece of paper as she's shoving her cleats on for practice.

"I've made a list of songs Becky will love."

"Okay."

"And I've described the family photos you need from the cloud for her video."

"Okay."

"And we want her video to be good, really good, like the one at Shelby's bat mitzvah, remember?"

"Sammy, you're doing it again. I've got this!"

She blushes as red as her cap. "Okay. Sorry!"

After she leaves, I settle onto the library pullout with my mom's laptop. I plug in the zip drive Uncle Mike slipped me, and the video he made for Becky loads.

It totally stinks! The slideshow's set to lame 80s music, with way too much falsetto and disco beat. The timing of the music is all off, and some of the photos scroll in complete silence. And they're not even grouped by theme!

Doesn't my uncle know his own daughter?

Disaster averted—lucky for Becky she has a cousin who's an artist!

It doesn't take me long to fix it.

Awesome music, check. Good transitions and fades, check. All the right photos, and even some great surprise ones, check.

When it's done, it makes a really great story.

Next I work on Becky's playlist. With the World Series starting this week, we hadn't even finished it.

I add all the songs Becky played in our studio sessions first, then I add the songs from Sammy's list.

When I get to the last song on my sister's list, I smile.

Sammy and I really are twins—she's picked the same song I was gonna pick for the last dance of Becky's bat mitzvah party.

My cousin's gonna love it!

I finish the playlist just as my dad pops his head into the library, home from his clinic.

He smiles when he sees my glove, which just happens to be on the table beside my bed with the Sandy Koufax book since maybe I'm rereading my favorite parts.

"How are you doing, Matt?"

I smile at him. "I'm good, Dad, really good now."

He raises his eyebrows. "How about them Astros?"

I raise mine back. "I think they've got a chance."

Dad says, "I think we all do," and winks.

He starts to shut the door to the library, and I say, "Hey, Dad?" and he pokes his head back in.

"Can I ride with you again to pick Sammy up from practice?"

He nods and doesn't say a thing when I grab my glove.

We get there, and Sammy's 14U team is just finishing up. For a minute, I sit in the car and watch.

The team's in the dugout, sore and tired and happy, packing up their stuff. The coach is loading the gear closet, rolling his eyes at a sudden yelp and game of keep-away that's just erupted with somebody's glove.

Sammy's talking to Ethan near the edge of the dugout, both of them all easy smiles. By the way she's standing with her shoulders back, leaning on her bat, waving her batting gloves around as she talks, it's been a day without a slump.

Ethan's up against the fence with his catcher's gear still on, mask under an arm. The sun lights the edges of his still-long, summer-bleached hair. He leans over Sammy and laughs at her quick, animated retelling. I could swear he's taller now.

It's all a really great picture.

I get out of the car, wave to them, and they jog over to us. I give Sammy a quick hug and give Ethan a longer one. When I finally pull away from him, my dad reaches over and pats his shoulder. "Hey, Ethan?" he says, and the chicken thing starts in his throat. "We've all really . . . missed you . . . around the house and . . ."

Dad puts his hands in his pockets, and I grin at Ethan.

"Thanks, Dr. Putterman," he says. "Maybe I can come over to Becky's soon."

Some of my teammates from our old 12U team call out when they see me. Some of the new players nod. It's not like we don't all know each other, since we've been playing each other in leagues since we were little kids.

I take a deep breath and nod to Ethan and Sammy. Then I hand my glove to my sister and walk over to the gear closet.

"Hey, Coach," I say.

He looks up from fiddling with the lock. "Matthew Putterman. What can I do for you?"

I look out to the edge of the ball field where the green, manicured grass line abruptly changes to mid-shin yellowing waves. I'm ready to be here again, but this is harder than I thought it'd be.

Ever since I threw my first pitch to Sammy, it's like my whole body's woken up. My right hand feels best in my new glove and my left hand doesn't feel great unless it's clutching a ball. My elbow feels best bent, stretching behind my shoulder.

In daydreams, I listen for the sounds I've missed. The sounds I'm about.

The *whoosh* a ball makes as it leaves my hand. The firm *pop* of a mitt catching it, the quick call of an ump, the sharp *crack* of a bat. My family's cheers in the stands and Sammy's cry, "Way to go, Matty! Way to go, Matty!" for the hundred millionth time.

These are the sounds I'm here for.

"Are you short any pitchers?" I say, looking at the dugout.

A tall, skinny kid glares at me. I'll bet he's Brandon, the kid who's been trash talking my sister. I glare back.

The coach says, "Season's almost over."

"Understood," I say back, my shoulders rounding down. I turn and walk away.

Everything goes quiet, then I hear it—the whizzing sound of a baseball in flight.

"Hey, Putterman!"

I whip around, just in time to barehand the coach's ball, coming fast at my head. It smarts, but not like it would've if it had hit me square on the nose.

He smiles. "You're on the bench. Then you're a reliever. Then we'll see."

I nod. "Thank you, sir."

He yells, "Goldberg, mask up! We're staying late."

And I grab my glove from Sammy then run to my place on the mound.

Becky

Friday night, I'm up at bat.

It's my bat mitzvah weekend, which I've been waiting for my whole life. It's the World Series, which my entire family, and every Houstonian has been waiting for their whole lives.

Needless to say, I won't be hitting any homers this weekend, that's for sure. I'm going to have to settle for a nice base hit.

If you can't beat 'em, join 'em. Isn't that the saying?

The out-of-town relatives arrive in Houston on Friday morning: on my father's side, Papa's brother, Milt, his kids and grandkids, and Bubbe's two loud-as-her sisters, Hazel and Fiona, from New York; and on my mother's side, my grandparents from New Jersey, the Blums, my aunt Naomi and her family from California, and my uncle Caleb from way up in Alaska.

They check into the hotel and head over to our house for the big Shabbat dinner/game three of the World Series watch party we're having tonight. Of course the game wasn't part of anyone's original plan for my bat mitzvah weekend, but it sure is now.

My grandmother, mother, and aunt have gone all-out with the backyard buffet, and they've even set up an ice-cream dessert station. And for a while, it's "Mazel tov, Becky!" and "We're so excited to be here!" It's food and family and celebration, just like Bubbe says we're about. And I feel special and shining, just like I wanted.

But then the game starts.

The Whole World parks in our living room on the sectional in full-on Astros fandom, and the out-of-town relatives follow suit. If this were one of studio my sessions, I'd say the ambiance is perfectly right.

The game's blaring, the family's cheering their hearts out, and I'm trying to cheer right along with them. The Astros lead 4–1 by the fifth inning, on track to win their first-ever World Series game at our Home Away from Home at Minute Maid Park, and George Springer even makes a dramatic left-center catch to prevent a run!

It's great. It's exactly what every Putterman always dreamed of.

All but one.

It's not that I'm not rooting for the Astros. I am. It's not that I don't understand how important the World Series is to my city after the hurricane. I do. It's not that I don't want to be a part of the Houston Strong team along with everyone else.

It's just that there's a part of me that feels disappointed, since I'm taking one for the team. Because for all these years, when I thought about what my bat mitzvah weekend would be like, I thought about three things.

Number one: my whole family would cheer for me.

Number two: my whole family would cheer for me.

Number three: my whole family would cheer for me.

And they are cheering for me, but not as much as I hoped they would, because they've got something else to cheer for now, too.

So I guess I'm going to shine a little less bright—just like always.

I leave them watching the game and wander to my room. I sit down near my studio, and Jess and Bartholomew immediately arch up from their cat bed and walk over to me, purring. I rhythmically alternate pets: fur, skin, fur, skin, fur, skin. And I feel a bit better.

At least I have two cats.

I open my social media page. I haven't posted a session in over a week, and my followers have noticed. They've saying things like, "Where are you, cat couture goddess?" "We want more tabby + sphynx!" and "Miss u lots @rebeccas-domesticcatfashions!"

I put together an impromptu session for them. Nothing fancy. Today's theme: the Ultimate Test, in honor of my bat mitzvah.

I choose lovebirds Katniss and Peeta from *The Hunger Games*, who face an unfathomable test when the Capitol decides they must duel each other to the death. But Katniss decides she'd rather they eat some poisonous berries and perish together. Then, in the face of Katniss's unbelievable inner strength, the Capitol comes around, and they both survive!

It's a super-easy session since all I need are a handful of blueberries from the fridge.

Come to think of it, *The Hunger Games* has an obvious connection with my Torah portion! Just like Katniss, the subject of my bat mitzvah speech tomorrow, Abram faces some serious tests, too.

There's a knock at my door. "Doll?"

"Hi, Bubbe."

My grandmother sits down on my bed. "What's all this?"

I explain my *Hunger Games* scene and how I might've just made some connections with my Torah portion like Sammy was talking about, but I can't quite put my finger on it. And that if I don't figure out my takeaway lesson for my speech *tonight*, I might just have to *wing it* tomorrow.

I explain that for me, the games this weekend aren't really Astros versus Dodgers—they're my bat mitzvah versus the World Series! And that I was hoping for a tie, but that's never going to happen now.

Heck, I'm not up against the Capitol or God, I'm up against the MLB!

When I'm done, she says, "You know, Becky, I had all sorts of ideas about what would happen when Papa retired. We were going to spend all this time together. We were going to be bridge partners! We were going to France!"

"Ooo . . ." I say. "I want to go to France, too!"

"But you know what happened? I got cancer, and I'll tell you, there weren't any crepes or macarons. Nothing turned out how I thought it would."

I reach over and squeeze her hand. "I remember when you were sick, Bubbe."

"Well, doll. The point is, sometimes we get dealt a tough hand."

I nod and squeeze harder.

"And while I skipped the fancy French desserts, I still got to spend lots of time with Papa, and we still got to play bridge. It was a big test—I had to find a different way of looking at things, and when I finally did, they ended up feeling okay. Not exactly like I wanted, but okay. And in the end, well, my cancer brought Papa and me so much closer, and that's what was most important."

I give her a quick hug, then my grandmother pops a blueberry in her mouth.

"Bubbe! Those berries are supposed to be poisonous!"

She smiles and offers me one. I pop it in my mouth, too.

She walks to the door, then turns back. "Doll, you and me, we can overcome just about anything, even a crazy weekend like this one. And just like your Bubbe, you've never been at a loss for what to say, so my instincts tell me you'll figure out your d'var just fine."

After she leaves, I finish my session with the cats and post it. It's an instantaneous hit.

As I'm falling asleep, my family's cheers carry up the stairwell, "We won game three! Way to go, Astros! Way to go!" And I can't help but smile.

The next morning at my bat mitzvah service, I stand tall. I stand strong.

I lead our congregation in prayer and read from the Torah without messing up once. I give my speech, and everyone sits forward on the edge of their seats to listen, especially the rabbi.

And I wing it.

I tell them all about how God tested Abram. I tell them how the Capitol tested Katniss. I tell them how cancer tested my Bubbe. Then I tell them how I'm being tested, too.

By having my whole family move in with us after the hurricane. By figuring out how to be friends with my cousins again after we hadn't been in such a long time. By having to share my bat mitzvah weekend with the World Series.

It dawns on me: even though all those things have been

tough, my real test isn't what I thought it was. Just like Abram, Katniss, and Bubbe, my real test hasn't been about what's happening on the outside, it's been about what's happening on the inside.

I say, "We're all being tested, all the time. But the biggest test is figuring out *what's most important to you* . . . that's the takeaway lesson. Katniss figured out her love for Peeta was most important. Abram figured out that God is most important, then God gave him a new name, Abraham, and made him the father of nations. My Bubbe figured out that being with Papa is most important." I smile. "I'm a Putterman . . . and my family's more important to me than anything else."

Afterward, during the luncheon, I stand beaming in line with my family and greet my congregation and guests.

Sammy says, "You picked the best theme for your d'var, Becky!"

Matty says, "You totally have a talent for public speaking!"

Papa says, "Honey, you were meant for center stage."

Bubbe winks and says, "She gets it from me!"

My father says, "The connections you made between that movie and the Torah, while only somewhat excellent, were highly innovative. Great job!"

And my mother says, "Becky, what an important takeaway lesson . . . for all of us." She nods to my father. "Especially for me and Dad."

Auntie Annie and Uncle Greggy give me a big hug, and

Yale comes up to me and whispers, "See you tonight!"

And when this guy says, "Mazel tov, and how about them Astros," I just smile.

And when this lady says, "Mazel tov, and I loved that newspaper feature about your superfan cousins," I still smile.

Even when someone says, "Mazel tov, and we got some last-minute tickets for game four tonight, so we'll drop by your party on the late side," I smile.

Because none of that is what's most important.

So, while this weekend isn't quite the home run I'd imagined, it's a hard-hit-to-the-wall double and I'm poised to slide on home at my party tonight.

It may not be exactly what I wanted, but just like Bubbe said, it still feels . . . pretty okay.

Sammy

Everyone's pooped after Becky's service.

The out-of-town relatives head to the hotel for some downtime before the party tonight, and the rest of us kick off our shoes as soon as we walk in the door to my cousin's house.

Bubbe says, "Ira and I are napping now."

"Us too," my dad says, yawning and nodding to my mom.

"Me as well," Uncle Mike says, and Aunt Deb glares at him. My guess is that she has to double-check all the party arrangements.

Becky has the same idea. "Can I help with anything, Mom?" she asks, and my aunt's eyes soften.

"No, honey, you go rest up for your big night!"

Matty and I take Bialy on a walk around the block.

"Becky's d'var was really great!" I say.

"Yeah! It was super awesome."

"But afterward, Matty, when everyone went on and on about the World Series, it seemed like Becky's decided she can't hit any homers this weekend, so she's settling for line drives."

We stop and let Bialy do his business, and Matty nods. "Agreed!"

"So even though it's game four tonight and we're up two to one . . ." I say.

Matty grins. "We have to help Becky hit her hardest!"

It's time to put our World Series fever aside! Our cousin needs to shine, too!

We start walking back. "Oh, Becky asked if we could get ready for her party together."

"Umm, I think that means *you*. She didn't ask *me*," Matty says.

"Gosh," I say. "She wants to start at three p.m., even though the party's at seven!"

He laughs. "You two are gonna have tons of fun."

That afternoon when I head upstairs, Becky's room looks like a cross between a fancy boutique and a beauty salon. It's a new kind of studio, complete with a dress station, a hair station, and a makeup station. She's even made a tray of yummy snacks and fruity fizzy water for us.

"I'm so excited we can get ready for my party together!" she cries.

My fingers instantly get tingly as I pull my new dress out of her closet and rip off the tags. During my oh-so-painful shopping trip to the mall with my mom, this dress was about the simplest, least frilly thing I could find. It doesn't look anything like Becky's dress, which has a shimmery skirt and tiny rhinestones covering the bodice.

"Oh no!" Becky says, gawking at my dress. She holds up her hand dramatically and shakes her head. "No, no, no, no, no!"

"What? What's *no*?"

"That dress is *not* party attire, Sammy." She points to her glossy bat mitzvah invitation on her bulletin board. "My invitations say *party attire*."

I remind myself that I'm Becky's superfan this weekend, and fans cheer for their team, no matter what. Even when they're being totally annoying and trying to get you to go way outside your comfort zone.

"Thank goodness we're about the same size," she says, rummaging through her closet. Then she tosses, like, ten dresses from all the bar and bat mitzvahs she's been to on the bed for me to try on.

Some of them are over-the-top frilly. My arms are going numb now! I sink into the geometric carpet while she waits for me to choose one.

"Don't I put the dress on last, so I won't wrinkle it?" I ask, hoping we'll move on to the next station and she'll forget about this one. Maybe I can slide into the not-frilly dress I bought right before we go.

"Sammy, *sheesh*! There is an order of operations to getting ready for my party. First we have to choose your dress, since its style and color dictate everything that follows! Hair and makeup can go in *so* many directions. Updo or down do? A soft, muted makeup palette or a sparkly bold one? Peach or pink lip gloss?"

I nod and put on the first dress.

Becky gestures to a stool that I should stand on so she can get a better look. "Well, maybe . . . a possibility . . . strong leanings . . . definitely no . . ." she says as I try each one on.

I look at Jess and Bartholomew and feel a sudden kinship with them. I almost want to kidnap them from her room and set them free.

Then I slip the last dress from the heap on her bed over my head. It's a simple green satin sheath, an outlier for sure. I can't even believe it was in my cousin's closet. "It's perfect!" Becky squeals. "It totally pops your hazel eyes, Sammy. Go look in the mirror!"

I walk into the bathroom. I'm sure that Becky's idea about what's perfect and mine will be totally different. Like always.

I flip on the light.

But this time, it's not! The dress shimmers in the light and my eyes catch the green color like the woods bordering the ballpark in the spring, when the leaves unfurl bright and new.

Becky really *is* good at this stuff!

My fingers get a teensy less tingly. I'm relieved that station one—the dress station—is over, and we're both happy with the outcome. One down, two to go!

"Next is hair, right?" I say, looking down at all the items Becky's put on the bathroom counter: clips and sprays and gels and brushes and dryers and irons. I won't need any of those. I pull the hairband off the end of my long braid and shake out my hair. It's bumpy, but I'll just brush it real well and rebraid it, then we'll go on to the third and final station, easy-peasy lemon squeezy!

She stands behind me. "You should definitely wear your hair down with that dress, Sammy. Your hair's so pretty . . . it doesn't have a bit of frizz."

"It is?"

She catches my eyes in the mirror, smiles, and plugs in her flat iron. "Hand me that brush."

She spends thirty minutes on my hair, and it looks amazing. Then we switch, and I brush hers out, too, and flat iron the parts she can never reach. I only accidentally singe her ear once!

She smiles the whole time. So do I.

And somehow, it all kind of feels like cheering.

"Now for makeup!" she announces. "Let's do smokey eyes, Sammy! Nothing Katy Perry, but just a little pop."

"I thought my eyes already popped from the dress," I say, one side of my smile drooping.

She laughs and points to a chair. "You're first."

We have so much fun. She does my makeup, then I do hers. Then she undoes everything I did since she decides I need more practice and it's her bat mitzvah party and all, so she's got to look great.

And when she's finished redoing her makeup, she really does. She looks like a shining star.

Then we both see it at once.

We resemble each other, me and Becky: the pale milky color of our skin and our full bottom lips. The narrow shape of our noses and our high cheekbones. We both have Bubbe's wide-set eyes, our dark eyebrows arched in the exact same way.

Becky tears up. "I always wanted a sister to do stuff like this: hair and makeup, getting ready for parties. To be there for me on days like today."

I squeeze her hand. "We may not be sisters, Becky," I say. "But we *are* cousins. It's the next best thing."

Then I tear up, too.

"Oh my god!" Becky says, fanning her face and reaching over to fan mine. "We can't cry, Sammy! Not after it just took us an hour to do smokey eyes!"

I laugh.

Even though they're happy tears, and not the least bit happy-sad, we can't cry, because it's time to celebrate.

I wrap my arm around her shoulders, then we stand in the bathroom like that for a while, hugging and smiling at each other in the mirror.

And I think . . . Becky and I . . . we're cheering our hearts out.

Our family loads up in the Suburban and zooms to Becky's bat mitzvah party at the hotel.

We pass flashing marquee signs for businesses that say, "Go Astros!" We pass people out on the streets of Houston in their navy-and-orange game-day gear.

And even though our whole family's dressed in our party attire, it's hard to forget that tonight our team is playing in the World Series.

Becky's dad turns on the pregame coverage for game four, which starts in an hour, and he, my dad, and Papa immediately start doing what they always do when a baseball game's about to start.

They review players' stats. They talk about who's hot at the plate. They run through the lineups. They discuss which Dodgers we need to pitch around.

Becky's oh-so-smokey eyes cloud over.

I clear my throat and my aunt turns around. She takes one look at her daughter's face and flips the radio off and wags her finger at my uncle.

We get there, and when Becky sees the ballroom, her eyes tear up for a second, but in a good way.

She gushes, "Oh my god! The tables are Rebecca's Domestic Cats! There's a stripy tabby-cat-themed table and an orange, black, and white calico one! There are Persian- and Siamese-themed ones and of course a hairless sphynx one, too! And look, Sammy! There's even a Maine coon table!"

My cousin throws her arms around her mom, and Aunt Deb says, "Honey, even though I've been busy at work, I'm trying to pay better attention."

Becky beams, then takes her mom by the shoulders. "Jess, Bartholomew, and I would *love* to meet a Maine coon in person! Can we please, *please* go on a road trip to Maine next summer after Sammy and Matty's camp session? We can take the *Whole World* in the Suburban! It would be so fun!"

Aunt Deb's eyes get big, but then she smiles and nods.

Becky's party starts ten minutes after the game at Minute Maid begins, and it's obvious right off the bat: some of the adults haven't gotten the memo that tonight's going to be all about my cousin.

They sneak looks at their phones under the tables during dinner and whisper. They take long bathroom breaks and walk out the main ballroom doors to a secret destination. A few tables even have some last-minute empty seats.

But Matty and I ignore all of it, and redirect Becky any time she notices. It's her bat mitzvah party, and we're here to celebrate.

We're here to hit it out of the park!

We sit with her during dinner, then we turn our chairs around and scoot them close together to watch the video Matty remade during dessert.

And it's so, so awesome!

It starts out with Becky as a baby, then scrolls to her as a pigtailed toddler. It runs through pictures of her dressing up Jess as a kitten, right alongside Itty Kitty. Then when it moves to all the pictures Matty found of the three of us on the cloud, the ones from our hallway, we each grab one of Becky's hands.

There are pictures of Mrs. Sokoloff and Bartholomew, and a bunch of amazing pictures from Becky's social media page. There are new photos of the three of us: at an Astros game, helping out in Becky's studio, and at Shabbat dinner.

As Becky's bat mitzvah photographer snaps away as we're watching her video, we have our own kind of telepathy. Maybe it's not exactly triplet telepathy, but I guess you could say it's family telepathy. Because family members can understand each other like no one else can.

And we know this is just the beginning—that we'll add the photos of the three of us celebrating Becky's bat mitzvah tonight to our walls, and soon enough, we'll add so many more. We'll fill them up with our friendship.

Because the three of us, together again—it makes some great story.

After the video's over, Yale and our religious school classmates, and some of the kids from Becky's school, take to the dance floor. We stand like a Sammy-Matty sandwich off to the side, thinking there's no way we're going to get on that dance floor with them.

Then Becky grabs our hands and drags us out there, and we dance around like total goofballs, laughing hysterically, while the photographer snaps away.

I look around, and some of the guests' faces look worried. I nudge the man next to me when I see him pull his phone out of his pocket and shake his head.

He says, "Still no score after five innings."

My heart throbs. For a second, I worry the Astros aren't scoring because of me, since I'm here and not rooting in front of a TV or at Minute Maid like I'd usually be.

Because superfan cheers reach your team wherever they are . . . as long as you're cheering for them. But I'm not.

I've been cheering for someone on a different team: my cousin, on my family team.

The crowd in the ballroom thins conspicuously. Suddenly Bubbe and Papa are gone, and so are the out-of-town relatives. Our parents are gone. Becky's parents are gone.

And the DJ's clearing the dance floor for the hora! We need our entire family here!

"Where are they?" I whisper to my brother, and he shrugs.

I send Matty out of the room to do reconnaissance, and a few minutes later, he comes back in. "They're all at the bar watching the Astros lose."

I gulp. The Astros are losing now! I send a message out to them, hoping they'll hear me: *I'll always be your super-fan . . . but tonight, my cheers are needed here.* I turn to Becky and hope she hasn't noticed what we have, that the rest of our family's gone missing and the DJ is positioning a chair in the middle of the dance floor—for her.

But she's gone, too.

"Did you see where she went?" I ask Matty.

He bites his lip. "She mumbled something about the bathroom."

Then our twin telepathy kicks in perfectly. We need to mobilize, again. It's an emergency!

I lift my chin and nod. "I'm going to the bathroom to get our cousin."

Matty lifts his, too. "I'm going back to the bar to get our family."

Just like our family has been able to turn around so many hard slumps this year, we can turn Becky's party around, too.

We can handle just about anything . . . when our team sticks together.

Matty

There's a big crowd glued to the row of TVs above the bar, trancelike.

Not just my family and our friends who are supposed to be in the ballroom, celebrating Becky's bat mitzvah for gosh sake, but literally everybody else in the hotel's planted there now, too.

The bartender is shaking a silver canister over and over. A waiter holds a tray of melting drinks in midair. The front desk clerk has left a short line at check-in. And the lady with the cleaning supplies cart has abandoned it against a wall.

Everybody's watching the Dodgers tie up the game in the seventh inning—miserable, feeling a lot less Houston Strong.

But for my family, tonight's not supposed to be about the Astros, it's supposed to be about my cousin.

I squeeze through the crowd, find Uncle Mike, and tap him on his shoulder. I whisper what's in my heart into his ear, the important things I've figured out during the time I've spent in his not-really-a-library/really-a-man-cave. The place where I learned . . . and I know this is gonna sound super corny, okay . . . where I learned what kinda man I wanna be someday.

His eyes get big, and he nods. He hugs me tight.

Then he whispers to Aunt Deb, who whispers to my mom, my dad, Bubbe, and Papa, and they whisper to all the out-of-town relatives.

My message overflows and spreads faster than floodwater: tonight, we've gotta be Putterman Strong.

'Cause just like Becky said in her awesome speech this morning, we're being tested all the time.

With an epic hurricane that flooded our city. With a kiss behind a dugout and broken twin telepathy. With a cousin you lose along the way, then find again. With a bat mitzvah party on the very same night as the World Series.

We're being tested about what matters . . . what we're about . . . what we're gonna cheer for. And we're gonna cheer for the people we care about. We're gonna cheer for our family. And tonight, we're gonna cheer for Becky the loudest.

Take it from me, you can figure anything out if the people who love you are behind you.

Becky's bat mitzvah contingent darts from the bar all at once, then bursts back through the ballroom doors. She's sitting on the chair in the middle of the dance floor looking, as she would say, très mauvaise. When she sees us all rushing toward her, she starts seriously bawling.

"Oh my god, Sammy!" she tells my sister, furiously fanning her face with her hands and blinking at the photographer, who's ready to shoot. "My smokey eyes are running!"

Sammy grabs a napkin and dabs the dark smudges away. "Don't worry, they still look great!"

The music for the hora starts, and Papa holds his hand out to Bubbe and does his little side-to-side shuffle. She grabs his hand, throws her head back, and does some moves of her own. The out-of-town relatives follow suit, and we all form a big ring around my cousin as the music speeds up.

My uncle and dad take two corners of Becky's chair, and Sammy and I take the others. Then we lift her up high.

Becky's tears turn to smiles and laughs as she brushes her hands over the multicolored balloons floating across the ceiling.

It's a really great picture.

When the hora's finally over, Sammy, Becky, and I head to the root beer float station to cool off.

Yale wanders over, and Becky grins at him. "Dance with me?"

"As you wish." Yale deadpans a perfect Westley from *The Princess Bride.*

"You *so* get me!" Becky squeals, and the two of them run to the dance floor.

We watch them for a few minutes, then notice Becky's frenemies Jenny and Rose a few tables over. Rose is crying big fat tears since Becky says she likes Yale, too, and Jenny's trying to console her. Sammy raises her brows and I raise mine back. I know exactly what she's thinking: *Yale has made a really smart choice.*

My sister hugs me. "How did you do it, Matty? How did you get everyone to come back from the bar?"

"I told them we had to follow Sandy Koufax's lead. That if he could skip playing in a World Series game on Yom Kippur, our family could skip watching a game on Becky's bat mitzvah."

She smiles and hugs me tighter.

Becky runs up to Sammy, super excited, and nods to the door.

Sammy says, "Don't be mad at us, Matty," and Becky grins.

I turn around, and there's Ethan with that smile that makes me smile back. That smile that says it's all okay. That I'm perfect. We're perfect.

"But it's your bat mitzvah party, Becky," I say. "You barely know him!"

"Don't you think it's time I did?" she says with a wink.

I leave them for a while and go hang out with Ethan. I'm not gonna say if there's another kiss or not, 'cause really, tonight's all about Becky.

But let's just say it's a more-than-good bat mitzvah party.

And it doesn't matter one bit to any of us later on when somebody whispers that our team lost game four of the World Series 6–2, giving up five runs in the ninth inning. 'Cause we didn't lose—not us.

Even though we kayaked down the street away from our flooded home. Even though everything we had left fit in a square shelter spot. Even though our house, Bubbe and Papa's house, and Mrs. Sokoloff's house are all being torn down soon.

Our team won, and we get that now.

We lived together. We wrote and drew our feelings into journals and speeches. We shared them and became strong again, Putterman Strong.

The crowd thins again when a bunch of the adults leave, but Becky, Sammy, and I don't care. All the kids stay.

Right before eleven o'clock, the DJ announces the very last song, the one Sammy and I chose for our cousin. Katy Perry's song "Roar" comes on, and we're out on the dance floor again, cheering so hard the adults who are left stand back against the walls and watch.

Then Becky, Sammy, Ethan, Yale, and I roar our heads off—all of us together.

Becky

"Bubbe and Papa are staying."

"That's not the same, Becky."

"Bartholomew is staying."

"That's not the same either."

"There's room here for everyone, Mom."

"Yes, there most certainly is."

"And it was great." I choke up. "It was really great, having everyone here."

"It was, honey. It was a real silver lining."

"And the Whole World feels that way, too."

"I would agree, Becky."

"So why aren't they staying?"

Sunday afternoon, after the out-of-town relatives head home, Auntie Annie and Uncle Greggy take my cousins to see the rental unit they're going to move into while their brand-new house gets built, high and dry.

My mother's designing it, so I'm sure it'll be amazing, but I don't see why they can't just keep staying with us: we all fit in this ginormous house—we fit together perfectly.

Life is a such a roller-coaster ride, with all sorts of unexpected twists and turns.

One minute, you're at the top in a hora chair waving your hands at your flippin' amazing bat mitzvah party . . . then the very next day, you plummet.

I plug in my hot glue gun and sift through the new pile of fabric scraps my mother dumped on my bed. I suspect she's trying to distract me this afternoon from the fact that I'm in my room alone again, without my cousins—stark foreshadowing of days to come.

"I got used to everyone being here," I say, tearing up.

My mother dabs my cheeks with a piece of fabric and says, "Me too, honey." She nods to the nightstand. "Aunt Annie told me you helped find that photo for Sammy."

I smile.

"It was such a nice thing to do, Becky. I'm so impressed by you lately." She pulls this gorgeous white crepe out from the bottom of the fabric pile. "This would be perfect for Princess Leia's robe!"

I run my fingers over the crepe. It's exactly what I envisioned for my last session with my cousins. I spend a few minutes cutting the shape of the robe, then I reach for my glue gun.

My mother says, "Here, let me help glue that together."

I hand her the glue and feel all runny and warm on the inside. It's the first time she's helped me get ready for one of my photo sessions. I don't say it, but lately I've been kind of impressed by her, too.

Maybe, just maybe . . . we're finally starting to bond.

We finish Princess Leia's robe and Han Solo's vest and V-neck chemise, and they look fabulous—even better than I envisioned. "Now I just need to find some faux fur for . . ." I clear my throat and grin at my mother. "Never mind."

I don't tell her Bartholomew will need some chest hair for this session, since Han sports an ample tuft in all the photos I've seen on the internet. For someone Leia's age, *a woman*, I imagine that kind of thing must be a draw.

I keep sifting, then I find it. "Got it!" I say breathlessly, setting some brown faux fur aside.

But really, back to my bat mitzvah. In the end, it felt way better than just okay. It felt like a bases-loaded home run since the Whole World cheered for me!

When I gave my speech and everyone loved it, that was cheering.

When Sammy and I got ready for my party almost like sisters, that was cheering, too.

When the three of us sat together watching the video Matty made for me with all its super cool surprise photos, that was cheering for sure.

When my cousins pried the adults from the bar TV and they lifted me on the hora chair and everyone danced around me, that was a ton of cheering!

When Yale and I danced, that was—you get the picture.

And when Ethan dropped in at the end to dance with us, and he and Matty smiled the whole time, well, even though that part wasn't about me, it was cheering, too.

Long story short: all the cheering felt great.

Bialy barks downstairs, and I know my cousins are back. They come upstairs, and Sammy's carrying a bag. I guess they went shopping.

My mother winks at them and leaves the room.

"How's the new rental?" I ask, sulking a little. I don't mean to hope it's terrible, but oh, how I do.

"It's a high-rise apartment in Uptown!" Sammy says giggling, excited.

Matty laughs, too. "My mom says for the next year, there's no way we're flooding again!"

I nod, turning my eyes back to my fabrics. The rental isn't terrible. They're happy they're leaving. Quelle catastrophe!

Sammy sits down on the bed next to me and pokes my shoulder. "Guess what I'm getting for my new room?"

I say, "Lots of shelves like my father has in his *library* for new signed baseballs?"

Sammy says, "Actually, yes. But I'm also getting something else."

I shrug and say, "I give up."

She grins at me. "Two twin beds for sleepovers."

I throw my arms around her. "Yay, yay, yay! It's going

to be so cool, sleeping in a high-rise! We can stay up late watching the lights over the city!"

Sammy hugs me back, and Matty sits down on the other side of me and pokes my other shoulder. "Hey, what about me?" he says. "Maybe I wanna sleep over!"

Bialy licks my knee like it's jerky. "Would he have to come?"

Matty raises his eyebrows. "He's going to miss you, too."

Now I'm grinning. I pet the top of Bialy's head. He's almost as soft as Jess. "Okay."

A quick, shiny-eyed look passes between my cousins, and they nod to each other. Sammy opens the shopping bag and pulls out a wrapped rectangular box. "It's your bat mitzvah present from the two of us!" she says, putting it on my lap.

The box has stripy orange, navy, and white paper—Houston Astros colors.

"Open it!" they say at the exact same time.

I rip it apart and pull out an official George Springer jersey, my favorite Astro! I'm back on top of the roller coaster.

"Oh my god, it's perfect! I can wear this to the game tonight!" I jump up from the bed and try it on, then I run to my bathroom to take a peek.

I look amazing, of course, almost like a bona fide Houston Astros fan like my cousins. *But am I really?* I push the thought from my head.

I love my new jersey and I'm so excited our family has tickets to game five of the World Series at Minute Maid tonight, courtesy of Sammy and Matty's picture in the Houston paper and the nice manager!

Matty says, "Are you wearing your Altuve jersey, Sammy?"

She smiles and looks away. "I was thinking I'd wear my new Alex Bregman jersey tonight, since he's Jewish and this *is* a bat mitzvah weekend."

I grin at my cousin, and her face goes red. I think Sammy Putterman might have a little crush! I mean, I'm sure Bubbe would approve of her choice. I'll bet Alex Bregman has a very nice mother.

"I'm wearing my new Keuchel jersey," Matty says, ignoring Sammy's blush. "The lefty starting pitcher!"

Sammy sits up straighter and gives us a determined look. "After last night's loss, we're split two and two. Our team really needs us to cheer."

"All of us? They need me, too?" I squeak.

Matty says, "Becky, the Astros need all their fans tonight! Every. Single. One."

Sammy

We're in Minute Maid Park the second the doors open. Our Home Away from Home.

Fan energy surges inside the stadium.

The retractable roof is closed, and even though it's not forty-thousand-plus fans full yet, the volume's rising fast. All our cheers are going to ricochet off the walls and ceiling tonight and go straight to our team.

Papa's giddy. He keeps kissing all of us: Dad and Uncle Mike, Mom and Aunt Deb, me, Matty, and Becky, then finally Bubbe, who blushes and tries to swat him away.

Then he starts all over again.

We find the seats the Astros manager has given us first thing. Matty and I grin at each other, and Dad and Uncle Mike give each other a big high five: they're ten rows up, smack between home plate and first, tossing distance to the batter's warm-up circle. I can hardly believe it—we've never sat this close. We won't need our gloves tonight since there's a big net in front of us, but that's okay!

When I see the official World Series logo painted on our field, I start jumping up and down and screaming. I can't help it. The logo here at our ballpark makes it all the more real.

Somehow, Mack knows just where to find us. He belly laughs and calls up the stairs, "Listen up y'all! The Putter-mans are IN THE HOUSE!" People turn around in their seats and smile at us.

Mack's tradition sure starts us off right.

My whole family stands for fist bumps and handshakes when Mack gets to us, then he sits down in the row in front of us.

"Sammy-Matty?" he says, all serious. "Y'all got your cheer on?"

I nod, all serious back. "Our cousin Becky does, too."

Becky grins at him and holds out her fist for another bump.

"We've got to break this split our way tonight," Mack says. "Thank the lord we're playing at home and . . ." He winks at me. "We've got our biggest superfan here, too."

Mack's words fill me up, and I feel my cheers building and rising. And now that Becky's celebration is over and she's cheering with us, too, now that Matty's part of my twin team again, there'll be no holding back.

We're so lucky to be here in person with our team. While my dad and mom talk with Mack, I hug Matty and whisper, "Thank you."

"For what?"

"For believing in this again . . . for cheering with me again . . . for drawing that picture of me . . . for being my brother. I . . . I . . . I . . ." I totally choke up.

He hugs me back. "I love you, too, Sammy."

My family talks with Mack for a while, then he stands up to make some more rounds. I've always had a feeling that there are other regulars "in the house" that are just as excited to receive his lucky greeting as we are.

A sea of Houston Astros fans fills in around us, dressed in orange and blue. People wave their rally towels and high five each other, and the game hasn't even started yet. I elbow Becky and Matty and point down our row—a man's setting up a small shrine of Astros bobbleheads under his seat. We all smile.

Finally it's game time.

We stand for the National Anthem and the ceremonial first pitch by former president of the United States George W. Bush. Then his dad, also a former president, announces, "Play ball!"

The Astros have a rough start. They give up three runs in the top of the first inning. I start cheering harder, but they give up another run at the top of the fourth.

I catch Matty's eyes, then he starts cheering harder, too, deeper and stronger than I've ever heard him before, and that's saying a lot. This game is louder than any game I've ever been to!

It's so right having my twin brother next to me, rooting for our team again. Over the last few months, I'd missed it so much.

Astros fans stay out of their seats the whole time and don't sit down. We just can't—our team needs us up and rooting for every single play.

And by the top of the fifth, it's a 4–4 tied game, but not for long. The Dodgers take the lead again with a three-run home run.

"Oh my god! It's a roller coaster!" Becky cries, covering her face with her hands for a second.

But then my favorite player, José Altuve, brings in three runs with a homer and we tie the game up again. The Astros train that runs the wall of the stadium sounds and takes off with a blast of fireworks!

Now Bubbe's clinging to Papa and my mom and aunt are sandwiched close together. I can barely look at my dad and uncle, whose faces rise and fall with each twist and turn on the scoreboard, El Grande.

In the top of the seventh inning, with the score still tied, George Springer dives and misses a ball hit to center field, and the Dodgers pull ahead again. It's a bad mistake. He hangs his head, and Becky covers her face again and says, "I can't watch! Why isn't my cheering working?"

I lean close and whisper, "Don't worry, Becky. He'll come back, just keep cheering. Superfans don't give up."

She grins at me, then starts yelling harder.

We're all on pins and needles during the commercial breaks when we do the seventh-inning stretch. Just as we finish singing our traditional Minute Maid stretch songs, "Take Me Out to the Ball Game" and "Deep in the Heart of Texas," Mack waves to us again from down the stands.

Then a lady with a microphone and a man with a big TV camera walk up to our row.

The lady flashes a pearly smile, and says, "Sammy and Matty Putterman?" and we nod. "It's so nice to meet both of you! I'm a sportscaster."

My fingers get tingly, the good way. I grab on to my brother.

The sportscaster signals to the cameraman to start rolling and says into the microphone, "I'm here with Sammy and Matty Putterman, the kids you might remember from the amazing drawing in the Houston newspaper two weeks ago, that a record number of Houstonians wrote in about."

She puts the mic in front of me. "How do you feel about being here with your family tonight at game five of the World Series, courtesy of the Astros?"

I peek up at El Grande. I'm on it!

I nod down the row to my family. "We're so excited and so thankful! We're cheering our hearts out! The Astros are going all the way tonight!"

She flashes another smile. "You heard it here, folks, from Sammy Putterman, a die-hard Astros superfan." She puts the mic in front of Matty for his comment, too, but he looks up at El Grande and shakes his head.

So the lady shifts it to me again and says, "So, Sammy, what does our team need right now, to put us ahead again?"

I catch Becky's eyes for a second: they're a little happy-sad, watching me and Matty, like she feels left out. That's the last thing I want her to feel on her bat mitzvah weekend! I pull her close to me, and say, "My cousin's an Astros superfan, too. Ask her!"

Becky looks at me. "I am?"

I nod. "You are! Big-time!"

Becky starts jumping up and down, waving her arms above her head. "Oh my god! I am! I really am! I'm a Houston Astros superfan!" she says, then she looks up. "And I'm on TV!"

The sportscaster steps back and blinks. She says into the mic, "Okay, well then . . . err, what's your name?"

Becky grabs the mic from her. "I'm Rebecca—I mean, *Becky* Putterman!"

The lady grabs the mic back. She seems a bit nervous, like this interview is getting away from her, but she recovers in a split second with another pearly smile. "Well, Becky Putterman, what does our team need right now to get back on top?"

My cousin doesn't miss a beat. She flips around and points to the name on the back of her jersey, then turns and looks straight at the camera and yells, "We need another George Springer dinger!"

The crowd around us goes wild, taking out their phones and recording the action in our section, chanting Springer's name. The lady can hardly ask Becky her next question over the roar. "You think he can come back from that big error he just made at center field, Becky?"

"Totally!" Becky says, grabbing the mic again. "You can never underestimate the power of sheer, undeniable talent!" She glances around our section. "And with all of us cheering for him, George is going to make it right!"

The sportscaster backs up and turns to the camera. "Well, Astros Nation, let's all root for another Springer dinger!" Then she waves to us and darts down the stairs.

Becky's still jumping up and down, grinning at everyone around us and giving high fives and fist-bumps. I turn around and look at Matty and the rest of our family. They're totally speechless, with wide-eyed smiley faces.

The commercial breaks end, and it's the bottom of the seventh. George Springer's up at bat at the top of the order.

And Becky gets her wish.

First pitch and GOODBYE! It's another home run, the hardest-hit ball I've ever seen! We've tied up the game again!

The train sounds and the fans go wild. The cameraman hanging out at the bottom of our section pans back to Becky and she's up on El Grande again.

She sees it, grabs me on one side of her and Matty on the other, and she starts jumping again. And then we're all jumping, cheering our hearts out together as George Springer rounds the bases home to a beyond-pumped-up dugout.

Everyone in the stadium goes berserk, and their cheers ripple like waves around and around the park.

Bubbe sits down, and Papa fans her. My dad has tears in his eyes, just like my nightstand photo from twelve years ago, and my mom hugs him tight. Uncle Mike waves his fists over and over like he's punching at the retractable roof, and Aunt Deb dances in the aisle.

It's all beyond exciting. It's baseball! It's the World Series in Houston, Texas!

Then Altuve hits a hard ball left and brings third baseman Alex Bregman home for the lead. In that same inning, another homer brings the score to 11–8 Astros!

The roller coaster keeps climbing and falling. In the top of the ninth, it's a tied game again. Then Alex Bregman drives in a run in the tenth inning, and the Astros win it 13–12! We're up three to two in the series, and the players storm the field!

We won! We won! We won!

We yell and yell until all our voices sound like my mom's raspy great-aunt Martha.

Finally some of the people in our section head to the

aisles, but we don't. I check the time on my phone. It's 12:45 a.m., five and a half hours from when the game started, but we're not ready to go.

"Let's just sit and rest for a while," my dad says. "Let the crowds in the concourse thin out."

We need just a little more time in our Home Away from Home.

We take our seats and we're quiet for a few minutes, breathing in the stadium. It's the last game of the season at Minute Maid Park, and we got to be here together. It's the fifth game of the World Series, and our team won. There will be at least one more game in Los Angeles, but we'll be watching on TV.

After a while, Papa says, "How about them Astros?"

And Bubbe says, "How about them grandkids?"

We all start laughing, and Becky's phone dings. Her mom winks. "Do with it what you will, honey!"

Matty and I lean toward Becky to see what her mom sent. It's the video of her Springer dinger call! "Wow," she says watching it. "I really am a fan." And we all start laughing again.

Mack comes back up the aisle, grinning. "That game was something," he says, sitting down in the row in front of us.

My dad grins back. "It sure was!"

Mack reaches into the big pockets of his jacket and pulls out three baseballs. "Here ya go, Puttermans!" he says, tossing the balls to Matty, Becky, and me. "The team sure was glad you were in the house tonight."

Becky's mouth hangs open. "I have my own signed baseball? I have my own signed baseball! Thank you!"

Matty stands up and fist-bumps Mack. "Wow, Mack. Thank you so much."

I jump out of my seat to give Mack a big hug.

Like my birthday baseball, these balls are signed by all the Astros greats, too—just the ones playing twelve years later.

Matty

The World Series roller coaster continues Tuesday and Wednesday the next week at Dodger Stadium.

The Astros lose game six on Tuesday 3–1 despite an early fourth-of-the-series dinger by George Springer. Then it's a three-all tie, forcing a winner-take-all game the next night.

On Wednesday's game seven, Springer scores the first run of the game, then he hits his fifth home run of the series, making it four homers in four consecutive games! The Dodgers never catch up, and the 'Stros clinch it, 5–1, and become World Series champs for the first time in their franchise history!

Becky's over the moon and back, a full-on Astros superfan.

Her parents watch her all-in cheering a bit wide-eyed.

When Springer becomes the World Series MVP, she even stands up in the middle of the living room and screams, "I love you so much, George!"

But yeah, we're all feeling it. We love our team. In a year where there's been so much total loss, this big win means everything.

Almost. For my family at least, there have been some other big wins, too.

I suit up Thursday after school for my first baseball game since playoffs last May.

I'm on autopilot putting my uniform on, just like I'm throwing a pitch: baseball briefs with a cup, knee-high socks, and my jersey, white baseball pants, and an elastic belt. Cap and cleats that I'll throw on in the garage.

I meet Sammy in the kitchen, and we make big jugs of ice water and grab a few protein bars like it's a regular thing, any game in the season.

But I don't think I'll work up a sweat, get thirsty, or hungry today. I'm hanging out on the bench, remember?

The whole family comes to the game. Becky even brings Bialy on his leash.

I'm nervous the whole way there, and I never used to be nervous about a game, for gosh sake. I'm pulling at my cup and moving my cap around on my scalp and itching at my jersey.

Sammy reaches over and puts her hand on mine, and it helps.

We get there and I put my bag on the dugout bench, and the minute I see Ethan, I breathe a little easier. As long as Sammy, Ethan, and I are here together, I don't have a thing to be nervous about.

It's same old same old, the way it's supposed to be, even if I am sitting this one out.

I warm up with the team, take a few practice throws from the hill. Not that I'm gonna need them. But it's a baseball game and I'm on the field and I'm a pitcher.

So that's just what you do, okay?

The game begins and oh, man, our starting pitcher, Brandon, is totally wild. He just can't get his stuff together, but Sammy says it's nothing new. It's painful to watch, and I bet it's even more painful to be him on the mound.

Not that I'd know, since my arm's never been *that* wild.

We go through three miserable innings like that, and we're down four–zip. Brandon's red and sweaty and breaking his motion, which you never, ever, should do in a game, even if yours isn't working right.

Baseball's a repetitive sport, and success is based on commitment to precise routines. That's why it's even more impressive that the 'Stros won against the Dodgers' star pitcher, Kershaw, since he's a master of that kind of dedication.

Then it happens real quick.

Brandon pitches two balls into the dirt at the bottom of the next inning and clutches his arm. He calls for Coach, and Coach glances back at the dugout. Today's scheduled relievers are playing keep-away with somebody's glove. He rolls his eyes and yells, "Putterman! You're up!"

I grab my glove, flash smiles at Ethan, who's catching, and Sammy, at first, and take my place on the mound. After some warmup pitches, the telepathy Ethan and I have takes over, just like old times. Sign, pitch, strike. Sign, pitch, strike. Sign, pitch, strike! You're out!

We hold the score to give our bats a chance to catch up.

And they do in the next inning, like I knew they would, since Sammy has her swing back. Even with the bigger distance to the fence, my sister's still got it: technique and power, catch and release.

She's right on time. She hits her first 14U dinger with the bases loaded. A grand slam!

And we're all up out of the dugout and yelling. I turn to the crowd, and Dad's spitting sunflower seeds and Mom's hugging everybody. Papa's laying a big kiss on Bubbe's lips and Uncle Mike's fist punching again and Aunt Deb's even doing it, too.

Becky's losing it, cheering her heart out, our twin team's biggest fan.

And after that, you know what happened? I kept throwing strikes and we won. 'Cause I dunno—anything is possible.

Like girls who hit home runs and best friends with smiles you wanna kiss. Like families who cheer you on no matter what. Like everything lumped together so confusing you wanna hole yourself up and say, "Sayonara, baby! See ya again . . . *never*!" But then you don't.

You open the door and put on a glove. You throw your hardest and catch what comes your way. You get back to your game. You watch the sun shine bright where the line of grass grows wild and it's okay. It's all gonna be okay. Then you get up and do it again.

I was made for this, all of it. I was made to be Sammy's twin brother and Becky's cousin and I was made to be a Putterman. I was made to be an artist and I was made to *like*-like Ethan Goldberg, a lot.

And I was made to pitch that game like I'd never left at all.

The city of Houston cancels school on Friday for the afternoon Astros parade through downtown.

The Puttermans go, of course, in full-on Astros glory.

We join nearly a million people cheering the players on as fire trucks carry them through town. Then we head back to my aunt and uncle's house for our last Shabbat dinner together before my family moves into our high-rise rental in the Uptown District over the weekend.

It's not like we won't be back next Friday for another dinner, but it won't be the same.

We won't be living together under one roof anymore, nine members Putterman Strong. Maybe it'll never be like this again.

And even though it's been hard not having our house anymore, not having my old room, I've gotten kinda used to my uncle's not-really-a-library/really-a-man-cave.

'Cause there was this shelf, up real high, where I put things for a while, things I wasn't ready to figure out. But they were never out of reach.

They sat there, waiting and safe, till I was ready to take them down.

The doorbell rings right as we sit down in the dining room. "I've got it!" I say, pushing my chair back. Everybody but Sammy and Becky raises their eyebrows.

Ethan and I walk back in, and there are *hello*s and *how are you*s all around. My aunt hops up to set another place at our table.

We all smile for a few beats without saying much.

Then we start talking about our 14U win last night and Sammy's José Altuve-style homer as we dig into our dinners. My dad and uncle go on and on about all Ethan's great calls and my strikes. And of course there's lots of talk about the Astros after that, just like there always is.

Finally my grandmother brings out her lemon cake. She cuts an extra thick slice, serves Ethan first, and says, "Doll? Did I ever tell you how much I like your mother?"

I mumble, "Jeez, Bubbe, I haven't even had my bar mitzvah," before I can help it.

Becky starts giggling, then it's contagious. Sammy busts up and I'm laughing next, and soon enough—Mom and

Dad, Uncle Mike and Aunt Deb, and even Papa are holding their sides. Ethan watches all of us, a bit confused, then he starts laughing just 'cause we are.

Then our laughter ripples around the table like the wave in Minute Maid Park.

Bubbe says, "What?" all innocent-like. Then she leans down and whispers in Ethan's ear, but we can all hear her since she has that voice that carries, "Dear, please tell your lovely mother hello."

Just like my grandmother, instincts run strong with me, too. Ethan and I—we stand a really good chance.

Becky

I'm famous. My Springer dinger call went viral and now I'm a star.

Not to seem full of myself or anything, but I owned that sportscaster lady's microphone like a natural extension of my arm. Sometimes you don't know you were meant for something until that go-big-or-go-home moment arrives.

And I went big—El Grande big.

Since it turns out, I've got lots of talents. I'm a fashionista, an entrepreneur, and an orator. I'm a Houston Astros superfan, just like my cousins. But of all my talents, there's one I'm most proud of: I'm great at cheering for my family.

While my cousins finish packing up for their move, I busy myself in my studio getting ready for our last session together.

Sammy's part of my closet is already bare; her drawers are empty. She wrapped the photo I found for her in one of her jerseys and put it in the middle of her duffel and carried it downstairs.

I stare at the empty spot on the nightstand and start to sniffle, I can't even help it. God!

Because having the Whole World here with us for the last two months felt, well, kind of . . . *whole*.

And I'm a bit worried that even with Bubbe and Papa staying, things are going to go back to the way they used to be—with my mother in one corner of this ginormous house and my father in the other, with me upstairs in my studio with Jess and Bartholomew.

That the family Matty says we've become—Putterman Strong—isn't going to seem that way without all of its members living under one roof.

But when I go downstairs to see if Sammy and Matty are ready for our session, my parents sit with Bubbe and Papa at the kitchen table, drinking their coffee. My grandmother's playing gin with my mother, and my grandfather's watching World Series replays with my father on his phone.

They all smile at me when I sit down, and my grandmother throws down her hand. "Deborah, I didn't know you were such a card shark!" she says with a wink.

My mother starts dealing to me. "Play with me, Beckele," she says. She hasn't called me Beckele since I was really little.

And I think, looking around the table, that just like Jess and Bartholomew's miniature outfits, we're wearing a smaller family outfit now, too. It's a smaller world, but it's still glued together tight, all sparkly and good.

We play cards for a while, then Sammy and Matty find me. I hop up to pour the last bit of morning coffee from the pot into a cup and we head upstairs.

Today's Rebecca's Domestic Cat Fashions theme—take a guess! My last session with my cousins is All About Love.

Because that's what taking in the Whole World can give you: lots and lots of love.

We watch some scenes from the Star Wars trilogy first, since getting the studio's ambiance right today is super important. We close my curtains and decide to create an inky night scene with flashlight spots from Matty and Sammy's phones to highlight the inner force of goodness in Princess Leia and Han Solo, our two featured characters.

Then we ply Bartholomew with a few laps of coffee and corral the cats to the corner.

Jess sits docilely while I slip on her white Leia gown and braided yarn side buns. Bartholomew only bites Sammy once as she wrestles Han's V-neck chemise and vest over his head and glues the faux fur to the skin on his chest.

Then we position them in the studio, but it's clear something's missing.

"We need Luke Skywalker!" Matty says. "I mean, Princess Leia and Han Solo are a great part of the story, but it's really about the three of them!" He looks at Sammy. "She needs her twin brother, right?"

She grins. "Definitely! And Luke and Leia even have telepathy like us!"

"Oh my god, you're right! What are we going to do?" I say, dropping my head to my hands. How could I, of all people, forget the powerful rule of three? "We only have two cats! Quel dommage!"

Matty says, "Be right back!" and runs downstairs.

He leads Bialy into my room a few minutes later with a hunk of raw hamburger, and he's carrying Sammy's new bat, too. "Light saber!" he says, when my eyes question the baseball introduction, and I nod.

Matty's brilliant. Bialy's actually perfect for Luke's part, with his flowing golden retriever mane!

Sammy and I tack some more white poster board on my walls to increase the studio size to accommodate our new actor. Matty throws a white sheet around Bialy and cinches it with one of my big-buckle Houston Rodeo belts, all the while feeding him marble-sized hamburger balls. Then he wraps the end of the bat with iridescent blue fabric from my scrap pile to fashion the saber.

We reposition the three of them in the studio and they look great, just how they're meant to be—like at the very end of the Star Wars trilogy after the characters have weathered lots of heartbreaking misunderstandings and even painful and lengthy separations, but come out fully committed to each other.

Then Sammy and Matty direct their phone flashlights on the scene, and the inner goodness of it all shines bright. The Force is clearly with us!

I start snapping away.

When we're done shooting, we add the best photos to my social media story, then add some hashtags.

#threesneveracrowd #threesthebestcompany
#powertrio

Really, I could go on and on since three's such a special number.

The story's an instant hit! Enthusiastic followers' comments pop up one after the other!

Jenny says, "Three friends like us!" and Rose posts three heart-eyed emojis. I *could* correct them about exactly *who* my theme refers to, especially after Rose's burst of envy at my bat mitzvah when Yale and I danced, but that wouldn't honor my very best self.

Just as we're dismantling the scene, my mother says from the doorway, *"Ahem* . . . Sammy-Matty-Becky?"

We look to where the rest of our family stands watching us with big smiles.

"I want to see those photos!" Papa says.

My father, Uncle Greggy, and Auntie Annie all say, "Us too!"

I grin at my cousins. "Then you're just going to have to be our followers," I say.

Bubbe winks. "Doll, I'd say we already are."

We clean up the studio, and after hugs and tears and

*thank you*s, my cousins leave for their Uptown high-rise. And yeah, the house feels bigger and emptier again, quieter for sure. It'll take some getting used to, but that's okay.

We'll all be here together again, full and loud, almost every Shabbat.

Until then, I have some alone time to process everything that's happened since Hurricane Harvey whipped through town and changed our lives forever, since the Astros won the World Series so Houston Strong, since now . . . I'm a Jewish adult.

I'm still working out some of the details of the aforementioned, but for now, it can all be summed up by the very last lines of my bat mitzvah speech.

Number one: I'm my very best self.

Number two: I have a flippin' amazing family.

Number three: I like to be called *Becky* Putterman.

After

Sammy

The commentator says, "High fly ball—goodbye! One pitch to Springer and we're tying the game!"

I'm sitting on my new bed in my new room in our high-rise apartment, watching my favorite World Series replay on my new laptop a few weeks later. I'm already dressed for my last 14U game of the season today; my baseball bag's packed and ready.

I press pause and head to my window. I squish my nose to the glass.

From way up here, I can see so much.

The city of Houston's tree line rises below me, lush and green even though it's already fall. Except for the constant stream of cars along the highways, the whole world lies almost still.

I squint to the distance. On the far left, there's a teensy corner of Minute Maid Park. To the south, there's the grassy line of Brays Bayou winding from Meyerland to Hermann Park. And just below it, I can almost pinpoint the exact spot where our lot sits, waiting for our brand-new house to be built since we decided to stay in our neighborhood.

My mom hit the home goods stores this morning again, since we need almost everything. The building's doorman helped carry up all her bags. She joked with my dad, "This place is the lap of luxury, Greg. I could get *so* used to this! Maybe we'll like living up high where the water can't reach us!"

He smiled and shook his head. "Annie, we're building that new practice cage in our backyard, remember? We've got two star ballplayers, and their cleats need some grass!" Then he nodded to Bialy parked by the front door again, his new lovey tucked into his cheek. "And so does our dog."

I sit back down and press play.

My favorite replay isn't the moment the 'Stros won game five in ten innings after coming from behind a third time for a three to two series lead, even though that was beyond exciting. It's definitely not a replay of game six two days later, when the Dodgers came back and won 3–1 and forced a game seven. And it's not even the very last game of the season, when the Astros took their first World Series title in Dodger Stadium after a 5–1 blowout.

It's the Springer dinger replay that Becky called. It's the

moment I realized that the real story behind Hurricane Harvey and the World Series was all about us.

I reach under my new mattress and pull out my feelings journal. I flip to a fresh page and write.

Once I was part of a twin team called Sammy-Matty. It was the greatest team ever. It was a team perfect for two. Then everything changed.

There was a kiss behind a dugout and some broken twin telepathy. There was an epic hurricane, and our home was lost in the flood.

We went to live with our cousin, Becky, and it wasn't easy at first, because we'd forgotten how to be part of a bigger team. But with a little help from the Houston Astros, we remembered how to cheer for each other and become like my brother says—Putterman Strong.

So each time I watch my favorite Astros replay, I remember my family at Minute Maid Park.

I remember Bubbe and Papa squeezing each other tight. I remember my dad with happy tears in his eyes, and they weren't happy-sad anymore. I remember how my mom reached over to wipe his face with her rally towel, how she was crying happy tears, too. I remember Aunt Deb and Uncle Mike holding hands and laughing.

And alongside everyone—all the fans in the stadium

watching the game that night and all the fans watching on their TVs in their gutted houses—were me and Matty and Becky, cheering our hearts out, together.

Because rooting for your team matters. It matters a lot. Just like Becky says: we're a family team that's glued together tight, and nothing can break us apart.

Maybe just like baseball, our great story will keep going forever.

I shut my journal and look around my room. There was hardly anything to unpack when we got here. There's the picture on my nightstand of me and Dad in the Minute Maid stands that Becky found for me, and I've hung a few new pictures on my walls, too.

There's one of Jess and Bartholomew in these adorable matching Astros jerseys. There's a bat mitzvah picture of me and Matty hoisting Becky up high in her hora chair. There's a picture that Mack took of my entire family in the stands at game five. And there's lots of room for more pictures.

It won't take long.

I have my new signed baseball on a shelf, of course, and some new clothes in the closet and a baseball bag full of gear. And oh, I have one more important thing! A second twin bed, for sleepovers with my cousin.

But even though my room's still pretty bare, I'm not tallying mental lists of haves and have nots anymore, because now I know—I have everything I need.

There's a quick rap on my door, and Matty peeks his head in. "Ready, Sammy?"

He's wearing the same uniform as me: grass- and clay-stained baseball pants, our team jersey and cap, and knee-high socks. He's carrying his cleats, since Mom said if we walked across the rental floors, we'd have to work off the bill for the damage. His jersey says PUTTERMAN across the back, just like mine.

Matty's our starting pitcher today, and the whole family's coming to cheer him on.

I smile. "Nice uniform. What do you think?"

He smiles back. "You know what I think."

Maybe I do. But sometimes I ask, just to make sure.

Our mom calls down the hall, "Sammy-Matty! Let's go, now!"

I shut my laptop, throw my cap on, and pull my long braid out the back. I grab my glove and cleats and grin at my twin brother. "Ready if you are. Game on!"

Acknowledgments

There was a time in my life when I couldn't have imagined writing a book about baseball. Before meeting my husband and his die-hard baseball-fan family . . . before having three sons who all became pitchers . . . and before attending countless games over the years at the Houston Astros' Minute Maid Park. Truth be told, I'm kind of like my character Becky—I've been surrounded by baseball for most of my life, and over time, I've absorbed the game and found myself becoming a superfan.

My heartfelt thanks to the following team of people for their guidance and cheer in creating and publishing this book:

To my amazing agent, Peter Knapp of Park & Fine Literary and Media, for your support of my ability to tell this story in multiple points of view, and to Stuti Telidevara for your instrumental behind-the-scenes assistance.

To my wonderful editor, Megan Ilnitzki at HarperCollins, for helping me find my story's center and for loving the Putterman kids as much as I do, to Erika DiPasquale for your keen eyes on this project, and to Toni Markiet, for your kind, continued support.

To the rest of my stellar team at HarperCollins—production managers Sean P. Cavanagh and Vanessa Nuttry; publicist Aubrey Churchward; managing editors

Rye White and Gwen Morton; marketer Vaishali Nayak; designer Joel Tippie; school and library marketers Patty Rosati and team; Andrea Pappenheimer and the sales team; audio art director Mary Keane; audio managing editor Pamela Lebedda; and audio producer Almeda Baynon—for helping to make this book the very best it can be.

To artist Abigail L. Dela Cruz, for bringing the world of this story to life through your beautiful jacket illustrations.

To the wonderful authors Michael Leali and Gary D. Schmidt, thank you for your early reading of my book and your first big cheers. Your words on the jacket mean so much to me!

To my first workshop leaders at Vermont College of Fine Arts, David Gill and Deb Noyes, and to all my workshop partners, for your enthusiasm for my first chapters, which inspired me to keep writing.

To my first faculty advisor at VCFA, Corey Ann Haydu, for your insightful comments that I read over and over while finishing my first draft, and for giving me the tools and confidence to write a prologue and epilogue.

To my sister, Jeneen, for reading all the chapters of this story that came your way, however disorganized, and finding things to cheer on in them even when I knew nothing quite made sense.

To my dear friend Raman, one of my biggest cheerleaders, for your reassurance that yes, I'm becoming a better writer, and I can do this.

To the Feldman family, for cheering me on over the years in just about everything.

To my sons, David, Isaac, and Daniel, for having been the sweetest little ballplayers in the whole world, and for being the best sons and friends a mom could ask for.

To my husband, Lowell, my forever teammate, my first and best reader, my expert baseball fact checker, and the real reason I wrote this fan book, for spending countless hours over the years patiently counseling me on the ins and outs of the MLB, and for encouraging me to put as many pieces of my heart as I can onto the pages of my books.

To the City of Houston community, for setting an example of how to come together in support of one another during a time of crisis. Houston Strong!

To all the boys and girls I've watched playing youth baseball over the years, for your inspiring sportsmanship, persistent striving, and never-ending cheers. Your voices are the ones I channeled when writing this story.

And finally, to the educators, librarians, and booksellers who put books into the hands of children, thank you, thank you, thank you.